"You Know a Good Exorcist?"

I didn't even know what an exorcist was, so I said, "You hear about the top hat at the beach?"

"My phone rang all morning."

I was about to tell Puffy I thought there was a connection between the flying hat and the leis that were now circling around her place when sweet, tiny voices began to sing, "On the Good Ship Lollipop."

Bill, my duck-billed robot sidekick, pointed at the souvenir case, where the mermaid lighters were singing.

"It's like some kind of cheap magic show," Puffy said.

A new voice, one that was low and cunning and full of sin, said, "It may *look* like magic, my dear."

Filling the bar doorway was a big bot in a white suit. Robots don't sweat, but this one gave the impression that his face was covered with it.

"What else could it be?" Puffy asked.

The bot said, "The science of any sufficiently advanced race—"

I finished the quote for him: "—is indistinguishable from magic. . . ."

WORLDS OF WONDER

☐ **BARROW A Fantasy Novel by John Deakins.** In a town hidden on the planes of Elsewhen, where mortals are either reborn or driven mad, no one wants to be a pawn of the Gods. (450043—$3.95)

☐ **CAT HOUSE by Michael Peak.** The felines were protected by their humans, but ancient enemies still stalked their trails to destroy them in a warring animal underworld, where fierce battles crossed the species border. (163036—$3.95)

☐ **LORDS OF THE SWORD by Hugh Cook.** Drake Douay fled from his insane master, a maker of swords. But in a world torn by endless wars, a land riven in half by a wizard powered trench of fire, an inexperienced youth would be hard-pressed to stay alive. (450655—$3.99)

Prices slightly higher in Canada.

HAWAIIAN
U.F.O.
ALIENS

by

Mel Gilden

A ROC BOOK

A Byron Preiss Visual Publications, Inc. Book

*Special thanks to Andrea Brown
and Josepha Sherman*

ROC
Published by the Penguin Group
Penguin Books USA Inc., 375 Hudson Street,
New York, New York 10014, U.S.A.
Penguin Books Ltd, 27 Wrights Lane,
London W8 5TZ, England
Penguin Books Australia Ltd, Ringwood,
Victoria, Australia
Penguin Books Canada Ltd, 2801 John Street,
Markham, Ontario, Canada L3R 1B4
Penguin Books (N.Z.) Ltd, 182-190 Wairau Road,
Auckland 10, New Zealand

Penguin Books Ltd, Registered Offices:
Harmondsworth, Middlesex, England

Published by Roc, an imprint of New American Library,
a division of Penguin Books USA Inc.

First Roc Printing, April, 1991
10 9 8 7 6 5 4 3 2 1

For Sidney Iwanter:
Friend in Need, Patron of the Arts,
And a Guy Who Knows a Good Idea
When He Sees One

Contents

8 **CONTENTS**

Acknowledgments

Thanks to Doctors Jon Davidson and An Yin of the U.C.L.A. Earth and Space Sciences Department for the geological information I put into the mouth of the man from Pasadena Tech in Chapter Twenty-Four. Any inaccuracies are my fault. I took lightning notes over the phone and may not have gotten all the facts down correctly. (The rest of the book, however, is definitely true. Really. Trust me.)

Also, thanks to Ms. Sandra Borders, librarian first class, who gave me a lot of information. I didn't use much of it, but that's not her fault.

"The science of any sufficiently advanced race is indistinguishable from magic."
—Arthur C. Clarke

"Every intelligent race in the universe has a semantic equivalent for the request, 'Pick a card, any card.' "
—Michael Kurland

Introduction

Whipper Will and I both decided we needed vacations. Detective work is not as easy as it looks, not even if you ignore the guns, the long hours, and the abuse; not even if you squint. So I figured I deserved some time off.

But all Will and his surfing gang did all day was hang around his beach house, get high on yoyogurt, and surf by proxy with their big, gnarly, party-size robots.

Don't get me wrong. I like Will. He's a smart, smooth guy who's learned how to keep other people's secrets by practicing with his own. He saved my life a couple of times, both metaphorically and literally. I just don't understand what a guy who seemingly makes his living goofing off does on his vacation.

But his friends and I gathered in front of his house to say good-bye, just as if he were an accountant or something.

Days before, I asked him about his vacation plans and he told me, "We're going to Hawaii for the waves, for the pure, unadulterated, unsweetened, island juice."

Now, we looked at the pod mall across Pacific Coast Highway while we made small talk to fill in the time before the shuttle came. Small talk made a nice change from saying good-bye again.

The shuttle came at last, and Will left for the airport with his girlfriend, Bingo. We waved at Will and Bingo until waving seemed pointless, and straggled back into the house.

I was now alone with the other people who lived there. Which meant that I was pretty much alone. Unlike Whipper Will, none of them seemed to have thoughts in particular. But they were all bitchen bros permanently stoked on each other, brewski, and ripping surf.

Flopsie (or was it Mopsie?), one of the redheaded twins, sat down in one of the permanent depressions on the lump of couch in the big living room. Mustard took up a position on the floor between her bare legs and lifted to his lips a small furled umbrella full of a substance that hodads and full hanks were not meant to know. He and Flopsie passed it up and back, each taking a turn sucking hard on one end of the umbrella and holding their breaths.

The thick curtains were closed, and the only illumination in the room came from the TV set. On it, healthy boys and girls were slammajamming in top-to-bottom tubes that were too fresh to be true. They were surfing. It was good surf, but that's all they were doing. I guess the novelty was that the surfers were real people, not robots. You didn't see much of that these days.

These days, a surfer's idea of a personal *mano-a-mano* type confrontation with the waves was to send out a big, waterproof robot that he could control from a remote box while standing on the beach. Most surfers never even got wet. It was as dangerous as checkers and took all the skill of a reasonably good taxicab driver.

Flopsie and Mustard watched the movie with the intense concentration of brain surgeons who were twiddling a ganglia with a knife.

Nobody else was in there, just a lot of pillows with gray spots where many heads had rested, surfing posters on the walls among seashells, blowfish and fishnets, newspapers from the past three weeks, plates encrusted with food so old and dry it didn't even smell any more, not even if you were sniffing with *my* relatively large, Toomler-size schnoz.

I was leaving pretty soon, too, but there were a few things I had to do before I took off. I went into the bedroom Whipper Will shared with Bingo, and found Bill standing in the back corner in front of Will's Rotwang 5000 personal computer. I was familiar enough with the house that I barely noticed the heavy smell of linen that had been too long without benefit of soap and water.

"Bill?" I said.

He didn't answer. Which was strange because he was a robot and programmed to pay attention. I tried again, with the same result. Small bits flashed and passed on the computer screen, like tiny green fish.

I crossed the room, avoiding the piles of clothing, camping equipment and junk that I *still* couldn't identify, even after months on Earth, and stood at Bill's left shoulder. A cable snaked from Bill's shiny, duck-shaped body and plugged into the back of the terminal. That's why he was even more engrossed than the two in the living room.

A game was in progress on the screen, but the playing pieces moved too fast for me to follow. The game was over in less than a minute and, without pause, another began. I pushed the ESCAPE key and waited. The screen went blank, and Bill looked up at me as if he'd been asleep. I am not a big guy compared to an Earthperson, and Bill would barely come up to my belly button, if I had one.

"Hey, boss," Bill said.

"I'm leaving."

"Back to Bay City." Bill laughed. He had absorbed my sense of humor, which is the kind of thing that happens to personal bots.

"Far from Surfing Samurai Robots and hostile natives," I said quickly, and before either of us could think about it, I slapped a sheet of flypaper on top of his head, stick-um side down. He stopped in mid-chuckle, and his eyes went dark.

I had done the kindest thing possible. I couldn't take Bill to, er, Bay City. Who knew what outrageous, perhaps even *true*, thing he might say to people? And I couldn't leave him to the warped mercies of Whipper Will's housemates. Instead, I had turned him off. I stood him in the closet behind a curtain of Hawaiian shirts that were so loud you could hear them from the next room even with the closet door closed.

I took off my shoes, put away my brown suit, the trench coat and the fedora. I put on my short johns, told Bill to stay out of trouble, and left the room.

In the kitchen, Thumper, the tallest of the bunch, was absent-mindedly using a spatula to tap a toasted cheese sandwich in a frying pan while he watched Captain Hook out the window. Captain Hook was standing defiantly at the edge of the water, controlling his surf-bot with a remote control box. The day was cold, and except for Captain Hook and a few diehard joggers, the golden sands of Malibu were deserted.

Mopsie (or was it Flopsie?) was sitting at the Formica-topped dining table at one end of the room, listening to Thumper discuss the quality of Captain Hook's hotdogging.

To me she said, "Going?" The fact that I was wearing a wet suit and not carrying any luggage did not seem to bother her.

"Yeah. Be cool, you hear?"

Thumper nodded at my sage advice, then happened to glance out the window. He jubilantly cried, "Wipeout!"

Mopsie shook her head and said, "Captain Hook'll be raw all day."

"Yeah, well, hang loose, dude," Thumper said, and clasped my hand in a complicated grip that the surfers had taken one hilarious evening to teach me. Mopsie bent low to hug me. Her tits were in my face. For that moment, I wished I'd been human so I could appreciate them.

I walked outside, through the small brick backyard, across the public blacktop walkway and across the sand. The sand crunched pleasantly beneath my feet as the cold wind whipped around my bare legs and arms. I could smell hamburger grease from miles away, maybe as far as Santa Monica. A guy had to be desperate to open his stand on a day like this. I didn't look forward to the cold swim, but there was no other way to get to my sneeve.

"Hang loose," I hollered above the wind at Captain Hook.

He waved in my direction, but he was too busy with his surf-bot to say anything.

Even wearing the short johns, I got a chilling shock when I stepped into the water, and for a moment, I couldn't breathe. I swam for a good long time, until I came even with a point I knew, and dived. Seconds later I was cycling the screw on my sneeve, the *Philip Marlowe*, and stripping off the abbreviated rubber suit. I wiped myself down with a handful of treated

tree sap that was not very much like a warm
dry towel.

So, I went back to T'toom.

No playing of recordings of *The Adventures
of Philip Marlowe* on this return voyage. I had
the complete books of Raymond Chandler and
a few other mystery novels that had been recommended to me. Trouble was my business,
oh yes. I'd proved that on Earth. But now I had
real trouble. I had to go home and face my rel-
atives.

The ride was not long, but it was longer than
the average Gino and Darlene movie, and my
attention span felt the strain. I had time to
check my cargo again. There was nothing new
since I'd loaded it and checked it the week before. I sat down to read *The Maltese Falcon*
and eat my own recycled wastes.

Sam Spade was an aggro dude, just like Marlowe, but without quite such an emphasis on
the smart mouth. Spade was good, but the
smart mouth appealed to me, too. I thought I'd
stick with Philip Marlowe for a while yet.

After a week of thinking like that, Spade and
Marlowe were having conversations right there
aboard the sneeve. They both looked like Hum-
phrey Bogart, and I had trouble telling them
apart. Evidently, so did they. In my dreams,
they traded quips with each other. I couldn't
think of a thing to say, and I woke up sweating.

My family never expected to see me again,
and my arrival on T'toom caused quite a stir.
Grampa Zamp rubbed my nose raw with con-
gratulations, and I would have avoided him if
I'd liked him less.

I hadn't realized how settled I'd gotten on
Earth until I saw the slick, wet-looking buildings oozing out of the soil of T'toom and
thought how much they looked like fruit-

flavored slugs. Another thing I was not used to was being the same size as everybody else. There was not a pug nose on the planet. I didn't know whether to be relieved or threatened.

Way back when, Dad had been against my going to Earth, but now he threw me a big Welcome Home party. I hoped T'toom Gravitational Products was doing OK, because just re-oozing the house for the event must have set him back plenty.

The day after, I knew the party was really over when I walked into the dining room and saw the family assembled. Dad was at one end of the table, and Mom at the other. Grampa Zamp sat between them, filled with so much curiosity I could almost see it frothing out of him. Their noses were quivering, meaning my family was ready for anything.

"We're not at a party now," Dad said. "Tell us what Earth is *really* like."

Terrific. I liked Earth, despite its obvious defects. Maybe I liked it *because* of its defects. But generally it was a pretty nice place. Kate Smith used to sing that it had purple mountains' majesty, fruited plains, that sort of thing. If I told anybody on T'toom the truth, entire families would be sneeving over there on vacation. Even if they didn't land, UFO sightings would be a nightly event.

So I made up such a story, my face is still red, or would be if I knew how to blush. According to me, Earth was a snake pit, a dark, dismal place full of cold rocks and hot-blooded creatures that would gobble you down in unexpected, unpleasant ways.

"You were there for a long time," Dad said.

"I wanted to make sure," I said.

Mom and Dad nodded, but Grampa Zamp looked as surprised and unhappy as if I'd dumped slaberingeo spine fixer over him.

"Besides," I said, "I wanted to stay long

enough to bring back my cargo." I pulled a plastic, leather-look bag from a pocket and poured a pile of small brown pellets on the table. Nobody moved. Grampa Zamp had the wit to ask me what they were.

"Chocolate-covered coffee beans."

"What does that mean?" Dad said.

"Try one."

Grampa Zamp was the only one who moved. As he picked up a bean, I said, "Suck on it. The outside is soft and will melt. The inside is hard and brittle and will take some chewing."

Grampa Zamp put it into his mouth, and his face lit up like Dodger Stadium at night. After that, the beans went pretty fast.

"You got these on Earth?" Dad said.

I nodded. "The storeroom on my sneeve is full of them. I figured you could sell them by the pound and make back the money I owe you." Dad got a faraway look on his face as he began to think about the possibilities.

"Earth?" said Mom. "Terrible old Earth?"

I put my hand on Mom's and said, "Once you've tasted chocolate-covered coffee beans, you've experienced the best Earth has to offer. Trust me."

I had been told that in Hollywood, "Trust me," means "Fuck you." But nobody on T'toom except me had ever visited Hollywood, so when I said, "Trust me," that's what they did.

A day or two later, the media discovered me and I became a celebrity. I was on shows explaining Earth's radio programs. I told the same lie about Terrible Old Earth, or variations on it, till I had it down pretty good. The photographs I had taken of Whipper Will and the other surfers caused quite a sensation, and a lot of biologists went back to their drawing boards shaking their heads. Dad's chocolate-covered coffee beans disappeared almost overnight. The loan was paid off, and Dad gave me the money that was left over.

After that, things got quiet. I'd had my fifteen minutes of fame on T'toom. I read my books and hung with my family, but very soon, I was bored. I didn't know if I had changed or life on T'toom was more placid than it had been, but I was bored. Then I realized that I wasn't just bored, I was hungry for Earth. Trouble is my business, after all, and there isn't much of it on T'toom.

I began to collect stuff to take to Earth with me: personal papers; pictures of the family; a little of the household ooze, just for old times' sake; boxes of Toomler stories; and a couple of extra slaberingeo spines—you never know when your sneeve might need a replacement.

I was listening to a Beethoven symphony on a recording of *Voice of Firestone* when Grampa Zamp caught me with all this stuff laid out on my bed. While he watched, I kind of moved it around, hoping the collection looked natural, like something anybody might have on their bed.

Grampa Zamp said, "Going somewhere?"

I looked at Grampa Zamp. My nose must have been twitching a mile a minute, but he was very relaxed. I took a chance and said, "Yeah. I'm going back to Earth."

His nose went up, then down. "I thought Earth was some kind of interstellar death trap."

"Depends on who you ask," I said. After that, I told Grampa Zamp the whole truth and nothing but the truth. I told him about Sylvia Woods and Surfing Samurai Robots and Whipper Will and the gang. He asked a lot of questions. I guess he found the story pretty entertaining because when I got done, he asked me, "Why did you lie?"

"I like Earth. I like it the way it is." I rubbed

my face with one hand and said, "Remember
the beginning of *Grand Central Station?* All
those trains heading for the same place. All
those people. All that confusion."

"I remember."

"I don't want Earth to become Grand Central Station."

He thought that over. "Too many handprints
on the ooze."

"That's right."

I waited while he nodded. He said, "I'll
square it with your parents. When do you
leave?"

"As soon as I can."

"Now's a good time. Everybody's at the
plant."

So I went back to Earth. I remember the kid
I had been the first time I'd gone there, afraid,
but not even knowing what of. I knew a lot
more about Earth now, but that didn't make
me any less afraid.

I dropped into Earth's atmosphere, and as I
descended through black clouds toward Malibu, they began to throw me around as if my
sneeve were a Frisbee. Lightning flashed, making sudden stark shadows in my ship. Rain
pelted the ship as if someone were throwing
chocolate-covered coffee beans at me. The
computer had a tough time navigating, but at
last, *Philip Marlowe* dived into the whitecaps
and suddenly everything quieted down. My
ship settled through the fish to the bottom. I
put on my short johns and cycled myself out
into the freezing water.

I swam toward the shore, but it was not always a sure thing that I would make it. I swallowed a lot of salt water, but there was plenty
left to slap me in the face and try to hold me
under.

1

Double-O Zoot — License Granted

At last, exhausted and thirsty for a drink of fresh water, I crawled onto the beach. It should have been daytime, but the black, boiling clouds kept out the sunlight. I lay on the sand, relieved that the rain and blustering wind were all I had to deal with.

I walked up the soggy mess of a beach and came at last to the house. As was always the case when Whipper Will wasn't around to remind them to lock it, the back door opened easily without a key.

The usual crowd was sprawled about the living room, watching a Gino and Darlene movie on TV.

"Hey, dude," Thumper called to me from the far side of the room, which was a compliment of sorts. I'd have guessed he was too busy with Flopsie (or was it Mopsie?) to notice my appearance in the doorway. Everybody actually looked away from the TV for a moment to acknowledge my existence. Hanger and whichever redhead wasn't busy with Thumper got up and gave me a friendly cuddle. You didn't have to be human to appreciate how warm and soft they were.

Mustard took a joint from his face and said, "Wet enough for you?"

"He likes it wet," Captain Hook said. "They all like it wet in Bay City." He never took his eyes off the TV screen.

The Captain was in one of his moods, so I obliged him with a low-grade zinger. "Sure," I said. "That's why Bay City is near the beach."

Thumper pounded the flat of his hand against the floor and shouted "Ahh-roooh! Zoot is *back!*" The rest of them took up the cry. All but Captain Hook. He was too busy watching Darlene jiggle across the TV screen.

At my feet was a puddle of salt water big enough to do laps in. I waved at the crowd, told them that I had to change, and walked along the dark hall to Whipper Will's room. As far as I could tell, nothing had been touched. Nobody had washed the laundry, that was for sure.

After pulling out a flat, waterproof packet and throwing it onto the bed, I peeled off my short johns, padded into the bathroom with them, and hung them on a hook, where they dripped rhythmically. I rubbed myself down good with a towel. Feeling more like myself all the time, I went back into the bedroom and put on my Earth clothes. The brown suit felt natural. I unwrapped the sheets in the waterproof packet and put them into my inside coat pocket. The trench coat and the fedora could wait.

In the kitchen, I found a glass that had not seen much action and drank tap water from it. I rinsed out the glass with a little soap and water and set it in the drainer, where it was all alone except for a fork that might have been clean. I was ready for anything now, so I went back into the bedroom and hefted Bill out of the closet.

Even in the dim light, Bill's silver body shone. I could barely hear a song about surfing and young love that was playing on the TV in the other room. Rain blew against the side of the house, went away, came back even harder. I reached down and pulled the flypaper off Bill's head. He blinked and said, "Bay City! Ya! Have a nice trip, Boss."

"I had a nice trip, thanks."

He computed that for a moment, then said, "How long?"

"A few weeks."

He nodded the way I might have. "What's the scam now?"

"I need a driver's license. You know where I can get one?"

"My meat, Boss."

"Wait a minute." I put on my trench coat and my fedora, figuring that the weather being what it was, wearing them did more than just put me in uniform. I followed Bill as he waddled from the room and down the dark hallway. We hurried through the rain and cold, across the small garden where Will grew the fruits for his yoyogurt, into the garage.

The Chevrolet Belvedere was waiting for me, looking like the ghost of a car in the gray air. Far away, thunder grumbled about how lightning got all the publicity. I lifted the garage door, letting in uncertain light and a good view of Pacific Coast Highway. A car swished by every so often, stirring up a big lonely sound, but the street was more deserted than I'd ever seen it. When I opened the car, it smelled musty and damp. I let Bill in the other side, and he sat near the window, his legs not quite long enough to dangle over the edge of the seat.

"You want the Department of Motor Vehi-

cles, known to its friends, of which there are
few, as the DMV.''

"I want it, all right. I'm tired of waiting for
the first cop with a little time on his hands to
pull me over and discover my terrible secret.
Where's the DMV?''

Bill told me, and I backed slowly onto Pacific
Coast Highway. Rain suddenly attacked the
windows with hard spatters, and we were off.
Soon I couldn't see through the cascade rolling
down the windshield. Driving was pretty exciting there for a while. Even Bill had a good grip
on the handrest. "Use the wipers! Use the wipers!''

"What wipers?'' I was busy at the moment,
trying to decide if the thing in front of me was
a truck or a sports car.

"Windshield wipers!'' His left arm tele-
scoped toward me, reached for the dash, and
turned a black plastic knob. Immediately, a
couple of arms came up on the outside of the
windshield and swept the water one way and
then the other.

"Cool,'' I said. "How'd you happen to know
about that?''

"Bubble memory,'' he said and tapped the
side of his little ducky head.

The DMV was a square yellow building with
a parking lot on one side. The gray, joyless day
complemented it so perfectly, I wondered if,
maybe, rain fell there all the time. The building had no class, no style, its only distinguish-
ing marks being the words DEPARTMENT OF
MOTOR VEHICLES in bold block letters on the
side, and a jagged chorus line of black marks
drawn along one wall.

"Graffiti,'' Bill said.

"Meaning what?''

"Meaning there's probably more action
around here when the place is closed.''

"I just want a driver's license," I said.

I had my pick of spaces in the nearly empty lot. I told Bill to wait for me in the car. He got busy betting himself which raindrop would reach the bottom of the window first.

Inside the DMV building was a single room, lit too brightly with fluorescent tubes. Following the Los Angeles tradition, the air conditioning was on, making the room even colder than the air outside. Bored clerks sat behind desks in the cubicles, making notes on papers that would probably be filed in boxes somewhere and never seen again. A lot of the clerks were wearing coats or sweaters. One guy had a knit hat pulled over his ears.

English and Spanish signs hanging from the ceiling told the multitudes where to stand, which line to wait in, whom to see. No multitudes were there at the moment, so I walked up to a counter that had an INFORMATION sign hanging over it. Arrows pointed downward just in case anybody entertained thoughts of standing in line on the ceiling. I stood tippy-toe so I could see over the top of the counter.

Nobody was standing on the other side, so I called out, "Am I in the right place to get a little information?"

A bored man looked up from his work. His shoulders sloped, and his hair was thin. But his white shirt was crisp, and his tie didn't clash with it. Astonishingly, his face drooped into an even more bored expression when he looked at me. "What sort of information?"

"Is this where I get a driver's license?"

"It is if you're eligible."

"Am I eligible?"

"I don't know. Are you? Read the sign." He pointed to another sign, this one taking up most of one wall. In English and Spanish it said that a driver had to be so old, had to pass such and such tests, couldn't be crazy.

"Sure, I'm eligible."

"Are you a citizen?" He kind of sneered when he said it.

I said, "I'd rather not shout. Do you have legs, or are you screwed into that desk?"

A few of the other clerks almost laughed. The guy I was talking to didn't like that, but he stood up—just to show he could do it, I suppose—and walked over to stand behind the counter. He was shaped like a bowling pin. Walking to the counter must have been quite a workout.

"OK. I'm here now. Are you a citizen?" He glared at my nose, which, truth to tell, is most of my face.

"The sign doesn't say anything about being a citizen."

"No, but you'll need a birth certificate anyway, to make sure you're over eighteen."

"Of course I'm over eighteen. Don't let my good looks fool you."

"No?"

"No. When I was a kid, I had a little accident involving toxic waste and a bottle of nose drops."

"Yeah?"

"Yeah. It could happen to anybody." I speared him with my best stare. "It could happen to *you.*"

The guy wearing the knit hat guffawed once, then caught himself. The guy at the counter almost looked over his shoulder at him, but didn't quite.

"You have a birth certificate?"

I took the folded document from my coat pocket, unfolded it on the counter, and waited. I'd done my homework, and I thought I was ready for this guy. Him and anybody else in that room, singly or in combinations. If homework were enough.

He looked at the document, turned it around,

turned it over. He studied me instead of the paper and said, "I hope this isn't a gag. The state of California wouldn't like it."

I was ready. I knew he wouldn't be able to make head or tail of the document because on T'toom, never having seen written English, we still used the letters of the local written language, which was called Gomkrix. But it really was my birth certificate. I'd just had to fiddle with the date and place of birth a little.

I said, "No gag. It's my birth certificate from the Bay City Hospital."

"It's not in English."

"Show me where it says the certificate has to be in English."

He took the document and talked to one of the other clerks. They buzzed to themselves while poking the document and watching me. I got tired of it and went to look out the window. The rain was so fine, it was almost mist. I could see Bill's dark shape inside the Chevy.

"Sir?" It sounded as if the word hurt him to say it.

I went back to the counter and the guy said, "OK. Let's go through this an item at a time." I spent the next twenty minutes explaining my birth certificate to him, making up facts to match what was written there. I didn't lie any more than I had to.

When we were done, he looked like a man with a bad taste in his mouth, but he gave me the written driving test anyway. He was not very happy when I passed, but we went outside and I drove him around the block while he made marks on a printed sheet on a clipboard. Bill sat in the back seat, thank Durf, not saying anything. I must have passed the driving test, too, because when we got back into the building, the guy took my thumb print, my picture, and forty-two dollars.

As he was writing up my temporary license,

he said, "If you're from Bay City, then I must be a Martian."

"Could be," I said, shrugging. "I've never seen a Martian." Which was also not a lie, despite Orson Welles. I picked up the temporary license and my birth certificate. The guy watched me walk out the door and hustle across the parking lot to the Chevy. Maybe he expected the Chevy to turn into a flying saucer and take off.

If he wanted to see a flying saucer, he shouldn't have been watching me. He should have been watching the news.

2

Beads and Trinkets

On the drive back to the surfers' house, I took a few more chances with the driving than I had before. Knowing that I had a license in my pocket gave me confidence. Bill seemed to enjoy the trip.

I parked the car in the garage and closed the door. Raindrops on the leaves and petals were tiny eyes that watched me and Bill walk across the garden to the house. Bill knocked into my legs when I stopped for a moment to inhale the just-washed smells and note that the clouds were breaking up into big, ragged piles of fresh laundry, the sun touching each with gold piping.

I went into the house and stood by the door listening. It was too quiet. The TV was talking, and nobody else. Nobody hissed as they inhaled smoke from one of those funny cigarettes. Nobody clattered a fork against a plate. Durf, it was quiet, and that's all. Everybody could have been sleeping, for all I knew. Bill and I walked into the living room and found Whipper Will and Bingo there, surrounded by luggage and their bros. Everybody was watching the TV. I watched it, too.

A short, grainy piece of film was shown over and over while a guy with a nice voice talked about it. The film might have been of a black fish moving through murky water. It might have been of a bird in a sky about like today's. The announcer said that it was an Unidentified Flying Object that had been spotted over the big island of Hawaii. He said it a lot and in different ways, but that was all he said. Pretty soon the special report went to a commercial, and the tableau dissolved as if we were statues that had just invented movement.

"Howdy, Will," I said. He was a very cool dude in his Hawaiian shirt covered with parrots, big, gaudy flowers and palm leaves, his white pants and his huarache sandals. Bingo stood next to him in very short white shorts and just enough tube top to cover her legal fees. With one hand, she brushed away her long, dark bangs, then gave me a hello hug.

"Zoot! You gnarly old hotdogger!" Whipper Will said. "The bros told me you were here."

We just stood there smiling at each other for a moment. Captain Hook dropped his nickel: "Maybe the old hotdogger has a fresh idea about this UFO stuff."

"Me?" I said, awfully surprised.

"Sure. The dude from Bay City." He laughed unpleasantly.

"We don't have UFOs in Bay City. Everything that flies around there is pretty much identified."

"Don't snake us, dude," Captain Hook said, not liking my answer much.

"Hey, dudes," Whipper Will said, "get cranked on these!"

"Presents," Bingo said, and began to pull small packages from a big suitcase that had been around the world a couple of times with-

out a friend. "Here's one for you, Captain." She
threw him a package the size and shape of a
brick. Captain Hook was distracted, and the
tense moment burst into nothing at all.

Everybody got a package, and soon we were
ankle-deep in brightly colored shreds of paper.
The surfers turned the stuff over in their
hands, liking it because it was new and given
to them by Whipper Will and Bingo. I didn't
know what any of the stuff was, but all of it
must have had something to do with Hawaii or
why bother going all the way there to get it?
There were small statues of crouching creatures with big eyes and tongues that hung to
their bellies, necklaces of tiny pink seashells
and others of plastic flowers, and bottles of
colored sand, poured in so as to make a simple
beach scene.

There were a lot of restless eyes among the
surfers then, and some polite appreciating of
other people's gifts. Trades were made.

All of that faded into the background when I
tore the paper off a white cardboard box and
looked inside. I stared at the contents, not be-
lieving what I was seeing. I could have been
wrong, and nothing would have pleased me
more. The cool, neutral scent rising from the
box didn't tell me anything. What I saw was a
necklace that seemed to be made from slaberingeo spines. They couldn't be real slaberingeo
spines, of course, or they would have floated
out of the box. Still, the resemblance was
astonishing.

While hoisting my slack jaw off the floor, I
stepped through the crowd to where Whipper
Will stood with Bingo, raking in the thank-
yous. He said, "Hope you're stoked about the
necklace, bro. In the store, it seemed to have
your name on it."

I nodded. "Gnarly for sure. What is it, exactly?" I said carefully, not wanting to damage

my sense of reality any more than I had already.

"It's a necklace made from blowfish spines."

"Uh huh," I said, studying the necklace.

Will smiled and went on, "I got it in Hawaii, if that's any help. It came with a certificate of authenticity, but we lost it somewhere between the store and the hotel."

"Sure," I said. "That explains everything." I bounced the pile of spines in my hand.

"What's the matter?" Bingo said. Both she and Whipper Will waited for me to say something smart.

Instead of doing that, I said, "The necklace just kind of reminds me of a little item I thought you could find only in Bay City."

"What item?" Whipper Will said.

"Sort of a piece of native handicraft."

When I didn't continue, Will said, "Anything you say, Zoot."

Will wasn't helping me. He might not be able to help me even if I told him that I'd thought the nearest slaberingeo spines were aboard the *Philip Marlowe*, somewhere off the coast of Malibu.

To change the subject, I said, "What is this other stuff?"

"Beads and trinkets for the natives. Household tikis for good luck, puka-shell necklaces, plastic leis, beach sand in a bottle."

"And a blowfish spine necklace."

"Cowabunga," Will said seriously. "I guess it really did have your name on it." He looked around the room. The little statues and bottles of sand had been lined up on the fireplace mantle. Hanger was wearing a shell necklace, and Mustard was on the floor again, a plastic lei draped casually around a foot beating time to the music on a TV car commercial that was otherwise being ignored.

A little too loudly, Will said, "Zoot, will you help us haul our traps into the bedroom?"

I slipped the necklace around my neck and flicked my tie over it. Matching Will's delivery, I said that I would be delighted, and picked up an overnight bag I could carry without dragging it on the ground. Will and Bingo and I manhandled the luggage into the bedroom. Bill walked to the Rotwang 5000 and said, "Anybody for a quick game of *Motorcycle Contra-Zombies?*"

"Not right now, Bill," I said. "Come over here."

He joined me at the doorway while Bingo and Whipper Will unpacked. From the bottom of one suitcase Will pulled a folded newspaper that he handed to me. Bill looked at it over my wrist as I read the big words at the top of the front page: *The Interstate Eyeball.* Under it were headlines that screamed, "Elvis is my Pool Man!" and "Chickens From Atlantis Lay Crystal Eggs That Restore Woman's Sight!" and, "Man Attacked by his Toupee!"

"Wow!" said Bill. "A lot happened while you were gone."

I said, "Yeah. A lot of creative journalism. Is this what passes for news in Hawaii?"

"Only in supermarket checkout lines. But take a look at this." He turned a few pages, folded the paper into a compact package so that even I couldn't miss what he had in mind, and handed it back.

At the top of the page was a grainy photograph that might have been a frame out of the film we'd just seen on television. Below that, it said, "UFO Buzzes Hawaii!" by somebody named Jean-Luc Avoirdupois, *Eyeball* Staff Writer. I swallowed hard. The picture was pretty clear if you knew what to look for. I said, "I guess anything that can make an island buzz is worth a little ink."

"Huh? Read the story."

I didn't have to read Mr. Avoirdupois' story, but I read it anyway, just to keep busy. As I knew it would, it gave the same facts as the TV special. Evidently this unidentified thing had come in low over Hilo, heading southwest. Nobody knew what it was, but certain unnamed experts were sure it was a vehicle from another planet. I let my nose twitch. Nobody on Earth would know what it meant.

I folded the paper and said, "It wasn't me, if that's what you have in mind."

He and Bingo were watching me carefully. Will smiled a little, as if he weren't sure it was OK. "I guess they don't have that kind of ride in Bay City." Bill took the paper from me and began to shuffle through it eagerly.

"No. Not in Bay City."

Will ran his hand through his long, dark hair and looked at Bingo. She shrugged and sat on the bed. Will said, "All right. How about this? On our flight into LAX, the plane was surrounded by fog heavy enough to fill cream puffs. Rumors circulated among the passengers that our plane was the only one that was having this problem. A couple of folks aboard the plane had nothing but trouble. Their dinners were not only cold but crawling with roaches. The light above their seats didn't work, and the air blower blew hot air instead of cold."

"That's pretty interesting if you're just telling me about your trip. Otherwise, why should I care?

"I'm thinking that the Hilo UFO and the fog and the bad luck all have something to do with each other."

"If they did, what would that be to either of us?" I said. It was a reasonable question, but it seemed to make Whipper Will angry.

"I thought we were friends by now," he said.

"Since when do friends ask friends embarrassing questions?" I fingered the spine necklace. It was its own embarrassing question.

Will smiled and began to unpack again. "If you didn't know something about all this, the questions wouldn't be embarrassing."

"Yeah. We embarrass easy in Bay City."

Will and Bingo kept unpacking. I took the *Eyeball* away from Bill, threw it onto the bed, and was about to walk out of the room when Mopsie (or was it Flopsie?) ran in and said breathlessly, "Come see what's new on the beach!" Nobody moved, so she stamped her feet and cried, "Come on! It's boss!" She ran away. Pretty soon our curiosity got the better of us and we followed.

3

The Magic Top Hat

Cool, groovy, jaunty-jolly, we walked through the house. No surprise, nobody was at home but us. If Flopsie (or was it Mopsie?) was so stoked about the thing on the beach, she probably wasn't alone.

The sun was making headway with the clouds; they'd parted like a curtain to let more sunshine through. The sand had dried and there were deep footprints where people had broken through the thin, fragile crust. But nobody was out on the rough water. No people, no robots, nothing but the occasional gull.

People in shorts and shades were cautiously peeking out of frame houses up and down the promenade. Some of them were wandering up and down the black public strip. A jogger went by, a radio plugged into his ears. He was sweating despite the fact the air was still cold.

We crunched through the crust of the dry sand, leaving footprints that might have been made by giants. A crowd was gathering down by the high tide line, and even from halfway up the beach we could see why. "Cowabunga,"

Bingo and Will breathed together. I just nodded. After the TV news and the article in the *Eyeball*, what I saw didn't surprise me much. But why here? Why now? Did it have anything to do with the spine necklace, or was my getting the necklace now just a coincidence? I wasn't so smart. The universe was filled with questions.

The thing stood about two stories high, was round, black, and shiny. The surfers were there, and a few other locals, talking in small clumps and never taking their eyes off it. I heard Mustard say, "It looks like an old Hollywood restaurant." A few people grumbled agreement.

As we approached the thing, I did a little experiment. I said, "What is it?"

Bill said, "From here it looks like a top hat."

"Top hat?"

Whipper Will said, "Don't you have top hats in Bay City?"

"Bay City? Top hats? Sure."

I guess I didn't sound sure because Bingo said, "You know. Like Fred Astaire."

"He makes top hats?" I said.

Will made one explosive laugh. Bingo just shook her head. Neither of them explained the joke.

A fat guy wearing a too-little T-shirt that said, DAMN, I'M GOOD, and a purple bathing suit he was funneled into, picked up a handful of sand and threw it at the hat. In any crowd, you can always count on somebody trying to see how much damage he can do.

In this case, the sand did no damage at all. It hit something solid and invisible a few feet away from the side of the hat, and slid to the ground. A lot of people threw sand after that, but as far as the hat was concerned, they might as well have been blowing kisses.

Carefully, as if they were trying not to hurt an injured animal, the surfers and a few other beach types began to dig down the invisible face of the force wall.

Bill ran across the beach and stirred up a convention of sea gulls. Calling out insults, one of the birds glided across and landed on the hat—on the actual hat, not on the force wall— and then flew away. Waves washed up onto the hat, leaving a wet smudge like the shadow of a reclining woman. I think it was the fact that only people and their tools were affected by the force wall that, more than anything else, led to Captain Hook's mishap. I don't think it was an accident, no. At least, not so far as the hat was concerned.

Bill came back and helped us watch Thumper and Mustard, but not too closely. They were still digging furiously, evidently having a contest among themselves to see who could fling the most sand into the air. The girls and most of the crowd backed off and watched. A few people even walked away. If the hat wasn't going to whistle "God Bless America," what good was it? Meanwhile, Captain Hook prowled around the hat like a hyena sizing up a dead zebra.

Thumper and Mustard were down to the hard-packed, wet sand now, and the going was much slower. Thumper looked back over his shoulder at Whipper Will and said, "I don't know, dude. This wall thing goes to Cronulla Beach."

"Is that far?" I said.

"Australia," Bingo said. "The other side of the planet."

Captain Hook marched over to us as if we'd personally offended him in some way—you never knew—and said angrily, "That thing really works me hard. I mean, I am seriously dogged." He turned around and looked at the hat. As Whipper Will spoke, Captain Hook casually threw sand at it.

Will said, "Don't be a full hank, Holmes. That thing doesn't even know you're here."

"Yeah?" said Captain Hook, throwing the sand a little harder.

"Sure. It's just a fancy piece of driftwood."

"Yeah?" said Captain Hook, throwing the sand even harder.

"Look, dude—" Whipper Will began, but was cut off when Captain Hook suddenly swept an old brown bottle off the beach and angrily heaved it at the top hat. Without even a "boink!" the bottle bounced off, followed immediately by a jab of red lightning that hit Captain Hook in the chest and crawled over him like nervous electric snakes, dropping him hard to the sand. He writhed there for a moment, then the red lightning seemed to burrow into the ground. Captain Hook didn't move.

We forgot about the hat and stared at the silent form as we stepped forward. I wondered if the red snakes were gone for good or only hiding momentarily. Whipper Will knelt over Captain Hook and listened to his chest. "Still alive," Will said softly. Captain Hook leaped to his feet with his hands in the air as if he'd just won a race. Surprised, Will fell back onto the sand.

The captain was smiling. It wasn't his nasty smile or his sarcastic smile or even the smile he used when he had one up on you.

It was good-natured. It had a lot of charm. Something was wrong. I think we all felt it. Even Bill looked at me and said, "Huh?"

Captain Hook declaimed, "Good afternoon, ladies and germs," and waited. Nothing happened. We were all too astonished to do or say anything.

Gamely, Captain Hook went on. "Anybody have twenty cents for a phone call?" He looked at the group earnestly, as if willing to be delighted by any answer. "No?" he said and strode over to me. I stood my ground, wondering if this was the moment when my curiosity would kill me.

He gripped the tip of my nose gently with one hand while he held the other under one of my nostrils. Something tinkled into his cupped hand, and a second later he held up two dimes. He laughed and said, "You know, sir, you ought to be more careful where you keep your change." He waited again. The fat guy in the T-shirt applauded slowly as if he were beating time. He looked more bored than entertained.

While Captain Hook enjoyed the applause and Bill stared up my nose, Whipper Will said, "That's not the captain I know."

"His interest in magic is new, too, I'll bet," I said.

"You're not just whistling 'Wipeout,' bro." Then in a voice that was almost too soft for me to catch, Will said, " 'The science of any sufficiently advanced race is indistinguishable from magic.' "

"No lie, friend," I said. "Back off, Bill." I didn't believe in magic, but I did believe in force walls. I'd seen them before. Never on a heap like this, but there were a lot of force walls I hadn't seen. The fact that this hat looked like the UFO in the smudge of a photo in the *Interstate Eyeball* just made the situation more interesting. Nobody else had noticed the similarity. But then, nobody else had my experience with interstellar heaps.

"Thank you, thank you," said Captain Hook. "For my next trick—"

Whatever Captain Hook was about to say was drowned out by an approaching siren. We looked around and saw a police car booming along the beach, kicking up clouds of sand. I came up alongside Whipper Will and said, "You'd better get the captain out of here.

Chances are he'll just confuse the issue, whatever it is."

Will nodded and took Captain Hook by the arm. Captain Hook looked surprised but still amiable. Will said, "Come on, Captain. I got some hats that need rabbits removed."

"Hey, great," Captain Hook said and went along quietly. Bingo took his other arm, which didn't hurt either. As they walked up the beach, the police car came to a stop a few yards away from us and the siren died. A couple of guys in plain clothes got out and walked our way. Behind the wheel, a uniformed cop picked his teeth while he waited.

One of the plainclothes guys was tall and the other one was short, for an Earthman. The tall one had straight blond hair lying across his forehead like rays of sunlight. He had the pleasant, open expression of a farmer who was having a lot of success rotating his crops. He never took his left hand out of the pocket of his overcoat. The short guy had a red face and a big red nose that was veined like a map of roads that nobody drove much. He was a peppery little guy who thought he was tough. I knew he thought he was tough because when he planted himself in front of the top hat, he looked around with disgust and then spit.

In a strident voice, the short plainclothes guy said, "I'm Police Detective Cliffy. This is Sergeant Robinson." He took a long time studying the top hat, as if it had a written message just for him all over it. His lips even moved. He said, "What the hell is going on here?" and looked at me. At least a dozen people were within interrogating distance, but he looked at me.

I said, "This thing showed up on the beach."

"What is it?" Police Detective Cliffy said as if he thought I ought to know.

"It looks like a spaceship to me. But I'm no expert," I said and shrugged.

Cliffy spit on the ground again. In a mild voice, Robinson said, "If you don't know, just say so."

"I thought if I didn't know, Cliffy would spit in my eye."

"I hate tough guys," Cliffy said and vigorously rubbed one finger under his nose. He chuckled at a funny idea he had. "Maybe you aren't so tough. And maybe you're a guy who knows a spaceship when he sees one."

"Not many spaceships in Bay City," I said. "I was just cracking wise."

"Cracking wise," said Bill.

"Yeah, well, this is a public beach and this thing can't stay here." He nodded at Robinson, who began to wave his hands at the crowd as if he were shooing chickens. "All right, folks. Move along. Nothing more to see here." People began to mill around and back away, but nobody actually left. Robinson looked at Cliffy as if he expected help.

Before Cliffy could explode in his face, a second car arrived, this one driven by a tweedy guy wearing thick glasses. He spoke with Cliffy and Robinson, all the while looking at the top hat and licking his lips. Robinson helped the tweedy guy unload all kinds of electronic equipment from the trunk and back seat of his car.

"What's happening, dude?" Thumper said to me.

"They're going to take its temperature."

As if it were some kind of show, we watched the tweedy guy point things at the top hat and touch the force wall with probes. He took readings and made notes. After a while, he got around to throwing sand at the thing, just like everybody else. Cliffy and Robinson watched him impatiently. Cliffy spent a lot of time on the two-way radio in his car.

While the tweedy guy was throwing his fourth or fifth handful of sand, loud, mechanical roaring came at us from across the beach. Big yellow machines were coming our way.

The machines were driven by robots, Surfing Samurai Robots if the trademark rags around their foreheads meant anything. SSR was the biggest manufacturer of robots in the world. Their advertising claimed that each of their robots had the agility of a surfer and the loyalty of a samurai. In my experience, it was true. Unthinking manufactured loyalty was one of the things that had finally tripped up Heavenly, the daughter of Knighten Daise, the man who owned SSR.

Surf-bots designed by SSR were slick, muscular things that had a rakish grace designed into them. The robots driving the machines approaching now were big, industrial jobbers with arms like pistons and heads like toasters. They looked about right for this gig.

"All right, folks, back off, back off," said Robinson. This time he had help from the slow advance of the big machines, and everybody cooperated. Cliffy and Robinson got into their car, and looked about ready to leave.

"Howdy, boys," Bill said to the work-bots.

The work-bots were not quick, but I guess they were programmed to have some basic social skills because they waved hands the size of garbage-can lids and grunted, "Howdy," back to him without being very excited about the introduction. After that, Bill watched them closely as they worked, but didn't try communicating again.

Under the tweedy guy's direction, a bulldozer tried to dig deep enough to get under the hat. The bulldozer's engine made a lot of very impressive, powerful growls, but the blade kept slipping. Evidently the big robot driving the rig had the same problem Thumper and Mustard had had earlier. The force wall seemed to go to the center of the earth. Then a crane, shrieking laboriously, tried to lift the hat, but there was nothing to hook onto or to catch a rope around.

Under the tweedy guy's direction, the robots tried a few more things, none of them very successful. After a while, the uniformed cop drove Cliffy and Robinson back the way they'd come, leaving long, delicate waffle tracks in the sand.

The tweedy guy talked things over with the work-bots, which must have been like talking things over with your refrigerator. People straggled away. Pretty soon, I straggled away myself.

4

A Fist Full of Rabbit

The house smelled funny when I walked into the kitchen. The stench was subtle enough at the moment, but I had the feeling that under the right conditions, it could grow to be a ripe old monster, with fangs and particularly with hair. It was an acrid odor that reminded me in an unpleasant way of the laboratory where Heavenly Daise kept her experimental animals.

In the living room, somebody was singing a simple melody over and over again. But he was singing it fast and breathlessly, singing it as if it mattered. Down at the beach's high tide line, optimistic heavy machinery was making monster noises from the dawn of time.

I took a step forward and stopped when a small furry creature with long ears hopped into the kitchen. When it saw me, its nose twitched in a provocative T'toomian way. Instinctively, I twitched back till I caught myself. The creature might have been molded from one of the clouds outside.

"What's that?" I said.

"It's a rabbit, doc," Bill said.

"What's it doing here?" The question took on new meaning when another rabbit joined the first, this one having brown spots. The two rabbits took slow, ungainly hops across the kitchen toward us. One of them stopped and left a deposit on the kitchen floor. What it left behind looked like boxed breakfast food, but it smelled the way the house now smelled.

In the living room, rabbits in assorted colors were everywhere. Great shoals of them covered the floor. A line of them was sitting on the back of the couch and another was on the mantle of the fireplace. A couple were even *in* the fireplace. Every one was twitching its nose. A few of them were gnawing on a sandwich that had been on the floor since before I'd returned from T'toom. Another one was working on some flowers that Hanger and Flopsie (or was it Mopsie?) had been nurturing on the window sill.

The surfers were sitting on the couch, watching Captain Hook with various levels of interest. As the captain sang the little song with enthusiasm, he threw a scarf over his palm, and a moment later, a long, slender shape grew under it. He pulled the scarf away. The big surprise was that under the scarf was not a rabbit but a flower on a long stem. With a theatrical flourish, he handed the flower to either Flopsie or Mopsie. Whoever it was giggled and took it.

As Captain Hook started another trick, Whipper Will said, "What's happening, dude?"

"Shouldn't that be 'what's up, doc?'" Bill said, and yocked as if that were funny.

A smile passed over Whipper Will's face like the shadow of clouds over water.

I said, "Los Angeles must have giant hats wash up on the beach all the time. This one brings out one squad car with a couple of clowns who'd make out parking tickets in

crayon, one half-bright scientist with a trunk
full of stuff out of a horror movie that told him
nothing a guy with two eyes and a brain didn't
already know, and a gang of tough bots from
the pothole brigade.''

Captain Hook lowered the sheet of newspaper that he'd begun to tear and listened to me.
But his hands kept moving as if they were all
grown up and had lives of their own. While we
talked, he walked dreamily around the room
and the hands kept dipping into things—his
pockets, the flower pot on the window sill, paper bags, coffee cups, shoes—and every time
one of them came up, it was full of rabbit. It
was some trick, really, but it got old fast.

Will took a rabbit away from Captain Hook
and found a place for it on top of the television. He said, ''The big hat is just too weird for
words—straight out of the Twilight Zone, dig?
Nobody wants to look like a lop if this is just
a publicity stunt or something—they could get
really dogged. So the big kahunas downtown
are just hanging loose and cruising. They'd
probably get more cranked about it if hats *did*
wash up on the beach every day.''

Captain Hook snapped his fingers and said
brightly, ''You know what I really need? I really need a tuxedo. And some doves, and rope,
and a set of linking rings, and a deck of cards,
and a little carrot guillotine.'' He held up his
hands to show how big—not very. ''I have to
make a list.'' He walked toward the kitchen.

Bingo said, ''Now I know he's really drilled.
Captain Hook never made a list of anything in
his life.'' The other surfers agreed.

''Come on,'' I said and pulled Whipper Will
out to the kitchen. Bill followed us and hopped
up onto a chair next to where Captain Hook
was sitting at the table licking the tip of a pencil. He'd put out a bunch of carrots, and the
three rabbits on the table were making loud

crunching sounds as they consumed them. Bill began to pet the rabbits, giving them each a turn.

Out the window, I could see that the work-bots had set up a barrier of yellow sawhorses to keep back the crowd. The machinery hadn't had any noticeable effect on the hat, but progress had been made. The tweedy guy had taken off his coat.

I slid into a chair on the other side of the captain and said, "How you feeling, dude?"

He got very haughty all of a sudden and said, "I ain't no dude. I am the Great Hookini."

Will and I glanced at each other. Will shrugged and did not look hopeful. I said, "How do you feel, Hookini?"

"With my hands, of course."

The bottom dropped out of any optimism I might have been feeling. If I was going to get old jokes instead of straight answers, things were even worse than Bingo suspected. Even worse than I suspected, and what I suspected was plenty bad enough.

Then Captain Hook—the Great Hookini—laughed and clapped his hand on my shoulder and said, "Pretty good, huh?"

Will and I smiled at him like idiots. Bill actually laughed.

Going by what had happened to Captain Hook, that force wall was not just a barrier, it was a sophisticated weapon. It not only put your enemies on ice, it also demoralized them by making them look silly. Darn clever. People that clever didn't just wash up here in Malibu by accident. I didn't, and I'm not half that clever.

"I feel great," said the captain. "Really fine." Suddenly he didn't sound sure. He looked at his half-finished list.

"You'd rather do magic than surf?" I said.

"Sure. Who wouldn't?"

"Cowabunga," Whipper Will commented. He looked at me accusingly and said, "What do you know about all this?"

"Just what's out there on the sand."

"Fer sher. No top hats in Bay City."

Will was in a tough spot. One of his people was hurting bad, and from his point of view, another one of his people wasn't helping very much. I said, "Look, Will. Think what you want to about my coming from Bay City, but believe this: If I could help the captain, I would."

Will looked at the table and made patterns with his finger. "I know. Sorry."

I went on, "But just because I don't know, doesn't mean I can't find out. I'm a detective, remember."

Will looked me square in the face and said, "I was wondering when we'd get around to that." He smiled as if what he'd said was funny.

"I cracked the Heavenly Daise case. Got that motorcycle gang off the beach too."

"Hang easy, dude. Don't get dissed. I was just waiting for you to offer."

"Consider it done."

"Then consider yourself hired."

We shook hands, a thing that still didn't make any sense to me but seemed to inspire a lot of confidence in Earthpeople.

"I like being a magician," said Captain Hook. "I really do."

Whipper Will nodded and said, "While you're out detecting, I'll try a little of the home remedy—genuinely gnarly amounts of yoyogurt." He leaned back, opened the refrigerator and pulled out a bowl full of creamy light brown stuff. "Oat-bran flavor." He set the oat bran flavor yoyogurt and a spoon down next to Captain Hook's list. "Try some of this," Will said.

"What is it?" said Captain Hook.

"It's yoyogurt. It'll make you feel bitchen."

"Bitchen? I already feel good."

"Bitchen is better."

What Whipper Will was telling the captain might even have been true. Yoyogurt was Will's own special yogurt made only in Malibu by hard-working bacteria like none other anywhere. The couple of times I'd tried it, the world got tied up in pretty rainbows that made everything fine. I liked the feeling for a while, but soon my brain got homesick for some thoughts.

As Captain Hook took his first spoon of yoyogurt, I gestured to Bill and he toddled after me into the living room. "Well?" Bingo said.

"I'm on the case," I said.

"Case?" Thumper said.

"You know. Trouble is his business." Bill yocked then, which kind of undercut the dignified effect I was trying to achieve.

5

Phantom Phone Calls
at the Malibu Bar and No-Grill

"Trouble is his business," Mustard mumbled from his place on the floor. "Business is his trouble. He's troubled by all this magic business."

"From the mouths of surfers," I said and walked out the door with Bill in my wake.

Pacific Coast Highway had come back to life with the appearance of the sun. People in beach clothes walked up and down, some of them followed at a respectful distance by robots carrying surfboards. Across the busy street, a line of shops sold anything a person at loose ends might need. Fried chicken, T-shirts, sunscreen, all the necessities. Everything but a clue. Any idea I had about where to start looking for a cure for what ailed Captain Hook was so vaporous it passed like the body odor of a ghost of an idea and didn't leave even the ghost of a calling card.

Bill and I walked for a while, taking the air, enjoying both the hustle and the bustle. The smell of hot grease coiled around my nose, and I was suddenly hungry. We didn't have hot grease on T'toom, and I didn't have any natural resistance to this kind of thing. I stopped at a counter that had "Arturo's World of Burgers" spray-painted on the wall over it and had one with everything. Bill wanted one, too, but I didn't see any point in spending the money. I turned away from Arturo's World of Burgers and almost ran into a ratty-looking guy with mud-colored hair down in his eyes. "Spare change?" he said.

"No such thing," I said and was going to give him a quarter and keep moving when an idea hit me with almost physical force. "Let's talk," I said and grabbed his thin arm with the hand that wasn't holding the loaded burger.

"No kinky sex," the guy said.

"Suits me," I said, which seemed to confuse him. I shoved the burger into his hands, and he looked at it with disbelief.

"No kinky sex. No drugs."

"Will you stop that and sit down?" I sat down on the brick wall dividing the walkway from the sand. Bill sat on one side of me, and this ratty guy sat on the other.

I don't know if there was a clean spot on him anywhere. He'd been walking on his cuffs for a long time, which was better than nothing, I guess, because his great knobby feet weren't wearing any shoes.

He inhaled the burger and licked his fingers. I guessed he was ready to listen now and said, "You sleep on the beach?"

"I told you. No kink—"

"You wouldn't believe how uninterested I am in kinky sex. You sleep on the beach?"

"Sometimes," the guy said, looking at me from the tip of his eye. He was mighty cagey. Yes, sir.

"You know about the big top hat?"

"I seen it," he said hurriedly, "but I didn't have nothing to do with it."

"Did you see it get washed up?"

He thought for a moment, and then said, "It didn't get washed up. It landed."

"Ah," I said. Bill said it, too.

"You see anybody get out of it?"

A little more confident now, the guy said, "How about a drink? All this talking's making me kinda dry."

"Drink?"

"I know a little place."

"Brewski," Bill said.

"Of course. I'll bet you know a place. OK," I said.

He loped off, kind of hitching himself forward with each step. Bill and I caught up with him, and the three of us walked along the walkway gathering stares, throwing the little ones back.

There were a lot more burger joints on the strand, but I didn't stop at any of them. Pizza also no longer interested me. I also didn't stop to buy a T-shirt, a pair of sunglasses or something being sold by a guy in a gray business suit who was attracting a lot of attention from a rowdy element. He watched coolly while two enormous women wearing very little but their personalities—a mistake, trust me—gyrated slowly to rhythmic music that blared from a pair of small speakers. Was he selling music? Gray suits? Kinky sex? I never did find out, but business was brisk.

When the music had faded in the background and I could hear myself think again, I said, "What's your name?"

The guy looked at me fearfully. "What's it to you?" he said and glanced at a hot blonde who was posing for an old guy who made his living drawing portraits in chalk. The blonde's over-muscled escort watched, seeming as proud as if he were doing the work himself.

I said, "Just taking an interest in the guy who

ate my burger and who soon will be drinking my brewski."

"Brewski?" the guy chirped.

"Forget it. What's your name?"

He still thought about the question, and I could see thinking wasn't easy for him. He said, "My friends call me Dweeb."

"You have friends?" Bill said.

"Mouthy robot, ain't it?" Dweeb said.

"We're sending him to obedience school. Where's this bar? I have a lot of bums to interview today."

"You shouldn't oughta call me a bum. It hurts my self-esteem. Besides, you're not even a real guy."

"You know about toxic waste?"

"Sure. The bay's full of it."

"I had problems with it myself."

"Gee, I'm sorry." He really looked sorry.

"That's OK. Where's that bar?"

Dweeb gave me a two-finger salute and loped faster. He looked back once to make sure Bill and I were following. We were.

I guess they knew him at the Malibu Bar and No-Grill, because when the bartender saw him, he ordered Dweeb to get out in a voice used to giving orders.

For a moment, Dweeb stood just inside the greasy black curtain that protected the bar from the outside world and let his eyes adjust. He whined, "No, wait, Charlie. My friend here has money." He walked across the dim room to the bar, knocking into only three or four tables as he went.

If it hadn't been for the despondent residual smell of cigarettes that had been smoked before Gino and Darlene made their first movie, you almost could have swallowed the thick odor of ancient brewski that filled the place. It was a free drink, but my nose didn't enjoy it.

On the wall opposite the bar was a painting of a woman surfing. She wasn't wearing any clothes, but a lot of convenient foam and spray. It wasn't a very good painting, but then, I suppose it didn't have to be. Under it was the legend, SURF NAKED. Signs stood on the molding that ran around the room halfway up the wall. One said, ABSOLUTELY *NO* SPITTING. Other signs suggested we not fight or bother the other customers or ask for credit. There were *a lot* of signs suggesting we not ask for credit. Charlie must have gotten a terrific crowd at the Malibu Bar and No-Grill.

Charlie stood behind the bar with his hands flat on it, not very happy to be watching us enter his establishment. He was a big guy with a previously broken face. His black butterfly of a bowtie was a little askew and looked lonely and small and sorry it had landed on the white expanse of his massive chest. "Just don't bother my customers," Charlie said in a voice a little kid might use to protect his pet frog.

The Malibu Bar and No-Grill didn't have many customers at the moment, and all of them sat at the bar. An old geezer not much more prosperous than Dweeb studied us with the mild eyes of a herd animal and attempted a smile. A fat guy didn't turn around. In his white suit, he looked like a giant marshmallow. Farther along the bar, where it was too murky to see who owned them, hands moved glasses of beer.

Game for anything, Bill hopped onto a stool. I stood on the brass rail and said, "Beer, please."

The old geezer and the fat man in the white suit were watching. The fat man in the white suit was not really a man at all, but a Surfing Samurai Robot. He had a chiseled artificial face that was all planes and angles. In that light—no better than the quality of the clientele—it seemed to be silver. Across his fore-head, just about where his white hat crossed it, was one of those samurai headbands. He had a glass in front of him, but I had no idea what he might have been drinking from it.

Charlie glared at me as if I'd asked for credit. "You got any ID?"

"ID?" I said.

He shook his head. "Identification." His hands never moved.

"Surely that isn't necessary," the fat man said in a low, gruff voice, full of sin and badly kept secrets.

"Surely you can butt the hell out," said Charlie without even looking at him.

I took my temporary driver's license from my wallet and laid it down on the sticky bar. Charlie looked at it without picking it up. "This thing don't have your picture on it. It could be anybody's."

"Look," I said, "if I promise not to drink any of it, will you give Dweeb here a drink?" I took the license back and set down a dollar bill. It must have been enough, because Charlie actually moved. He took the dollar and replaced it with an open bottle of beer and a glass. Dweeb reached for it hungrily and began to carry it away.

"You'll drink it here with these nice folks," I said. I wanted everybody to hear our conversation. You never knew when somebody might have something to contribute.

Dweeb moved his fingers nervously, then put the beer and the glass down again. With a shaking hand, he poured the beer, not getting much of it on the bar. Charlie moved slowly to mop it up and slide a paper coaster under the glass. It said, SURF NAKED, and had a picture of the woman on the wall.

While I let Dweeb take a long sip of his brewski, a young man emerged from the gloom at the end of the bar, walking toward me splay-footed as if he expected me to hand him a diploma. He managed to look thin and soft at the same time, and his skin was the unhealthy color of mushrooms. Hair as gloomy as the shadows he'd emerged from hung in strings to his shoulders. The clothes he wore were neither clean nor new, but very neat, as if he'd ironed his shirt and pants without washing them first. The brown tie that hung around his neck like a flat wrinkled worm—the color hiding who knew how many terrible stains?—was tacked to his shirt with a tiny pearl sitting on a golden tripod. The tiepin was the only bright spot on him.

"Excuse me, sir?" he said, piping like the upper registers of an organ.

"Sure," I said.

He shuffled his feet for a moment and then went on. "I was just admiring your necklace."

"Oh?" I'd forgotten I was wearing it. I resisted touching it now.

Dweeb put down his beer and said, "Nix. These guys are all over the place. Everywhere you go, one of these Medium Rare freaks wants to buy your spine necklace."

"Why is that?" I said to the freak.

The freak didn't say anything but pulled a folded sheet of pink paper from a pocket. I unfolded it. It was some kind of flyer advertising spiritual advice. At the top it said, HAPPY DAY! MEDIUM RARE LOVES YOU!

"Does this mean anything?" I said.

"I let Medium Rare into my life. She asks so little from each of us, yet gives so much."

"How much does she give for this necklace?"

"A free reading when you come to her retreat in Changehorses."

"Reading?"

"Your fortune."

Bill laughed.

I said, "I know what my fortune is. Trouble is my business. No sale."

Charlie growled, "Get out of here before I throw you out." He took the flyer from my hand, ostentatiously balled it up, and dropped it behind the bar.

"Medium Rare loves you," the freak said and scrammed.

The door curtain fell back into place, and I looked at Dweeb. "You were saying?" I said.

"Huh?" When Dweeb put down the glass, there was foam on his upper lip.

"About the passengers who were on the hat. The hat on the beach. You remember the hat on the beach?"

The geezer apparently couldn't follow the ins and outs of our conversation because he hummed a little tune over and over to himself as he stared at the dusty bottles behind the bar and sipped his beer with a small lapping sound. Charlie was rinsing out his gray rag. The fat robot was watching me as if I were a puzzle box he was trying to figure out. Down at the dark end of the bar, beer glasses rose and fell, making cozy thumping sounds as each touched the bar in its turn.

"I remember. I was just gathering my thoughts."

I had something clever to say, but it didn't seem to be worth the trouble. I just waited. We all did. The only sound in the place was the slow whish-whish of the big fans turning in the ceiling.

"Thoughts all in place?" I said.

"Yeah." Dweeb looked worried. He'd always look worried, even if he was just talking about the weather. He said, "The two that got off the hat were kind of Oriental types. Slanty eyes, big, wide faces, you know."

"I know." I'd seen a Charlie Chan movie

once. It didn't make me an expert, but it would have to do. "Did you see them get off the hat?"

"I didn't see them getting off, exactly, but near enough. They walked right by it as if they saw giant hats on the beach every day. Is that natural?"

"I guess not. What else?"

"One of 'em was a good-looking babe with long blond hair. The other was a guy with short hair like a brush."

For some reason, our conversation seemed to be making Charlie the Bartender nervous. His fingers drummed the bar, which for him was almost a screaming fit.

The fat robot said, "Excuse me, but I couldn't help overhearing. I've never encountered a blond Oriental." A guy like that would say excuse me when he slid the knife between your ribs.

Dweeb shook his head and said, "Yeah. That's funny, isn't it?"

"I seen one. Real recent, too." I looked around in surprise. The geezer who I thought was asleep had spoken. His voice had been used hard all its life. It was just tin cans kicked down a gutter, but it was more intelligent than I would have expected. Charlie was wiping down the bar as if he wanted to buff a hole through it.

"Yep," the geezer said, still looking at the dusty bottles. "I was down at the Sparkle Room relieving a powerful thirst when these two came in."

"How were they dressed?" I said.

"Casual. Like a couple of tourists back from the islands."

"That's them," Dweeb said.

Charlie burned him with a look.

"Anyway, they come into the Sparkle Room, the woman in particular getting a lot of attention. They asked the bartender-bot for the

phone number of a taxi service. They talked
pretty." He smiled, savoring it. He savored it
long enough that I thought maybe he'd fallen
asleep. Charlie was leaning down at the curve
in the bar, drumming his fingers again, watching us as if we were cockroaches.

The geezer shook himself and said, "Well,
that bot mixes a hell of a drink, but he don't
talk much. He just pointed at the books hanging by the phones back near the johns. We all
kind of watched these two when we weren't
watching nothing else. I saw them look up a
number, but I never seen them use a phone.
Nobody around me saw them use a phone.
When it was all over, I checked."

"OK," I said. "Nobody saw them use the
phone. Make something out of it."

'OK, buster. You asked for it. A few seconds
after these two don't use the phone, a big black
guy with a mustache you could hang birdcages
from and wearing a Big Orange Taxi Service
cap comes in looking a little confused, wanting
to know if anybody had called for a cab."

He waited for applause. He didn't get it, but
he had everybody's attention. He finished, "So
these two Oriental types walk out with the cab-
bie just as casual." He shook his head.

"You expect us to believe that?" Charlie said
from his station at the turn in the bar.

"God's truth," the geezer said, making an X
over his heart with a finger.

"You guys give me a pain. First that Rare
freak, and now you guys with your blond
gooks and your giant hats and your phantom
phone calls." He didn't seem to move, but a
second later he smacked something down on
the bar.

Everybody but me jumped. I had only the
vaguest idea what the thing was, but no one
else seemed to be in doubt. The customers at
his end of the bar sort of began to drift away.

Charlie gripped the thing as it lay on the bar, smooth and deadly—a weapon of some kind but too long even for Charlie to carry in a pocket. Charlie glared at me, almost smiling. Then the smile was gone, and he was looking at Dweeb hard enough to push him over. "You get out of here. And take your friends with you."

"I'm a customer," Dweeb said, showing more crust than I would have suspected he had.

Charlie hooked his thumb over his shoulder at a sign that said, WE RESERVE THE RIGHT TO REFUSE SERVICE TO ANYONE. He slid a dollar across the bar and shouted, "Get out." Dweeb grabbed the dollar and ran. Charlie gave another dollar to the geezer. The geezer mumbled, "There are other bars in this town. Guy knows when he's not wanted." He climbed from his stool and followed Dweeb out.

"Yeah," I said. "This is a classier establishment already, now they're gone. I can feel it. I'll recommend this place to my friends." I grabbed Bill around the neck and walked out dangling him. When we got outside, I put him down and he kind of straightened his beak. The geezer was gone, along with Dweeb and my dollar. That was OK. I'd gotten my money's worth.

Bill and I walked back the way we'd come. Quietly, I said, "What was that thing?"

"What thing?"

"The thing on the bar everybody seemed so afraid of."

"Sawed-off shotgun."

"Sawed off from what?"

"Haw!" said Bill, giving me another sample from his menagerie of laughs.

"Haw," I said. I suddenly felt dirty, just having been inside the Malibu Bar and No-Grill. I probably wouldn't have liked the place any better when it had been Surf Naked. "Let's get out of here," I said and walked faster.

The sun was sliding slowly toward the far edge of the Pacific, turning the few clouds a pink I'd never seen on a T-shirt. The crowds on the walkway thinned as the air cooled. I couldn't get the geezer's story out of my head. Somehow it fit with Captain Hook's problem and with the top hat itself. Those two Orientals were worth a closer look, if only because of that. But there was more to the story. Orientals, blond or not, don't just climb out of hats unless they have a reason. It might all just be innocent good fun, but I doubted it.

On a hunch, I stopped to look in the window of a place selling little animals made out of seashells glued together. Not far away, a big robot in a white suit was looking in a window, too.

I said, "Somebody's following us. Any ideas?"

"Better scheming through electronics," Bill said and laughed as he waddled off.

6

Progress Happens

I stopped once or twice to see if maybe the robot in the white suit had given up. But no, he was determined to make more work for us, and that's what he did. Bill strolled off the walkway and into a parking lot the size of a small country, full of gleam and dazzle. It had been jammed earlier in the day, cars even parked in the lanes between rows, but now it was merely full, and growing emptier by the moment.

I followed Bill to the middle of the lot, where we looked as natural as a mustache on a chorus girl. An aisle away, the fat bot pretended to unlock a car door. He took a lot of trouble with the door, but it wouldn't open for him in a million years, not with that house key he was using. Every once in a while, he glanced at us and began with the door again.

"Are we going to wait for the real owner of that car to show up?" I said.

"That's entertainment," Bill said. A flat, circular antenna rose from the top of his beak. As it clicked into place, a lot of excitement began all around us at once.

On every car I could see, and I could see plenty, headlights came on and glowed, making no more distance against the late afternoon sunshine than candle flames. They stayed on while windshield wipers started squeaking across dry glass like old men rubbing their eyes. But what really attracted everybody's attention were the radios and the horns. Frantic DJs tossed the time, weather and stereo ads into the hard, cloudless sky. Over that, rock 'n' roll fought with the tinkle of piano sonatas. And over it all, repeated in car after car, blared the mating call of the irate motorist. All together, it was too loud to be merely noise, more like somebody rooting out my ears with a stick.

The fat bot looked in my direction as if I'd called his name. He frowned, a strange effect on that mechanical face, then made a move as if he wanted to walk toward me. But we were washed apart by crowds of people pouring off the beach, each of them pawing at their cars as if they were life preservers.

I grabbed Bill around the neck so as not to lose him in the crush and forced my way back to the walkway, bucking the crowd that was gathering to point, watch and laugh.

I put Bill down, and we walked away quickly, stopping only a few times to check for the bot in the white suit. Either all of a sudden he'd gotten a lot better at tailing, or Bill's trick had worked.

"Pretty good, huh?" Bill said every time I checked. The fifth or sixth time this happened, I said, "Good enough, but it gets a little old in reruns."

He blinked at me and said brightly, "Right, Boss."

By the time we got back to Whipper Will's house, the sidewalks were nearly empty. The bot would have had to be invisible or I'd have seen him. I didn't see him.

* * *

We let a couple of rabbits out the front door when Bill and I came in, but that didn't matter. The floor was covered with them. What wasn't rabbits was rabbit pellets. And what wasn't rabbit pellets was long-stemmed flowers. Captain Hook—the Great Hookini—had been busy while we were out.

The captain was all by himself—not counting the rabbits—glumly sitting on the couch in the living room with a big steel ring in each hand. The TV was not on, which was about as normal as the captain making lists. He tapped the rings, and suddenly they were hooked together. He spun the one that was hanging, and it made a noise like a softly ringing bell. Then, in a bored voice, he said, "Abracadabra," and pulled the rings apart. He looked at the rings as if he'd never seen them before and tapped them together again.

I said, "What's happening, Holmes?"

The captain studied the hanging ring as he spun it again. Without looking at me, he said, "People got no appreciation for magic. It's a beautiful art form."

"You've been performing all afternoon?" I said.

"I'm a magician," he said as if he wished he weren't.

"Where's everybody else?"

"Gone to a movie." He shrugged. "No accounting for taste."

Bill had picked up a rabbit and was stroking it. I said, "Anything in your bubble memory about the Big Orange Cab Company?"

"It has connections with organized crime."

"What is that, criminals with their own filing cabinets?"

Bill didn't laugh, so what I'd said must not have even remotely been a joke. Gamely, I went on, "I was thinking more of their phone number."

Bill gave me the number. I said, "Don't get rabbit fur in your machinery," and walked into the kitchen. Out the window over the sink, the top hat sat on the sand, surrounded by yellow sawhorses as if they were trying to get autographs. A convention of seagulls was being held on its top. The sun squatted on the horizon, lowering itself into the cold Pacific with all the care of an old woman entering a swimming pool. Still looking at the top hat, I dialed my number.

"Big Orange Cab Company. Will you hold?"

Before I could say anything, she was gone and I was listening to music that had no more character than a slice of white bread. It was polite music wearing polished shoes, mouse-gray gloves and a small, self-satisfied smile.

Before my brain had a chance to sit down to tea with that music, the girl came back, sounding a little harried, and said, "Big Orange Cab Company. May I help you?"

"My name is Zoot Marlowe. I'm a private detective, and I'm looking for one of your drivers."

"Why?"

"He picked up a couple last night. They might know something about a little problem my client is having."

"We don't give out that kind of information." She knew I wasn't a customer, and the tone of her voice let me know she knew.

"He's a big black guy with a mustache. Know him?"

"We have a lot of black drivers, and some of them have mustaches."

I said, "You know, you're cute when you're rude," and hung up. If it had been earlier in the day and I'd been thinking straight, I'd have been able to predict that conversation, down to the punctuation and my snappy retorts. Back in the living room, Captain Hook's hands were still linking and unlinking rings. The captain himself didn't seem to be much involved. Bill was watching the rings closely while he petted the rabbit. I said, "I'm going out. Don't let anything happen."

"Nothing happens. Right, Boss."

I had thought it would be months at least before I'd need my short johns again, but I got into them now. They were still a little damp and difficult to manage, but I got them on and walked out to the beach. A deep trench circled the hat, and some signs told people to stay away from it. Whether the police were afraid of somebody hurting the hat, or of the hat hurting someone, I didn't know. I hoped no one else had been turned into a magician. Malibu couldn't take any more rabbits, not without cracking off into the Pacific.

I plunged into the water and swam for my sneeve.

The water was cold, of course. And salty. And just for the record, it was wet too. When I got inside my sneeve, I felt disconnected from it, as if it were somebody else's apartment that I'd only seen pictures of. I dug around in the emergency gear, found what I wanted, and then stood in front of the screw, looking the place over, making sure I hadn't forgotten anything. I'd left a copy of *The Maltese Falcon* on the pilot's seat. Sam Spade stared at me from the cover. When he winked, I knew I'd been avoiding the swim back too long and went out into the water through the screw.

I changed out of the short johns and back into my brown suit just before the gang got home, eager to tell me about the monster picture they'd just seen. They were nice to Captain Hook, but nice the way they'd be to someone with a terrible disease. It's not really the guy's fault, but you still don't want to go near him.

"Enough magic is too much," Mustard said and sat down on the floor to roll dry grass into a line of his smoking umbrellas. One by one, he dropped them into a plastic bag as if they were shotgun shells and then put them into a pocket. Everybody else milled around. I think some of them changed clothes, but the difference was not apparent.

"Wanta go dancing, dude?" Whipper Will said.

"Not if you want to see progress on this case. Big day tomorrow."

"Progress?" Thumper said, sounding surprised.

"It happens," I said and shrugged.

Soon after, they all bubbled from the house. Some of them were carrying rabbits. "Everybody likes rabbits," Hanger said. She was carrying a black one like a baby.

"Better you than me."

"Huh?"

They left me alone with Bill and Captain Hook. It was so quiet, I could hear the surf banging its head against the shore. Bill was no problem. He hooked himself into the Rotwang 5000 and played with himself. I sat down in the living room with *Farewell, My Lovely*, but didn't get far with it because Captain Hook was full of, "Pick a card, any card." Eventually I took refuge in Will and Bingo's bedroom.

For a while, I was afraid that Captain Hook would follow me. Time drifted by and he didn't. Maybe he taught one of the rabbits how to pick a card. I was tempted to check, but I wasn't stupid enough to actually do it.

7

Bay City Manners

Whipper Will and the others came in late, still laughing and singing. When I cracked my eyes, I saw them doing little dance steps at each other. I waited them out, and soon it got quiet again.

When I woke up the next morning, they were still asleep. Whipper Will and Bingo were snoring romantically into each other's ears, and they didn't seem to be bothered by my getting dressed, eating, and sneaking out with Bill.

Sunshine had returned to Malibu and the Southland. Pacific Coast Highway was crowded, but I didn't mind. The streets were dry, the Belvedere had a full tank of gas, and I had a temporary driver's license. I drove along the coast, the water looking like wrinkled cellophane beyond the white sand.

It was a little early yet for the snowcone and sand-pail crowd, but a lot of supposed grown-ups were out there, getting tanned before the rush. A small black Toyota truck, with its cab raised so high the driver probably had a pilot's license, was in such a hurry that it kept forcing narrow escapes on other cars and attracting curses and horn blasts. Despite all the extra work it did, the truck got stopped one car ahead of me at the big light at Sunset Boulevard. That was the kind of joke traffic played on drivers, but a lot of them never got it until they *really* got it, knotting themselves around a light pole or, worse yet, taking somebody else with them. That was another joke traffic played on drivers.

I had fewer fancy wheels to worry about as I rolled through Santa Monica and into Culver City. It hadn't changed much since I'd been there last, and it wouldn't, not as long as landlords could rent storefronts without having to repaint them.

A few minutes later, I pulled up in front of a square, squat building with the words Acme Robot Company painted over the brown door. The place was a lot livelier than it had been when Surfing Samurai Robots had rolled over in its sleep onto their business. Trucks with the silly Acme logo—a robot with a hat like a funnel—rumbled self-importantly out of the paved yard and through the open front gates. Somewhere inside, machinery shrieked as it turned metal into robot parts.

One of the gates made the fourth wall of a cage for a skinny black dog that, at the moment, was very busy sleeping. As I got out of my car, the dog awoke, stretched, and barked at me. Bill and I looked at the dog. An Acme truck went by, not taking much of the dog's attention.

"That's Benny," I said. "Any minute now, he'll do his trick for you."

"He pulls rabbits from hats?" Bill said.

"Watch."

A second later, Benny got tired of barking

and sat down to have a good scratch. Bill didn't say anything, so I said, "That's it."

Bill laughed, but he always did that. We went into the small building through the brown door.

The dimness and smell of age were familiar, but at the desk where Mr. Harold Chesnik had given me the address of Surfing Samurai Robots sat a tall, thin woman with a long, sharp nose—not quite a Toomler nose, but close. Her bony fingers moved quickly over the keys of an old mechanical adding machine. She pulled the lever and tore off the tape.

She glanced at me and said, "May I help you?" as if she'd memorized the sounds but the words had no meaning for her. The tape was what really interested her, but she took another look at me anyway. I was worth a look, I guess, if you hadn't seen me before.

"Mr. Chesnik here?" I said as I walked farther into the office. I'd checked the overstuffed leather chair where he usually slept, and nobody was in it.

Now I could see he was at the other desk, with one hand against his forehead and the other turning over sheets of paper. His face said that he wasn't happy with what the papers were telling him. Either that, or his stomach hurt. One knee was pistoning up and down a mile a minute. He wore the same heavy black framed glasses, and what could have been the same gray sweater, as the last time I'd seen him.

"Mr. Chesnik?" I said.

Mr. Chesnik looked up and smiled. He adjusted his glasses and cried, "Zoot! Marsha, this is the Zoot I was telling you about."

Marsha nodded as if she'd expected that, and in a voice as sharp as her nose, told me without convincing me that she was pleased to make my acquaintance. She watched me narrowly, as if she thought I might walk out with a chair under my coat.

Mr. Chesnik sighed and said, "You never call. You never write." He saw Bill then and waggled a finger at me. "You still owe me plenty for that robot." He chuckled, inviting me not to take his accusation too seriously.

"I need more," I said.

The chuckle disappeared down a drain, and Mr. Chesnik shook his head. "Bay City manners," he said. "How much?"

"A couple hundred bucks."

"And expenses?"

"Mostly for the office bourbon bottle."

He laughed easily, as if we weren't talking about money, and said, "So all right, already. You can still do the Chandler patter. That butters no parsnips with me."

"I have something you might want to buy."

"Like what?"

"Can we go somewhere and talk?"

Marsha reacted as if I'd slapped her in the face. She said, "Mr. Chesnik has no secrets from me."

"Bay City secrets," I said.

Mr. Chesnik ran his tongue over his lips and stood up. I still came up only to the middle button of his sweater. "Come on. We'll talk."

I followed him down a short hall, Bill clattering behind me. Through the wall, I could feel Marsha simmering slowly over low heat. We passed a bathroom that had seen a lot of use and a storage room full of boxes big enough to hold cockroaches from the bathroom—though there may not have been enough boxes.

At the other end of the hall was the garage, brighter now with a garage door open. The air compressor began to chug. An Oriental guy in gray work clothes was standing at a low rough table, banging on a piece of machinery with a big hammer. He stopped long enough to smile at us, then went back to work. He couldn't have been the Oriental guy I was looking for. Nobody could get that greasy since the night before.

Mr. Chesnik said, "Marsha wants to see you."

The Oriental guy nodded and put down the hammer before he walked back into the office. Mr. Chesnik took me to a corner of the garage and turned on a light hanging by a cord over a small workbench on which insect-like electronic parts were strewn. He sat down on a low, worn stool with a cracked leather seat that may once have been red.

"Nu?" he said.

"It'll be new to you," I said, hoping I didn't sound like the idiot I felt myself to be.

Mr. Chesnik laughed, but Bill didn't. Go figure. I said, "I need some money, about a hundred bucks, but I don't want a loan. I want you to buy something from me."

"I'm suspicious already. Go ahead."

From my coat pocket, I took the slaberingeo spine I'd gotten from my sneeve. I kept a hold on it so it wouldn't float to the ceiling. Bill watched Mr. Chesnik take it from me and study it as if it were a diamond. He let it pull his hand upward, where it bobbed like a sea gull on water. Except for the occasional truck going by, the garage was quiet. Marsha hadn't fired up her adding machine again. Maybe she was done adding. Maybe she and the Oriental guy had their ears to the wall with hope springing eternal.

"What is it?"

"Sort of a craft from the simple native artisans of Bay City."

"It could be that, I suppose. Why is it worth a hundred dollars? Money don't grow on trees—obviously not even in Bay City."

"I don't know. But a little bit of anti-gravity must have its uses."

Mr. Chesnik grunted and turned toward the bench. He took something from his pocket and unfolded it into a small, sharp knife that he used to hack off two bits of the spine. He put a bit into the heel of each of his shoes and stood up, a smile growing on his face, blossoming on his face, absolutely blooming on his face. "I'm dancing," he said and shuffled his feet about stiffly. I got the feeling that he didn't dance very often.

I said, "What do you say?"

"We could sell these. Call them Slice O' Heaven Shoe Pads."

"You know we can't. Not even if it were a good idea."

He kind of bounced on his heels, enjoying it. "OK, Zoot. The money is yours if you'll tell me more about this stuff."

"It don't grow on trees."

He considered that before he said, "I didn't know we got secrets between us."

"Do *you* tell *me* everything?"

Mr. Chesnik shrugged and turned the spine over and over in one hand.

I said, "I can tell you this: If you begin to have a run of bad luck, get rid of the spine. All of it. Even the bits in your shoes. What you'll be having is not bad luck, but statistical anomalies caused by an unbalanced spine."

"Statistical anomalies," he said, enjoying the way the words felt in his mouth. "You won't tell me any more?"

"No."

"I must be going soft in the head." He folded his knife, put it in a sweater pocket with the spine, and buttoned the pocket. On his way back to the office, he walked pretty light for a guy as old and tired as he had been a moment before.

As we got to the office, the Oriental guy came in the front door carrying three cups in a cardboard box. They smelled like coffee. Not good coffee, but even bad coffee smells pretty good. He put a cup in front of Marsha and another on Mr. Chesnik's desk. He and Marsha watched while Mr. Chesnik opened a heavy desk drawer with a key and took out a pile of bills. He counted one hundred fifty dollars into my outstretched palm, each one personally etched by the incredulous stares of Marsha and the Oriental guy.

I folded the money away, and Mr. Chesnik shook my hand as he wished me good luck. "Knowing you, you'll probably need it."

"Yeah. I'm always walking into a door or something."

Mr. Chesnik enjoyed that.

I nodded to Marsha and the Oriental guy. They were still using their mouths for flycatchers as Bill and I went out.

In the car I said, "The address of the Big Orange Taxi Company." Bill gave me an address downtown and then directions how to get there.

We were driving east on Adams Boulevard when he said, "I never saw anything like that spine before."

"You don't want to know what it is. Trust me."

"Sure. I'm built that way."

That's the main difference between a robot and a human.

8

Con Carney's Lucky Day

I took Adams downtown. Since it was the middle of the morning and not rush hour, the traffic was only hideous and not impossible.

We went north through a not-very-exclusive residential area with houses that looked as if they'd been blown there by the wind but had probably been there for years. Pale paint was flaked and patchy, as if the houses had the mange. Lawns were thin and yellow, and the few stunted trees looked not very happy to be there. A lot of wild kids were running around the streets, and clumps of discontented adults gathered on corners drinking from brown paper bags, smoking cigarettes and talking.

Then the houses were behind us, and we were gliding past warehouses decorated with graffiti and marred by broken windows. The warehouses farther on were in better condition and belonged to people who told you all about it with big signs painted in bold, manly letters.

Traffic thickened up again, and Bill told me to turn onto a side street, where there was a garage with an open door not quite as wide as the Santa Monica Freeway.

I drove into the cool, dim building and parked in an empty space near a vest-pocket office that was tacked onto a side wall like an afterthought. Outside it were three blocky chairs with chipping hide, held together by curved metal tubes and good intentions.

Through the glass walls of the office, I could see two women and a man. One of the women was talking into a microphone that rested on a little table pushed against the wall, and the other was at a desk, laboring over some complicated forms. The guy was leaning back in his chair, looking lazily through cigarette smoke, memorizing the cracked yellow ceiling. I wouldn't like the cigarette smoke. I never did.

The garage was full of pale green taxis, each with the words BIG ORANGE TAXI COMPANY on the side. Bill and I got out of the Belvedere and slammed our doors. Each slam made a big boom in the vast place. Anything that moved would make a big echo in a place like that. There was the same smell of ancient grease as filled the garage at the Acme Robot Company.

Bill and I went into the office. No friendly bell tinkled. We stood on our side of a beat-up counter and waited for somebody to notice us.

The woman at the microphone was small and slim, and had short dark hair. She whispered into the microphone and kept notes. I cleared my throat, and the woman at the desk glanced at me as if I were a window shade moving in the breeze, just something that distracted her now and then. The guy never moved. He was settled into his chair like a lump of clay. His round, fleshy head was nearly bald, but where I could see them below the rolled-up sleeves of a glaringly white shirt, his arms looked as if they were covered in black carpeting. I had been right about not liking the cigarette smoke.

"Excuse me," I said.

The woman at the desk dropped her pencil and said, "May I help you?" It was the same voice I'd heard on the telephone.

"I'm a little embarrassed, actually. One of your drivers was nicer to me than he had to be, and I'd like to thank him. But I don't know his name."

The guy at the back desk said, "Why didn't you thank him at the time?" He never looked at me. Maybe he wasn't memorizing the ceiling, but the cigarette smoke. It would be a big job.

"I was," I laughed nervously, "not quite myself when he picked me up."

"Are you quite yourself now?"

Bill said, "Yock!"

"Look: all I remember was that I was at the Sparkle Room in Malibu and I needed a ride home because I wasn't quite as sober as I had been when I walked in. A taxi took me home. It was driven by a big black guy with a mustache like a pair of buggy whips." I'd seen buggy whips in westerns. You can learn a lot from TV. "I have a couple of bucks here that belong to him."

"Sounds like Con's lucky day," the woman at the desk said.

"Yeah." The man leaned forward in his chair and his feet loudly struck the floor. "Just leave the money, sir. We'll see that he gets it."

"I'd like to give it to him myself. More personal that way."

The guy frowned and moved his lips in and out. "There seems to be a distinct lack of trust in the air," he said.

"How can you tell with all the cigarette smoke?" The man glared at me, but the trick at the microphone shot a warm smile in my direction. The man said, "You got your damn nerve sticking your nose in here and making judgements."

"Nose," the woman at the desk said, chuckling.

"Look. I don't care what you smoke. What has that got to do with trust anyway?" I tried to make it sound as if I didn't suspect Con would never see anything I gave this guy.

"OK," the guy said. He leaned back in his chair and said, "Be smart. It ain't Con's shift, and he don't live so close. It'll take a while for him to get here."

"When's my next appointment?" I said to Bill.

"Appointment?" Bill said.

I told the man, "I guess I'm open for the next few hours."

The woman said, "Actually, Con's here. He came in early today." That was clever enough to make her laugh.

"Sure," the man said. "I forgot."

"So do we whistle or rub a lamp or what?"

"Call him, Dinah," the man said.

Dinah flicked a switch on her microphone and spoke softly into it. Outside the office, her voice boomed, "Con Carney to the office. Con Carney to the office, please."

I nodded. Nothing happened. The guy blew a long lungful of flannel into the air. Nothing happened some more. Nobody even looked in my direction. It was quiet in that office. The woman at the desk jumped and put her hand to her throat when I said, "There's something about your company I don't understand."

The guy had gone back to holding up the ceiling with his gaze, but the woman at the desk said "What's that?"

"Shouldn't all the taxis run by the Big Orange Taxi Company be orange instead of green?"

The guy laughed as if he were clearing his

throat and actually looked at me again. The ceiling didn't fall down.

The woman behind the desk smiled. At last she was enjoying something. She said, "It's not orange like the color. It's orange like the fruit. You know, sometimes L.A. is called the Big Orange." She must have noticed the stupefied expression on my face because she went on, "You know. Like some people call New York the Big Apple?"

The guy said, "Where you from, you never heard of the Big Apple?"

"Bay City."

"Oh?" said the guy. "I'd have guessed farther than that."

"You'd guess wrong. My little problem with toxic waste and nose drops always throws people off. I win a lot of bar bets. Where is this Con?"

"He'll be along. If you and your bot waited outside, people could get their work done."

"Sure. You probably have another pack of cigarettes to go through before quitting time."

His glare pushed me and Bill out of the glassed-in office. Bill plopped himself down on one of the ancient chairs, and I settled beside him. They were as comfortable as a couple of sacks of cement. I asked Bill about this fruit business and he tried to explain it to me, but one of us was too dumb. I ended up saying, "You might as well call Malibu the Big Yoyogurt."

We watched Big Orange taxis go in and out. Somewhere in the garage, somebody was running machinery that sounded like animals fighting and dying. Not more than ten minutes later, a sturdy-looking black guy walked up from the back of the garage. He was wearing a Dodgers T-shirt and cap, jeans, and some ancient shoes held together by their scuff marks. He was no bigger than the guy in the office, but his muscles had actually seen some use. He had a wide, intelligent face and hair cropped so close that it looked like a pattern of iron fillings. Under his flat nose was the famous mustache. It was even bigger than I'd imagined it, and curled at the ends like loose springs. He could have been the guy I was looking for.

Bill and I stood up, and he said, "You the guy looking for me?" You could polish your car with that voice.

"That's me."

"Do I know you?" He didn't seem inclined to shake hands. The three people in the office were watching us as if we were taking off our clothes.

"People always ask me that. I have one of the eleven average faces."

He laughed as if he meant it. "Sez you. With that beezer I'd remember." He suddenly looked grim. "And I don't."

"I guess you would at that. I was never in your taxi, but I need some information."

"Phyllis said you'd make it worth my while."

"Trust Phyllis."

He studied me, not hiding it. Something happened behind his eyes, and he suddenly became as cagey as three kids dividing a candy bar.

I said, "I'm looking for the driver who picked up a pair of Oriental tourists from the Sparkle Room in Malibu last night."

"What's the beef?"

"No beef. No chicken, either. Just information."

"Are you for real?"

"Sure. Want me to pinch you?"

I surprised him with that, but he took it well. He said, "We could dance like this all afternoon. What do you want to know?"

"Where did you take them after you left the Sparkle Room?"

"That stuff's confidential."

From my pocket I took the money Mr. Chesnik had given me and counted off fifty.

"I could lose my job."

"Not if you keep your mouth shut. They think I'm paying you off for good service."

Carney thought about that for a moment and then said, "I took them to a place over on the west side called Kilroy's." He frowned as he took the fifty and made it disappear. He said, "You know anything about them?"

"Not much."

"Nobody called me but I knew they wanted a cab. It was like ESP or something."

"ESP?"

"Extrasensory perception," Bill said. "Mind reading."

Top hats. Mind reading. What next? I said, "I guess the other guy didn't know much about them either."

He jumped as if I'd jabbed him with a fork. "What other guy?"

"The guy who got you to come down here early in the first place. The girl in the office said this was your lucky day."

Carney grinned. "OK. So you're good. Maybe you're very good. But you still got taken. I told the big robot in the white suit about Kilroy's for twenty-five."

"*You* got taken. The information's worth fifty."

"I wish I'd known that earlier," Carney said and shook his head. "Need a ride to Kilroy's?"

"No thanks. My car's out in front."

We shook hands. He even shook hands with Bill. Bill liked doing it, and after a while, Carney had to kind of like unwrap his hand from Bill's grip.

When we got into the Belvedere, I said to Bill, "Do I have to tell you where we're going or do you want to guess?"

9

Blowfish Spines of the Gods?!

I took the Santa Monica Freeway west and got off at Overland. From there, I took Pico under the San Diego Freeway to where a lot of men in work clothes were standing more or less in a line up and down the block. While they sucked on cardboard cups of coffee, they casually watched a few others climb into the back of a dull green pickup truck already too full of picks and shovels. I passed some restaurants—each of them "world famous"—and a low, square building surrounded by a forest of potted plants.

Then, at the corner of a funny, three-legged intersection, I saw Kilroy's for the first time. It was a rambling place that looked as if it were made of a lot of small buildings shoved together without anyone being too careful how well they matched. Among them, raised like a defiant finger, was a lighthouse. The walls were mostly an off-white, except where they had been painted with scenes of thick brown guys surfing, and chunky brown girls who each had one hip cocked high enough to sit on. The guys had towels wrapped around them, and the girls wore grass skirts and knots of color over their boobs. The pictures had been splashed on with more enthusiasm than skill and were not much gaudier than a birthday cake. The sign out front said Kilroy's was world famous for its drinks and its Hawaiian barbecue.

I parked out back in the lot where there were only three other cars. Bill and I followed arrows painted on the walls to the front door. Inside, it was cool as clean sheets and smelled of liquor and fruit. More fruit. I think it was pineapple. The Big Pineapple. Faint voices bubbled from the darkness as if the darkness itself were talking. The illusion was broken by a female voice shrieking into laughter, followed by somebody applauding wildly.

I walked along a dim hallway papered in palm leaves and came to a shadowy open area. Whoever'd decorated that restaurant didn't know any more about Hawaii than I had gleaned from Whipper Will's travel folders and the souvenirs he and Bingo had brought back.

The restaurant was lit by dried fish with electricity in their bellies. They were suspended from the ceiling, and their great, round eyes and half-open mouths made them look as if they were astonished to be there. Where there were no dried fish, there were big, shiny birds sitting stiffly on perches. I think the birds were fake. Either that or very ill. In a corner under a pink light, a waterfall made of big seashells chuckled to itself about how cute it was. Paddles and more dried fish were attached to curtains of fishnet.

Leis of plastic flowers hung from wooden pegs on an awfully rustic wall behind a lit case full of tiny bottles, each one containing a colored sand sculpture, keychains and coffee cups that said "Kilroy's," mermaid cigarette lighters and bloated fish paperweights. Also in the case, lying out on dark cushions, were spine necklaces. In that light I almost took them for slaberingeo spines. They weren't, but they made me sweat anyway.

A loud speaker croaked once, loud enough to bust an eardrum, and ukulele music began. Gino had once serenaded Darlene with one while singing a sappy song called "Pipeline Lullaby." The strumming was not more frantic than a foot dangling from a porch swing.

"I like this place," Bill said.

"The effect is kind of charming if you like Hawaiian garage sales."

It was a clever line, but it wasn't clever enough to cover what happened next: One of the plastic leis lifted off its peg all by itself. It turned horizontal, spinning faster and faster, then began to soar around the room like a Frisbee, like a sneeve. If I hadn't been so busy watching it, I'd have seen the other leis take off. Soon there was a squadron of them swooping through the air.

"Anything in your bubble memory about that?" I said, diving to get out of the way.

A pudgy whirlwind of a woman not much taller than me hustled around a corner with menus clutched to her thick chest. She was wearing a loose gown of some kind, and even in that light the pattern of dancers, surfers and palm trees on the gown were bright enough that they seemed about ready to leap for freedom. Sort of blonde hair was piled on her head. She opened her wide mouth and cried in a voice that could remove paint, "Zoot!" She rushed at me like a football player and took me in a hug I am only now recovering my breath from.

We hugged each other tight enough to break bones, then she let me loose. "How are you, Puffy? Bill, this is Puffy Tootsweet, the Empress of 'Bu."

She nodded at Bill and said, "I haven't seen you since the night Heavenly Daise was shot."

"I've been busy. You work here?"

"You might say that. I own this joint."

"I like your floor show. Except it won't stay on the floor."

We bobbed and feinted as the leis continued to circle. Puffy said, "They'll stop pretty soon. They always do." She grabbed at one, but it climbed out of reach.

"How long has this been going on?"

"Just tonight. No, yesterday. Seems like forever. The customers come in here, take one look and are no longer customers. You know a good exorcist?"

I didn't even know what an exorcist was, so I said, "You hear about the top hat at the beach?"

"My phone rang all morning. Everybody thinks I'm in charge."

"You wouldn't like it if they didn't."

"Yeah, and besides, it's true." She shook all over when she laughed. I was about to tell her I thought there was a connection between the hat and the flying leis when sweet, tiny voices began to sing, "On the Good Ship Lollipop."

"What th—" Puffy began.

Bill pointed at the souvenir case, where mermaid lighters were singing.

Puffy began, "I never saw that—" but was interrupted when the dead fish paperweights and ceiling lamps took up the bass line. "Doom de-doom. Doom de-doom," they sang, way down in the basement somewhere.

"It's like some kind of cheap magic show," Puffy said.

A new voice, one that was low and cunning and full of sin said, "It may *look* like magic, my dear."

Filling the bar doorway was the big bot in the white suit. Robots don't sweat, but this one gave the impression that his face was covered with it. Maybe it was the shine of the metal.

"What else could it be?" Puffy said.

The bot said, " 'The science of any sufficiently advanced race—' "

I finished the quote for him: " '—is indistinguishable from magic.' "

The bot and I appraised each other as if we were about to go three rounds. "You know this guy?" Puffy said.

I said, "No, but I guess we have the same writer."

The bot laughed. It was a deep, round laugh that seemed to have been brought up in the scoop of a steam shovel. He handed me a card that said he was Jean-Luc Avoirdupois of *The Interstate Eyeball*. I started to hand the card back, but he said, "Keep it, my good sir. Keep it. There are plenty more where that came from."

"Thanks."

"Perhaps you will join me for a drink? I believe, sir, that we have many important things to discuss."

"What sort of things?"

"Please." He bent slightly, and with one arm made a sweeping motion like a headwaiter showing a fat tip to a table.

The mermaid lighters and the fish stopped singing, then one by one the leis hooked themselves gently over their pegs. In less than a minute, it was as if the world had been normal all afternoon.

Puffy and I shared a knowing look that didn't know anything, and I walked ahead of Avoirdupois into the bar.

The bar was darker than the restaurant, but that couldn't hide the fact that it was decorated with the same tacky Hawaiian tourist bait. A bartender stood at one end of the bar helping a man and woman watch cars race on TV. He nodded to us when we came in.

Taking tiny steps, almost dancing, Avoirdupois weaved among the tables, leading me to the darkest corner of the room. He bowed to me again, and I sat down with my back to the wall. Avoirdupois dredged a chuckle up from somewhere and sat down next to me. Bill sat down on my other side and began to swing his legs.

"And now, sir. What will you have?"

'Brewski," I said and watched him.

"Hah. You are a card, sir." He snapped his fingers in the air and called over his shoulder, "A beer for my friend."

I said, "You get around, don't you, Mr. Avoirdupois?"

Avoirdupois shrugged and said, "It's my job."

"*Interstate Eyeball.* I know. I saw your piece on the Hawaiian UFO."

"You're very kind, sir."

"Isn't writing a strange job for a robot, even a Surfing Samurai Robot?"

He grunted and said, "Indeed not, sir. I was designed as a journalistic hack-bot to the exact specifications of *The Interstate Eyeball.*" He patted his expansive rotundity with both hands and said, "I contain many accessories not normally associated with robots."

"That tells me a lot about the *Eyeball.*"

He chuckled like an idling diesel truck as the bartender put down a paper coaster and a glass full of beer. Avoirdupois paid him, and he went away.

"That UFO article had more tap dancing than information."

Avoirdupois laughed and shook his head. "You have the best of me there, sir. Tap dancing is all I had, and a bot must make a living." He lowered his voice. "To tell you the truth, sir, this UFO business is why I have sought you out."

"Sought me out? I didn't know myself until an hour ago that I was coming here."

"Perhaps. Perhaps. But it is likely that two men following the same trail will cross paths sooner or later."

"What path?" I said. I thought about Con Carney and his comment about a fat bot dressed in white.

"I must admit that our meeting at the Malibu Bar and No-Grill was by chance, but I recognized you instantly."

"How's that?"

His shoulders hunched up and down as he laughed. "You are a corker, sir. That is certain. Word gets around when someone cleans up the beach, if you get my meaning, sir. You were described to me more than once. And, if you don't mind my saying so, few would mistake you for anyone else." He smiled, his lips pressed together. He was pleased with himself, that was for sure.

"What about our paths?" I sipped the beer. It was cold and bitter.

"To tell you the truth, sir, it began with the Rare freak. When he attempted to purchase the spine necklace, my interest was piqued. Yes, indeed it was, sir. I see that you are still wearing it. Your luck, as they say, is holding."

"So it's holding. So what?"

"So spines are being stolen all over town, sir. That Rare freak was not the type to use force, but Medium Rare has other agents who are. You may meet one of them soon."

"Oh, my. Threats."

"Not at all, sir. Merely an informed prediction."

I took a big swallow of beer. It did nothing to clear my mind, but it loosened me up enough to make probing remarks. I said, "I'm still waiting to hear what all this has to do with me."

"It is simplicity itself, sir. From the conversation you had at the Malibu Bar and No-Grill, I know you are interested in that top hat on the beach. I have a professional interest in UFOs. I believe that there is a connection between that top hat, aliens from space, and the spines you wear around your neck."

Somehow Avoirdupois had put the puzzle together in much the same way I had. He didn't know about slaberingeo spines or Captain Hook's problem, of course, but if he had, he'd have seen how it fit right in. Evidently Avoirdupois was a better reporter than the *Eyeball* article showed. Either that, or he was lucky. Maybe he had a luck generator in his stomach along with a Teletype, an eyeshade and a pair of arm garters. Maybe—Durf, the beer had let some strange beasts loose in my mind. They prowled around, kicking over things I'd have to clean up later.

I yawned and said, "Assuming any of that is true, how do I fit in?"

He rumbled with amusement and said, "Oh, it is true, all right. I assure you, sir. I used one of my accessories to download a selection of clips over *The Interstate Eyeball*'s satellite link." Something in his stomach began to whine, and a sheet of white paper stuck out like a tongue from under his vest. It rolled out of him and dropped into his hand. By the time he gave it to me, another sheet was already on its way. Then another. Each one was a photocopy of an *Eyeball* article. They had titles like "Blowfish Spines of the Gods?!" and "Experts Claim Blowfish Speaks Old High Martian," and "Woman Plays Elvis Records With Space Spines, Says, 'He Has a Message For Us All From Beyond.'"

I glanced at the papers, not appearing to be

too interested, and said, "You may not believe this, but I'm still not convinced."

"Convinced or not, sir, I will tell you this: Frankly, I am at the end of my rope. I've followed every clue I have to its terminus and have discovered vacuum. You, on the other hand, are a man—if I may call you such—of singular talents and abilities." From his pocket he took a check made out to me for a thousand dollars. Enough money to pay Philip Marlowe's rent for a year. Enough to make him go so far as to raise an eyebrow. "Perhaps you will accept this as a retainer in hopes that you can find the crew of the top hat. It should not be difficult for a man of your, shall we say, *bon mot*, to find two Orientals, one of them blond."

I said, "What do you want with them?"

"An interview, nothing more."

I handed him back his clips and his check and said, "I can't promise you anything."

"Still, you are a man of character and nice judgment. I make no secret of the fact that I would feel better knowing you were working on my behalf." He held the check in my direction.

"Keep it," I said.

Avoirdupois smiled as if I'd agreed to everything. "You are a corker, sir. No doubt about that." He stood up and growled down at me, "I must leave. I have an appointment to interview a man who claims he can predict earthquakes by telepathically communicating with rocks." He shrugged a bemused look onto his face and extended a hand to me. Bill tried to shake it, but I pushed Bill's hand out of the way and took Avoirdupois'. It was cool. I couldn't say whether it was damp or not, but that was my impression.

He walked away from me lightly and turned at the door to say, "An alien may yet try to steal your necklace. I will keep in touch just in case."

10

Here Today — Gone to Maui

I sat there drinking the dregs of my beer while
Bill made patterns with one finger in the stuff
I had spilled. Avoirdupois was smart, but like
any smart guy, he needed help to look that way.
The clips from *The Interstate Eyeball* had told
Avoirdupois that he could connect spines with
the aliens from space who arrived in the top
hat. It was likely that what passed for journalism in the *Eyeball* would, at some other rag,
be no more than a suggestion scrawled on a
bathroom wall. My conversation at the Malibu
Bar and No-Grill told Avoirdupois he could
connect the spines with me. Who could I connect them to? Unless somebody told me something pretty quick, my trail would be just as
cold as his.

I swallowed the last of my beer, left a buck
on the table to thank the bartender for leaving
us alone, and walked back into the restaurant
proper. Bill trotted after me shouting, "I didn't
finish my picture."

"You can stay here if you like."

"No thanks. I'm programmed to be with you."

"Like Avoirdupois said, my luck is holding. Come on, then."

I found Puffy back by the silverware, talking to one of the waiters, a tall, gray-haired gentleman in white pants and shoes and a print shirt. He was scrubbed and neat as a box of new crayons. He took a bite out of me with his eyes, but Puffy told him to go see if table seventeen needed water.

When the guy was gone, I said, "Avoirdupois didn't get anything out of you, did he?"

"Who?"

"The bot in the white suit."

"I don't know him. Why should I tell him anything?"

"Do you have anything to tell?"

"He asked me about a couple of Orientals, one of them blond. Is that what you had in mind?"

"That's a good place to start."

Puffy looked around, then gestured with her head that I should follow her. We walked among the empty tables. The tall, neat waiter was sitting at table seventeen, drinking a glass of water. Puffy pounded on the table and said, "Stay awake, Harvey," as she passed. Harvey showed a set of teeth that belonged in an elephant's graveyard.

Puffy took me into a room that was no larger than a broom closet but had the advantage of having a door she could close. Photographs of girls wearing grass skirts and smiles were tacked to the wall among very businesslike charts and beer advertisements.

Puffy made the chair sing when she sat down behind a desk with a drift of papers piled high around a lamp that was too big for it. She tortured the chair some more as she turned around to face me. The chair behind me looked as sturdy as two twigs and a bent nail, so I sat down pretending I weighed no more than one of Dweeb's ideas.

Puffy said, "What about those two Orientals?"

I looked at Bill, who was sitting on his feet in front of the door, gazing at the girls as if his little mechanical heart would break. I said, "My guess is they are the crew of that top hat."

Puffy's eyes got big and she blew air between her lips. When she was done she said, "Well, in the first place, they're not Oriental. They're Polynesian."

"I knew that."

"In a pig's eye. You don't even know what it means."

"All right. I shouldn't try to kid a kidder. What does it mean?"

"It means they come from one of the Pacific islands."

"Hawaii?"

"Maybe."

"Maybe my foot. This case is soaked in Hawaii. Only they don't *really* come from Hawaii. Not unless flying top hats have become all the rage."

Puffy chewed on that for a moment. Dreamily, not even looking at me, she said, "I've never heard of a blond Polynesian, either."

I let her dream until it looked as if she'd forgotten I was there. To snap her out of it, I said, "Were they here?"

"Who? Oh, the two Polynesians? Yeah, they were here. Came in dressed for the big number at any Hawaiian night club and ordered one of my fancier drinks, the kind made with pineapple juice and rum and served on fire in a plastic coconut shell. And they were none too polite about it, either."

"I'll bet that was about the time your souvenirs went into show business."

"Actually, it didn't happen till after the two of them left."

I frowned and said, "Is that all?"

"Hard to say, not knowing what's important. But I serve those fancy drinks with little paper parasols and plastic mermaids. Usually people exclaim over the toys for a moment and then toss them aside, eager to get to the alcohol. But these two studied the trash as if it were the nail clippings of a dead rock 'n' roll star—"

"Hey, that's good."

"Thanks. Anyway, they spent a lot of time with the trash and then drank up. But before they left, they bought out my entire souvenir case."

"Even the fish paperweights?" I said, astonished.

"Don't be snobby. Fish make great paperweights."

"If you don't mind being stared at all day."

"Yeah, but they work for scale."

"Huh?"

She shook her head and said, "If you're going to make it as an Earthman, Zoot, you're going to have to learn the language."

"I do all right."

"He does all right," Bill said. But he was still staring at the girls.

I said, "If we could just kind of delicately get back to the subject. Your souvenir case is full at the moment."

"Yeah. I had a lot of things in stock."

"Where do you get it?"

"The Here Today—Gone to Maui Souvenir Company. Is that a clue?"

"Could be. Our two friends seem very interested in Hawaiian souvenirs. It would make sense for *me* to go where *they* might go to get a lot more of them." I stood up and noticed that Bill's eyes were roving again. I said, "I thought Heavenly Daise cured you of lusting after humans."

"I'm cured, but I'm not dead."

"Not as long as your batteries are fresh."

I led him through the lobby, where the water in the clamshell waterfall was changing color as it poured from shell to shell. From each color, matching tiny birds, no more than puffs of cotton with wings, flew into the air, making boisterous conversation among themselves that sounded like thousands of tiny bells ringing. It was a lot to take, but I took it. At least the mermaids and the fish weren't singing.

The Here Today—Gone to Maui Souvenir Company was in Venice, not far from Kilroy's but complicated to get to. We glided among a lot of shabby neighborhoods chockablock with frame houses in various states of repair. A well-painted house with a green postage stamp of a lawn likely as not would be next door to a tumbledown place whose front yard was being used to store a rusting automobile. Though Bill was navigating, we got lost more than once. Bill was not happy about that. Even a bot has his pride.

A stiff wind was blowing the smell of seaweed in from the ocean. I wondered if the landlords included that in the rent.

After an exciting twenty minutes, I turned off Washington onto Glencoe and found that the Here Today—Gone to Maui Souvenir Company was one of a row of new warehouses, most of which were very secretive about what went on inside.

I parked in the new lot and stood a moment watching cars go in and out of the big shopping center across the street. It was just a shopping center, not much concerned with top hats on the beach and blond Polynesians. I sighed. Just because trouble is your business doesn't mean you don't need a nap now and then, or the chance to visit a store just to buy something normal, not because you were shopping for clues.

The glass doors of the warehouse opened by themselves as I approached, fascinating Bill so much I could barely get him inside. A veil of soft music floated through the air without disturbing anything.

The ceiling arched in a simple curve high over a single room just small enough not to have its own zip code. The air was cold and did not smell of seaweed. It didn't smell of anything. There were cash registers in the front and wide aisles farther back, just as if the place were a supermarket. One of the registers was open, with a clerk lounging at it reading a magazine. He didn't even look up as I passed him. I almost lost Bill again when we went through the turnstile.

This place would be heaven to the two Polynesians. I saw plastic mermaids in a variety of sizes and colors, napkins with clever sayings on them, coasters, plastic sticks with planets on top, glasses in more shapes and sizes than I'd have thought possible, from teardrops up to Greek columns big enough to water elephants. Plates, matchbooks, plastic silverware. I probably missed a thing or two. In a place that size, it couldn't be helped.

The place was not crowded, but it wouldn't have been crowded even if it had been only the size of the Taj Mahal. A couple of fat people of indeterminate gender—you didn't have to be a Toomler to be confused—peered over the top of a stack of boxes loaded on a flatbed cart they pushed while referring to a shopping list and gaping at the things every good civilization needs before it can begin to decline.

Bill said, "Let's buy something."

"Pick something and we'll see."

"My meat, boss," Bill said, but even so, he seemed intimidated by the wide selection.

I found a small, thin guy dressed in jeans and a Here Today—Gone to Maui shirt big enough to camp under, loading boxes of cocktail toothpicks onto a shelf. They were in assorted colors, and you could buy them in lots of twenty. He seemed awfully engrossed in what he was doing. He didn't look at me until I said, "Isn't a cocktail a drink?"

He looked at me from under bushy black eyebrows that matched his mustache, and said, "If you mix it right."

"Even if you mix it wrong, you shouldn't need a toothpick in assorted colors to help you swallow it."

He looked me over as if I were a display with a can out of place and said, "Say, what planet are you from?"

I said, "The planet of the inquisitive customers. Does it matter? I'm looking for spine necklaces." I touched the one around my neck. "Like this one."

"Aisle seven."

"Thanks."

Bill followed me to aisle seven, where we found what would have been a fortune in jewelry, if it had been real. But it was more gaudy than real, and more plastic than gaudy. We walked slowly down the aisle. I don't know what Bill was looking for, but I found what I wanted. Or, I didn't find it, which in this case was the same thing.

A card in the rail said, BLOWFISH SPINE NECKLACES: $1.00/@. Over it was a lot of empty shelf. I stared at it, but an empty shelf is only an empty shelf, even if it's a clue. The Polynesians had been here. I was getting closer, but I was still a half-step behind them and not sure what I'd do when I caught up.

I went back to the guy stocking toothpicks and said, "I'd like to talk to the manager."

"Did you find them?"

"Yeah, I found them. I need the manager."

He looked at me along his nose, suspicious-like. He didn't want anybody complaining about him. He said, "In the back," as if he were telling me where the dangerous drugs were stored.

I said, "Thanks," and strolled along the back wall until I found a pair of metal swinging doors that looked as if they'd been through an air raid, and on the losing side.

Beyond the doors was a cool room piled high with crates and cardboard boxes that gave their flat, earthy smell to the air. It was actually, cozy if you liked that kind of thing. Fluorescent tubes dropped a harsh light sharp as broken glass and buzzed with a sound that would give you a headache after a while.

I wound between walls of boxes, following the sound of subdued voices until I found a woman not much older than one of Will's surfers. She was holding a clipboard in her hands and a pencil in her teeth, watching a very tall, brown-skinned man count packages as he touched them with a hand big enough to squeeze a cantaloupe dry. They were each wearing official shirts, but both fit better than the one on the stock clerk. The big man turned to glance at me, and something glinted on his collar. He started to count again. I waited till he was done and the woman had recorded the number.

"Manager?" I said to both of them.

"May I help you?" said the woman. She was short, compact and trim, with blond hair that was smooth over her head and then hung in ringlets around her ears. The lipstick she wore made her look as if she'd been sucking a cherry

Popsicle. Her eyes tried to look worried, but were too tired.

"I'm looking for spine necklaces—"

"Aisle seven—"

"But there aren't any more in aisle seven."

"Oh." That upset her entire day. "We'll be getting an order in soon."

"You don't make them here?"

"No. We don't make anything here. We're just a distributor. We get the spines from the Sue Veneer Novelty Company."

The big guy who'd been counting the packages was watching me as if he didn't want to but couldn't help himself. Or maybe that was just his idea of being polite.

"Thanks," I said, nodding. I began to walk away.

"But they won't sell them to you," the manager called after me. "They're a wholesale outfit."

"That's OK. I just like to look," I said.

Bill and I were halfway out to the Belvedere when I heard footsteps behind me. I turned just in time to see the big dark guy swing something toward where my left ear would have been if I'd had ears.

Bill squawked. There was a roaring like a train going through a tunnel, and somebody turned down the contrast on the world until it was black.

11

A Certificate of Authenticity

I awoke in the miserly shade of a small tree in the parking lot. The air was full of stars that sparked and died and sparked again. Bill was sitting next to me. He looked around when I grabbed the side of my head and moaned.

"You should carry a gun," he said.

"I suppose so. Then I could blow my foot off just to show everybody how tough I am." What I'd said didn't make sense, but I was pleased to be able to talk at all. I tried again by saying, "What happened?"

"Before or after he hit you?"

"After. I'm pretty clear on what happened before."

"He took your necklace. I tried to stop him, but he wasn't impressed."

"He wouldn't be."

I thought about the necklace as I touched my chest where it had so lately hung. The guy who'd stolen it could have been an alien, but I doubted it. Avoirdupois would be disappointed. This whole situation was wrong. It stank on ice. It was trying to tell me something, but I didn't feel well enough to listen.

Instead, I looked around. There were other cars in the lot but none of them close. Anybody in the lot of the shopping center across the street had business of their own. It was likely that, even in daylight in the middle of a parking lot, the guy had been as safe sapping me as he would have been in the middle of Griffith Park at midnight. I love it when everybody minds their own business.

I could report the guy to the police. I could talk to the manager and get him fired. Either way, I'd have to answer a lot of questions I'd rather not have asked. Still, the guy didn't know when he hit me that I wouldn't press charges. He'd taken an awful chance for a cheap necklace just like hundreds of others in the Here Today—Gone to Maui stock. A quick check of my pockets told me he hadn't taken anything else. The guy wasn't just a thief. He was a thief with a mission. Finding out what it was would be interesting.

I knew that eventually I'd have to go see Medium Rare. But right now, it seemed like a bigger job than I could manage just to get to my feet. I was quite a guy, though. Using the tree as a crutch, I managed it. I stood there with my hand resting lightly on Bill's head. He didn't move. He was good at that. I listened to the traffic. It was a normal noise, comforting enough if you'd been raised with it. I hadn't but took comfort where I could.

According to Bill and his bubble memory, the Sue Veneer Novelty Company was a good deal south of where we were, in Dominguez, one of the brood of independent cities that sucked up to Los Angeles and wouldn't exist without it.

I drove with one hand, the other probing the growing squash on the side of my head. Though it hurt when I touched it, I couldn't help touching it now and then. The pain made me a little sick, but I managed to keep everything where it belonged. I ran little amateur theatricals in my head in which the guy who'd done this to me was variously tarred, feathered, and hung up by his thumbs. It was nice but not as satisfying as I'd hoped. I thought again about calling the police or getting him fired, but it still didn't seem like a good idea.

As early as it was, the afternoon rush hour had already begun; fortunately most of it was going the other way. Without braking more than a couple of times a mile, I boomed down the Santa Monica Freeway through neighborhoods of which I saw no more than the tops of trees that seemed to move like an ocean until you saw the real ocean, a gray line at their far edge. The trees stopped abruptly, as if somebody had trimmed the forest with a scissors, and soon I was driving through factory complexes that sprawled like masses of arthritic plumbing.

The sun was hurrying home through the haze by the time I left the freeway at Dominguez, the slanting rays making my headache seem more like a spike in the eye. I crossed some railroad tracks, then rode between them and a line of plain buildings whose main charm was that they weren't sure whether they were offices or warehouses.

"Here it is," Bill said, and I pulled into a parking space in front of a candy-red truck big enough to carry my Belvedere away without even breathing hard. It seemed to be looking at me with the extra lamps that gleamed from the top of the cab. Fancy white script on the door said, "Cash and Carry."

The Sue Veneer Novelty Company was a big block of cement painted what might have been yellow in a former life but now looked like the mortal remains of many years of city dirt. Bill and I went in through one side of a double glass door, and stood before a couple of crowded desks in an office crowded with papers and furniture. Maybe they just expected a lot of company, but there were three or four chairs too many in a space that could not even stand one. The air was cool and had the flat smell of distant, impersonal death. Nothing was on the walls but landlord-white paint.

At one desk, a harried-looking guy wearing glasses pecked at the keys of a typewriter. When he saw me, he stopped typing and began to shuffle papers that were already typed on. Behind the other desk was a middle-aged woman who thought she looked younger but wore a lot of makeup as insurance. She wore a pale-blue suit with dark-blue piping, and her hair—almost, but not quite, brown—was waved above a face carved from a baked potato.

She looked up from a list on which she was making check marks, and smiled as if she wasn't sure it was OK. "May I help you?" she said in a pouty voice, like a little girl being made to recite.

I smiled, hoping mine looked more realistic than hers, and said, "I'm looking for a little information."

She folded her hands on her list and said, "What sort of information did you require?"

"You people make those blowfish spine necklaces?"

"Sometimes." She watched a lot of TV and knew never to admit anything.

"Have you any idea why anybody would be interested in collecting them?"

Her eyes got furtive, as if she expected my gang to leap out from under my coat and attack at any moment. Bill was trying to see what

the guy had been typing and I said, "Stop that."
He froze, then backed off.

The woman said, "One moment please." She
cried, "Harry," putting a jagged hole in the air.

"What is it, Hilda?" It was a man's voice:
nice, but right now a little miffed at being interrupted. It came through a short hallway that
led to another office.

"Harry, a man out here wants to know about
blowfish spine necklaces." Her voice was loud
enough to be the lunch whistle.

"What?" came Harry's voice. Maybe he was
chained to the floor back there. With his fingers in his ears.

"Blowfish spine necklaces," she said slowly,
carefully pronouncing each syllable as if she
were trying out for radio announcer of the
week.

In the other office, squeaky wheels rolled,
followed by footsteps. A tall man came up
through the hall, bouncing a little with each
step, and stood in the doorway with the backs
of his hands on his hips, fingers out like
chopped pink wings. He was dressed neatly, if
casually, in a short-sleeved cotton shirt and
blue pants that almost matched the piping on
Hilda's dress. A little black was left in his gray
hair, like hummocks of rock under snow.

"What is it, Hilda?" he said. His chin was
out, pointing arrogantly at her.

I said, "Blowfish spine necklaces."

He looked at me for the first time, and his
mouth opened in surprise. He pointed at Hilda
with one hand and played arpeggios in the air
with the other. He said, "Hilda can take your
order."

"I'll bet she can. I'll bet she's faster than a
squirrel after nuts, but I don't have an order.
All I have is a head holding too much pain and
the name Medium Rare."

He frowned and nodded. This was serious business. "Come on into the office," he said and walked back the way he had come, still bouncing.

I followed him into a sunny room that was used as much for storage as for thinking. On the walls were brass plaques and photos of boys in uniform. In each, Harry stood to one side, smiling so hard the photographer wouldn't have needed a flash. Along the baseboards were piles of paper and stacks of small boxes of white cardboard. On his desk was a card file and a heap of plastic items—novelties. I saw a comb and a clothespin you'd use to hang mouse clothes out to dry, but most of the bits were bizarre enough to be from another planet. A planet like Earth. We certainly didn't have stuff like that back on T'toom. One wall of the office was glass, with a sliding door in it. Through it, I could see a couple of men wearily carrying cardboard boxes from a loading dock into a truck that said Pantages Transport on the side.

Harry sat down behind his desk and grinned at me. It was the same grin he used in the picture. Old dependable.

Bill and I were still standing. I pointed to one of the photos and said, "All these kids wear the same style clothes."

The smile slipped a little, but he concentrated and jacked it up again. "Little League. I'm an athletic supporter." That made him laugh. It was either a real laugh or he'd been practicing it along with the smile. Bill laughed, too, and stopped before Harry did. When Harry noticed he was laughing alone, he looked at me earnestly and said, "No Little League where you come from?"

"No leagues at all."

"No baseball?"

"Oh, baseball. Sports. Sure. But no leagues. Not even tiny ones."

"I get it," he said and winked.

Bill winked back by flashing the light in one eye.

Harry got it. He was one up on me. I said, "Why would Medium Rare want necklaces made from blowfish spines?"

He knitted his fingers together on the desktop and said, "Who's Medium Rare?"

"If you don't know, why am I in here?"

"Just being polite. I thought *you* were Medium Rare." There was that smile again.

Out front, a train went by slowly, breathing hard, as if each chuff would be its last. Everything in the room shook a little. Bill jiggled but had no trouble keeping his balance. The heavy sound rolled into the distance, and I said, "All right. What about this? Tell me about the necklaces."

"We have the license in California."

"You need a license to sell blowfish spine necklaces?"

He got very serious and intense. "In a manner of speaking, we do. We pay big bucks to use the Hands Tell a Story Tourist Bureau necklace design."

"Anybody in California using a different design?"

"Not that I know of. Why would they?" He smiled.

"For the money?" I said, guessing.

"No reputable dealer would do business with them. It isn't worth the hassle from the Hands Tell a Story people. And before you ask, there are no unreputable dealers."

"So anybody who wants a blowfish spine necklace has to come to you. You ship them to Hawaii, and tourists bring them back."

"That seems to be the arrangement." The arrangement pleased him. Smiling, he picked up a circle of purple plastic and flicked the edge with a thumbnail.

"OK. So, it's a swell souvenir. Why would Medium Rare or anybody else want a lot of them?" An idea raised its hand. It had been there all the time, sitting in the corner of my brain not making a noise. I hadn't noticed it before, but I noticed it now. It excited me. It was brewski. It was pizza. It was chocolate-covered coffee beans. I said, "Or maybe they just want one special one."

"There are no special ones," Harry said. "They're all the same. Made from the highest quality mold-injected plastic."

So much for my exciting idea. I said, "Not even real spines?"

"You know what real spines cost?"

"I know," said Bill brightly.

"Keep it for later," I said. "So you sell necklaces made from fake blowfish spines. And they're all the same. What about the certificates of authenticity?"

"Then you *do* know something about the necklaces."

"Just enough to be dangerous, evidently. How authentic can the necklaces be if the spines are fake?"

"They're not fake. Each is an authentic reproduction. It's like having a print of a piece of art."

"Sure it is. Just the same."

"Look," he said. He got up, took a sheet from the top of a stack of papers, and handed it to me. Bill looked over my arm at it. The paper said:

THIS IS A GENUINE SUE VENEER NOVELTY COMPANY BLOWFISH SPINE NECKLACE, AN INCREDIBLE SIMULATION OF THE KIND USED BY THE ANCIENT HAWAIIANS FOR MONEY AND GOOD LUCK.

Below that was a signature. To one side was a small photograph of a pretty woman with high, round cheeks and a cloud of light, curly hair. It was a face that would smile easily, but it was not smiling now. At the moment it had the serious expression of somebody who could authenticate fake blowfish spine necklaces and make it stick. Her name was Busy Backson.

I said, "I'd like to visit Ms. Backson."

"I don't give out that information."

"It's all right. I'm a private detective. I'm a professional."

"I don't even know if you're human." He smiled his smile. It was just a joke between us girls.

"I'm human. I had a little problem with toxic waste and some nose drops."

Bill started to say something, but I was able to grab him around the throat before he could ruin everything.

"Sorry," Harry said. He stood up. He thought the interview was over, but the fun was just beginning. People began shouting outside, and we looked through the glass wall. A man and a woman were out there. The man wore white pants and shoes, and the most riotous flowered shirt I had ever seen—louder than the design on a twelve-year-old's skateboard. The woman wore a slightly more sedate print dress and red pumps. A human male would have enjoyed the legs rising out of them.

The man and the woman each wore a pile of flowered necklaces that rose, one atop the other, right up to their eyes. You couldn't see what they looked like, but their eyes could have been Polynesian, and the woman's hair was a blonde cascade that puddled around her shoulders.

At the moment, each of them was flinging magic.

12

It's Magic

Or maybe it wasn't magic. The science of any sufficiently advanced race, you know. Whatever it was, it did the job.

Wherever the man pointed, a green worm burst out of the ground, quickly became a green arm exploding with thorns. The arm became a trunk, and the trunk spread to become a wall. In seconds, a thicket of thorns taller than the building surrounded the truck and the two Polynesians.

Wherever the woman pointed, a spout of flame lifted a box out of the warehouse and loaded it into the truck as if the box were a spaceship in one of those cheap fifties sci-fi movies. She was a perfect shot. Never missed.

Bill was fascinated, of course. Harry seemed astonished at first, but then his face hunkered down into a mask of self-righteous anger.

The laborers were shouting in a foreign language that may have been Spanish. They prudently backed off, but once they saw they were safe they called encouragement and blew noisy kisses. The two Polynesians took no notice.

Harry cried, "Those people are stealing from me," and slid the glass door open so hard it bounced against the end of its track. I couldn't tell whether Harry was upset because the two were stealing, or because they were stealing from him. He ran outside but was stopped pretty quick by sword-length thorns and vines that appeared to be tougher than telephone cord. I could see only his back, but his body language was pretty clear, even to me, a guy with a different type of body altogether. As he watched, he became as despondent as a melting snowman, except for his hands, which were balled into fists; his fingers might as well have been bananas.

He ran back to the open door, called, "Hilda, get my rifle," and looked again through the roughage at the two loading the truck. Either they hadn't heard, or gunshots did not concern them.

"What?" Hilda cried. Bill and I looked in her direction.

"My rifle, Hilda. My rifle," Harry cried. Bill and I looked in his direction. We weren't learning anything, but the level of entertainment was rising.

"What?" Hilda cried. She strutted into the office and at first was surprised to see me there alone. Then she saw what was going on outside. Her mouth opened wide, and she covered it with one hand.

Harry ran into the room, and quickly, as if ordering a stubborn child to bed, said, "Hilda, get my rifle right now." Hilda ran off, clattering a sloppy cadence with her high heels.

It wasn't long before the blonde Polynesian woman was done loading the truck. The man swung up under the steering wheel, and she swung up beside him. The thorn bush wilted where the truck went through. The truck turned left at the alley, and a moment later was gone.

Hilda ran into the office gripping the rifle. "Excuse me," she said as she ran past me and Bill and out the door.

Harry turned around and looked calmly at Hilda and the rifle she carried. As if reasoning with that same naughty child who still would not go to bed, he started in on her. He flattened her with the steamroller of his words, then backed up and did it again. According to him, it was all her fault that the hijackers had gotten away with a truck full of his merchandise. Everything was her fault. If it wasn't for her, the entire world would be free of war, starvation and sickness.

Then she gave it back to him, whining that it wasn't her fault, that she'd had trouble hearing him, then trouble finding the rifle, then trouble finding the ammunition. She never suggested that he hadn't done anything either, that he might have gotten the rifle and the ammunition himself.

They were a fine pair, and just watching them work each other over made me want to go back to T'toom. I walked out to join them.

I said, "Are you two dandelions about done?"

"Excuse me?" Hilda said. She wasn't angry, just confused.

"Because if you are, it's not too late to call the police."

Harry's eyes narrowed. He looked tough with that rifle in his hand. Oh, yes. Tough as one of his Little Leaguers holding a baseball bat. He said, "Have you called the police, Hilda?"

"Why, no. I didn't think—"

"Well, don't just stand there, Hilda. Go do it."

She walked back into the office, mumbling in a shrill voice how she was going as fast as she could and that she hoped the 911 number worked.

I strode to the nearest thorn and Harry called after me, "Where are you going? This is private property."

"Just taking a look," I said pleasantly. "Aren't you curious?"

A moment later, he was beside me, watching me touch the thorns and the vines. I bent a thorn and it sprang back like a spring, even making the kind of comic spring sound you'd hear in a cartoon.

The whole thicket seemed to be made of some kind of rubber, and it was already sagging and evaporating into the air.

"I'll be doggoned," Harry said.

"Sure. And while you're doing that, Bill and I'll have a look in your warehouse."

I could hear him behind me, but didn't turn around. When I got into the warehouse I found the laborers yammering around a hole just wide enough for one of them to jump into without touching the sides. Maybe it wasn't a hole. But it was round and seemed to have no color at all, not even black. You couldn't look right at it without going a little crazy. Rising from the hole were heat and a noxious vapor that drilled up into back tunnels of my sinus cavities that were previously unknown, even to me. Neither the look nor the smell seemed to bother Bill, who walked right up to the edge of the hole and looked down.

"Fire?" I said and made a motion like a crate sailing through the air.

The laborers didn't say anything I understood, but they nodded.

Harry said, "This where the explosions came from, Haysoos?"

The laborer named Haysoos said, "Si, Harry."

Evidently the holes were handy little do-it-

yourself volcanoes that the woman had flung
under crates in Harry's warehouse by science
or magic—take your pick. It was a nice effect
either way. Controlled eruptions had blasted
the crates into the truck. I hoped the holes
wouldn't start to erupt again.

Bill leaned over a little too far. He squawked,
flapped his hands, and was gone before anybody could catch him. I looked into the hole,
blinking against the bad breath rising from it.
Bill tumbled as he fell, getting smaller and
smaller.

"Bill," I cried, feeling a sickness that had
nothing to do with my knock on the head or
noxious vapors.

Bill was now no more than a point of glim-
mering light. "Get a rope, Haysoos!"

"I don't think we have one long enough."

"Get a rope!"

Haysoos went away, as much to get away
from me as anything else, I suspect. I kicked
at the hole, expecting this to be a useless, emotional act. I kicked at the hole, and one side of
it curled back like a circle of rubber and laid
back flat on the ground with a slap. I looked
closely. The hole was still just a hole.

"What is it?" Harry said.

Saying nothing, I reached for the edge of the
hole as if it were a snake. Gently, I took it in
two fingers and lifted a little. It was easy. I
lifted some more, and saw that the dirty cement under the hole looked and felt just like
the dirty cement anywhere else in the garage.

"I'll be doggoned," Harry said. The laborers
grumbled among themselves and more than
one of them made a cross on their chests.

I pulled the hole up more and found Bill. He
was just standing there blinking and wobbling
a little. In my hand I held a thin black sheet. I
reached into one side, and my hand disappeared into something hot. I touched the other

side, and felt something cool, but smooth and real.

"Where were you, Bill?"

"I don't know, Boss. I was falling, and then I wasn't."

"I'll be doggoned," Harry said.

I rolled up the hole, smooth side out, and handed it to Harry. At first, he didn't want to take it, but then his tongue watered his lips and he took it eagerly, hungrily. "This would make a great little item," he said.

I grabbed Bill around the neck and held him just tightly enough so he couldn't run away.

I took a deep breath and said, "OK. What was taken?"

"Haysoos?" Harry said.

Haysoos gave orders to his crew and they climbed over the boxes remaining in the warehouse, noting what was missing. One of them called to Haysoos. Haysoos said, "Only blowfish spine necklaces, Harry."

"Isn't that what you were asking about?" Harry said suspiciously. He almost pointed the rifle at me.

"I was expecting something like this to happen. That's why I'm here."

Bill squeaked out, "Gee," as if he were impressed.

"I have a different idea about it," Harry said. "I think you should wait till the police come." This time he raised the rifle. He was close enough not to miss me or the crates behind me.

"It's more important that I see Busy Backson."

"I told you about that."

"Don't you want your stuff back?"

"The police will get my stuff back."

"They will if they believe your story about giant thickets and convenient explosions."

"I'll show 'em the holes."

"Look at the one in your hand." It looked like a melted candy bar. Harry tried to unroll it, and it dripped to shreds. In a second, it was no more than something to wash off your hands.

Harry frowned and pulled at his lower lip. "You're a witness," he said.

"You saw the same thing I did."

"What does Busy have to do with this?"

"It's a long story. Every moment we wait, that truck gets farther away."

"Can I trust you?" he asked, and gave me the old dependable smile.

"Look," I said, "I don't know why you think I had anything to do with the heist. It's no secret that you have blowfish spine necklaces here. Everything would have gone pretty much the same if I hadn't been here. I'm already on this case, while the police would be just starting. What are you losing by trusting me?"

"What about your fee?"

"Don't worry about that. I'm being well paid by my other client." Sure. Whipper Will would call me an aggro dude and let me stay in his house some more.

Harry nodded, and I followed him back to the office. The thorns were just about gone, leaving not so much as a green puddle. He ducked into a tiny bathroom off his office and wiped his hand. The sludge had evaporated, just like the thorns.

Harry looked up a phone number in a card file. A moment later he was talking into the phone, laughing, having a wonderful time. He was so slick I'm surprised the receiver stayed in his hand. When he hung up, he said, "She'll see you as a personal favor to me." He gave me her address and began to tell me how to get there.

"I'll find it," I said. "Oh, yeah. When you tell the police your story, would you kind of leave me out of it."

"Why?"

"Don't you think my presence might confuse things?"

He thought about that for a moment and nodded.

When Bill and I went through the front office, Hilda was making check marks again, and the harried kid was typing. Business goes on. With a guy like Harry, it would always go on. I wished the police luck. That, and a strong stomach.

13

Harry Sent Me

Busy Backson lived in Hermosa Beach, a pastel place that existed only to charge people for parking when they went to the beach. If it was like other water-front communities, there would be no parking space without its parking meter.

Traffic was heavier, and the sun had disappeared in the bank of unwashed cotton wool that covered the western sky. It showed through the clouds like a dime. The side of my head throbbed, and moving suddenly still made me dizzy. Feeling better should not feel this bad.

Bill was still dazed from his experience with the black hole, but I kept reminding him of Busy Backson's address in Hermosa Beach, and his bubble memory came around at last.

We had plenty of time, maneuvering along narrow streets between new apartment buildings that grudgingly allowed me a free glimpse of the Pacific between them. I asked Bill to explain again what being in the black hole was like, but he never said anything more descriptive than what he'd said at first. "First I was falling, and then I wasn't."

Neighborhoods that could have been anywhere slid by. I let them. I had other things on my mind, like the growing popularity of blowfish spine necklaces.

The first group to be interested in the spines contained two Polynesians who might have been the crew of the top hat and, therefore, were responsible for Captain Hook's sudden preoccupation with proving that the hand is quicker than the eye, and, therefore, the sooner I found them, the better. It was a mystery why they wanted souvenir necklaces that were all the same. Maybe they were going to start a business back home. That was my bump on the head talking. I rubbed my nose with a free hand and kept thinking.

Then there was Avoirdupois. As far as I could tell, his interest was purely journalistic. The rumors, wishful thinking, and outright but colorful lies his paper called news connected the spines to space travelers, and he thought they might lead him to the Polynesians, whom he also thought were connected with the top hat. He wanted to get *the story*. That was all. That was all he would admit, anyway.

Then there was Medium Rare, some kind of fortune teller with enough clout or pull or whatever to attract a certain type of people, and then order those people to acquire spine necklaces in any way they could. Why she wanted them was the little man who wasn't there. I would have to go see her eventually. Soon. I didn't have a necklace anymore, so I guessed I was safe.

And then there was Busy Backson. To my knowledge, she had no interest in blowfish spine necklaces beyond her employment at the Sue Veneer Novelty Company. But she did things as a personal favor to Harry. That told me more about her than I liked.

I let the Belvedere ride the engine down a long hill, and turned more or less left at a five-way intersection that didn't have a stop light. I found a place to park in front of a small grocery store that had a couple of blond guys wearing T-shirts down to their knees who were horsing around in front of it. As far as I could tell, each of them was trying to shove an ice-cream wrapper down the front of the other. Maybe that's a sport in Hermosa Beach. Maybe they even have a league.

I was going to put some quarters into the meter, when Bill said, "Hold it, Boss." I stepped aside, and he shot a wire out of his little spherical belly and into the slot where you're supposed to put the money. He felt around inside for a minute, with a kind of fixed expression on his face, as if he were feeling around in a rat hole, and a second later, the VIOLATION sign went down and the little black arrow swung up to two hours.

"That's pretty good," I said.

"I can do laundromats too."

"I'll tell Whipper Will."

We strolled along to a wide walkway between the buildings and followed it to an alley a block away. The walkway was inlaid with bricks so you'd have something to slip on in wet weather. The alley was clean and, in another part of town, might have qualified as a street. I could hear the ocean booming close by. Its strong smell filled the air.

I found the number I wanted on a blue, two-story building that faced the other way—toward the ocean. I walked over some uneven cement to get to a stairway that led to a second floor, where I knocked. There was a nice view from here: energetic kids slugging a ball over a net, more sand, and then the sun setting through a prism of clouds into the Pacific, which was preening itself as if it knew I was watching.

"Who is it?" came a nice voice.

"Zoot Marlowe. Harry sent me," I said, feeling as if I were delivering Prohibition whiskey to Jimmy Cagney.

The door opened, and I was looking at Busy Backson. She was tall and slim, wearing a long-sleeved turtleneck shirt that followed her curves with the determination of a race-car driver. They were good curves, too, a selection of the best from a guitar and a bowl of fruit. On the upper rise of her left breast was a small golden comet, its tail making an arc. Faded blue jeans were a second skin.

She was barefoot. A cloud of yellow hair shined as if sunlight were behind it. Her smile was enough to make me wish I were a real boy.

"Come in," she said and held the door open wider.

Bill and I stepped into a small room that was crowded but not fussy. The place was mostly bookshelves, and when she'd run out of room, Ms. Backson had shoved the books in any way they would fit. There were some shelves she'd kept empty on purpose, and on them were seashells, glass unicorns, and some small tikis like the ones Will and Bingo had brought back from Hawaii.

One long shelf held a tank full of fish. They came in all colors, shapes, and sizes. They chased each other from one end of the tank to the other, where bubbles bounced together as they rose eagerly from a small plastic man wearing a diver's suit and struggling with a treasure chest that was too big for him to carry alone.

Above the books, posters were tacked to the wall. Some of them were of waterfalls hidden in dim, mysterious rain forests that didn't quite drip onto the apartment's walls. Others showed green landscapes that were too green to be real. One poster—dark and drab by comparison—showed fanciful Hollywood designs of alien space ships. Not one of them looked like a sneeve or a top hat. On the floor were some rugs with complicated geometrical designs. They were clean, but worn enough to show they had been there a long time.

"Sit down," she said and pointed to a couch woven of stiff yellow sticks and covered in gray pillows. When Bill and I sat down, the couch creaked as if we'd sat on a live thing. Bill jumped off, causing it to creak again. You couldn't move on it without it creaking.

Busy Backson dropped into a big armchair that matched the couch and folded her legs up under her. She said, "Harry tells me you're interested in blowfish spine necklaces."

"That's right." I crossed my legs, and the couch told everybody all about it.

"There's not much to tell. The ancient Hawaiians used them for barter and because they were considered to be good luck."

"That's what it said on the Certificate of Authenticity."

"That's all there is."

"Anything special about the spines that Harry makes down at the Sue Veneer Novelty Company?"

Busy Backson shrugged. "They're plastic. Not very good plastic, I suppose, but they don't have to be. We're not making space capsules here."

"Still," I said, "I understand they're being stolen all over the city. Somebody stole a whole truckload of them from Harry."

She nodded, frowning as if she'd broken a fingernail. "I know," she said. "Harry told me."

"Did he tell you how it was done?"

"He mentioned a couple of Hawaiians. One with blonde hair."

"That mean anything to you?" I said.

She wasn't looking at me. She wasn't looking at anything in the room. "Scarcer than hen's teeth," she said.

"Scarce as all that, hmmm?"

The lights came back on behind her eyes, and she looked at me with the seriousness she usually reserved for authenticating. "You're a pretty scarce kind of guy yourself, Mr. Marlowe."

"Toxic waste and nose drops will do that to you."

"I'm sorry," she said, and looked it. She leaped to her feet, said, "Come on, I'll show you something," and marched out through a doorway. I caught up with her in a dim room, obviously the bedroom, in which some blinds were lifting gently in the breeze off the beach. On the wall over the bed were some very dangerous-looking clubs and spears. On a stand to one side was a huge, arched thing made of yellow feathers that fluttered in the breeze.

Busy Backson was standing near a dresser that had a lot of spines on top. She held her fists out to me, knuckles up, and said, "Turn on the light."

I was reaching for the switch when Bill's eyes went on. "Look over here, Bill," I said, and Bill looked at what Busy Backson was holding, shining his light on it.

Ms. Backson said, "Here. You tell which is real." She opened her hands, showing that in each was a blowfish spine. Looking at them told me nothing. Bill pointed to one of them and said, "That one."

But he was wrong. The other one gave off a faint reek of dead fish and kelp. No one but a

Toomler would have been able to pick it up. I pointed to the same one Bill had.

"No. It's the other one." My guessing wrong didn't make her particularly happy. It was just part of the demonstration. Busy Backson was a lot more adult than I would have expected from a friend of Harry's. "So you see," she said, "the Sue Veneer spines are pretty good. They deserve a Certificate of Authenticity."

"That still doesn't explain why anybody would steal a truckload of them."

"Well, they are valuable." She put both spines back on the dresser and scanned the room quickly.

"Like diamonds?"

"Well, of course not."

"Then why not steal diamonds?"

"You're the detective."

"Having a title doesn't always make things easier."

"No." She bit her lip as she walked back into the crowded living room. The biting of the lip was nice, but she had no reason to do it. Not if the spines were somebody else's problem.

She was watching the fish. I stood behind her, watching fish, too. They swam up and back with the same concern for the two of us as sales girls on Rodeo Drive.

I said, "You heard about the top hat on the beach in Malibu?"

Without turning around, she said, "Sure. It was in the news: the Martian Hat."

"Among the crew was a blonde Polynesian woman."

She turned around, mangling her lip again. It was kind of endearing, actually. "The news didn't say anything about that."

"I'm a detective, remember?"

The lip got free, and she said, "Do you know anything about Hawaiian mythology?"

"Only that there are probably no top hats in it."

That brightened her right up. The smile almost gave me a sunburn. She said, "Hey, you *are* a detective, aren't you?" She folded herself on the gray chair again and went on: "One of the main gods in the ancient Hawaiian pantheon is Pele, goddess of volcanos. Sometimes she's pictured with red hair, sometimes with blond—the colors of volcano fire."

"If Pele existed, what would she want with blowfish spine necklaces?"

She shrugged, lifting her shoulders almost to her ears. "You ought to talk to my brother, Gone-out."

"Is he a personal friend of Pele?"

"No, but he's a big Raymond Chandler fan. I bet you two would fascinate each other."

"Look, Ms. Backson—"

"Call me Busy. Don't deny it. Why else the uniform? Why else the patter? I'll bet trouble is even your business."

I sighed and said, "Sometimes it turns out that way."

Busy snapped her fingers and went on, "And now that I think about it, if Gone-out didn't once date Pele, he probably knows someone who did."

I looked at Bill. It was possible he was the only one in the room who wasn't crazy. I was wrong. He said, "You could use a guy like that."

"Yeah. I could use a guy with an imagination able to take more abuse than the Santa Monica Pier."

"You'll see," Busy said and went to get him.

14

As Plain as the Nose on My Face

Somewhere in the apartment, voices were raised. I couldn't understand what they said. They were just voices, sounds rising and falling as if animals were discussing a bone at the back of a cave.

While Bill stood before the fish tank, transfixed, I went to the front door and opened it, allowing a cold, damp wind to shoulder its way past me and begin to search the room. In the short time Bill and I had been in Busy's apartment, the beach had emptied almost entirely. The ocean was gray as an old pot, except where an orange road led to the sun, which rippled like a snake going down a ladder as it dropped through the hazy air.

"Mr. Marlowe?"

As I shut the door and turned back toward the room, I said, "Call me Zoot."

Busy was standing next to a tall thin man with a beard and hair the same angelic color as hers. From behind thick glasses blinked eyes such a pale blue they were nearly a strange kind of white. They never stopped moving as they studied me. He used his lizard lips to make a crooked, knowing smile. He wore brown pants and a shirt with a smoky brown stripe. Something gold was pinned to his blue tie, which was loosened a little as if this were his day off.

Busy watched us to see what we would do with each other. I felt like a new fish in her tank. She said, "Zoot, this is my brother, Gone-out."

"Charmed, I'm sure," he said as we shook hands.

Nobody shook hands with Bill, and he put his down.

"Busy told me she had an interesting visitor, and I see that she was right." His smile became more crooked. If he wasn't careful, it would slide off his face. "You are not of this Earth, are you?" His bright, flickering eyes skewered me as if I were already a specimen mounted in his collection.

I'd heard of people like Gone-out. UFO nuts. Men who received messages from space through their teeth; women who had close encounters with star princes who looked like movie actors. UFO nuts: righter than they knew, but for all the wrong reasons. UFO nuts. Nuts was right.

On a whim, I decided to take a chance on an idea I would not have considered five minutes before. But Gone-out's personality gave me confidence, and the gig was too good to resist. I guess I was a little nuts myself. Call it an experiment in human relations.

I said, "Is it that obvious?" Poor little me.

Busy didn't disappoint me. She groaned theatrically and sat down again, this time with her feet on the floor. She rested her boobs on her crossed arms and watched us with tolerant good humor. Gone-out stepped toward me eagerly, and I got a good look at the pin on his tie. It was not the same comet Busy wore, but a pearl sitting on three crossed golden sticks.

Then something dropped out of my mind like a toy dropping down a chute in a penny arcade. I remembered the glint on the collar of the guy who hit me. But it wasn't just a glint any more. It was a small pearl on a golden tripod, the same kind of pin Gone-out Backson was wearing, the same kind the freak in the Malibu Bar and No-Grill had been wearing. I had the feeling Medium Rare was stalking me, though there was no reason in the world she should be. No reason in *this* world.

Gone-out gripped my shoulders and cried, "Brother."

"I don't think so," I said, and tried to step back.

"No, wait," he said. "I am also of another plane."

"Plane?" I said. "As in big silver bird?"

Gone-out laughed as if over tiny, crustless sandwiches at a tea party. He said, "Another plane of existence, a place wiser than ours."

I nodded and said, "Is that what the dingus on your tie means?"

He seemed pleased that I'd noticed. He said, "In a manner of speaking, yes. The 'dingus,' as you so quaintly call it, is a honk, an ancient Krybassinian symbol of knowledge and universal balance, now taken by Medium Rare as her own."

"Would it be too difficult for you to give me my shoulders back and tell me about Medium Rare at the same time?"

I think he'd forgotten where his hands were. He took them away, and held one finger in the air as he declaimed, "She is the beginning and the end. She is the Serpent of Time biting its own tail. She sees all, knows all, tells all."

"She's bigger than a bread box and she 'knows what evil lurks in the hearts of men.'

All you have to do is cross her palm with silver. OK. I got it."

Gone-out squinted at me, and his crooked smile went up again. He said, "Busy guessed you were a follower of Raymond Chandler's. I can see why."

"As plain as the nose on my face," I said, taking another chance. It was a good evening for chances.

Busy and I were both watching Gone-out. He sat down on the singing couch and twined one leg around the other. He was as casual as the changing of the guard at Buckingham Palace. He said, "I am Chandler come again. I've been debirthed many times, and I know it."

"You're too old. You had to have been born before Chandler died."

"That's what *I* told him," Busy said.

Gone-out smiled and crossed his legs the other way. His legs were very thin. It was astonishing how many times they'd go around. Calmly, he said, "The Universe is a mysterious place, is it not?"

"The Universe has nothing on Hermosa Beach, " I said.

Gone-out actually laughed at that, but it was a harsh laugh that did not enjoy anything. "Of course mysteries are nothing new to me." Proudly, he went on, as if reciting the names of awards he'd won. "I also study New Age music, astral projection, harmonics, crystals, channeling, and reincarnation."

Bill said, "I'm the reincarnation of a '54 Chevy."

Busy squashed a laugh behind a hand, but Gone-out looked at Bill with wide-eyed interest. "Mechanical reincarnation. I've not heard of this."

"It's a new one on all of us," I said. "I'd like to meet Medium Rare."

Gone-out closed his eyes, and held his open

palm in my direction as he nodded. "Yes. Yes.
I can see it."

"A lady's yellow handkerchief with the ini-
tials ZM?"

His eyes snapped open like shutters. His
mouth looked even more as if it belonged on a
lizard. He said, "You scoff, yet I sense that you
and Medium Rare were tightly bound together
in a former life. That is why this unexplainable
urge to see her."

"I knew one of us was bound a little too
tight," I said. "When can I see her?"

"She will be at the Aquaricon, a New Age
convention at the Airport Stanton Hotel this
weekend."

"I'll be there."

"I know," Gone-out said.

15

A Sentimental Geek Thinking Wishfully

We agreed to meet in the lobby of the Airport Stanton Hotel the next day. The door clicked closed behind Bill and me, and he trotted down the stairs, marveling at what a mysterious guy Gone-out Backson was and how amazing it was that he knew I'd be going to the Aquaricon.

I stood there with the door behind me, looking past Bill, and let the blackness beyond the promenade lights suck me out into the night. I could hear the big machine of the ocean out there, working and grinding, grabbing the land and trying to pull it under. Far out were some points of white light that didn't move. A smell of popcorn came on the cold wind and curled around my nose like a warm scarf. It occurred to me that I hadn't eaten since that morning. I pulled my trench coat around myself and said, "After I said I was going, it was easy for Gone-out to say he knew it ahead of time."

"Yeah, but," Bill said and waited for me at the bottom of the stairs.

"Yeah, but nothing." We argued amiably about Gone-out Backson's psychic powers all the way back to the car. In it, I started the engine, and had the Belvedere rolling toward Malibu when Bill said, "Wait a minute. They found it."

"Who found what?"

"They," he said excitedly. "The police. They found the Pantages truck with the spine necklaces in it."

We were at a stop sign with no one behind us. Thin fog was moving in like the ghosts of new neighbors. I was cold and wanted my dinner, but the car didn't move. I looked at Bill and said, "How do you know?"

"I get the police calls."

"All the time?"

"Sure. It's easy."

"How come I never heard about this before?" I grumbled. Bright lights reflected into my eyes from the rearview mirror, and the guy who'd pulled up behind me tapped his horn. I drove. "How come?" I said again as the guy swerved around me and roared up to a red light.

"It was never important before."

"You may even be right about that. Where?"

"Where what?"

"Life without nouns is confusing, isn't it? The truck. Where's the truck?"

"Dominguez. Near the Sue Veneer Novelty Company."

Artesia Boulevard moved surprisingly well considering how solidly it was packed, and the San Diego Freeway south looked like a road race. Northbound looked like mud being forced through a pipe. There must have been an accident behind me. It could as easily have happened in front of me. Sometimes you get lucky.

I followed Bill's directions through a maze of dark side streets, illuminated only by the rectangles of yellow light that hung against the darkness like paintings in a gallery. I was a block away from the truck's location when I heard the sharp grunt of police calls hammering the neighborhood like a pile driver. Farther on, red and blue lights swept the nearby houses from behind a police barricade that kept out a clump of curious neighbors.

Beyond the barricade, a searchlight was focused on men in uniform who were crawling like ants over the Pantages truck. More policemen were standing with Police Detective Cliffy and Sergeant Robinson. A little to one side, Harry and Hilda stood, looking cold despite their heavy coats. They were not arguing, but I was sure it would be just a matter of time.

I backed up my car and found a place to park on a dark street about a block away. Bill and I walked toward the excitement. A woman dressed as if she were going somewhere fancy walked quickly in my direction, and I asked her what was going on.

"Truck full of drugs," she said, pained as if it were her truck.

By morning the word on the street would be that the truck contained the yearly heroin output of a mythical but real-sounding South American country and enough weapons to overthrow the government of your choice. So much for hearing it through the grapevine. I nodded to her and walked on.

With Bill at my heels, I bobbed under the barricade and joined the confusion. Some giggles from the watching neighbors may have been for me. A man in uniform strolled over with a flare in one hand. He smiled pleasantly enough, and said, "Sorry, sir. This area is temporarily closed."

I said, "I'm a friend of the guy who owns the truck. He'll be glad to see me."

"That may be so, sir, but nobody gets in here without the OK of Lieutenant Cliffy."

At this point, Philip Marlowe would have flashed his buzzer, but I didn't have one. I said, "If he saw me, I'd get it."

The policeman nodded, but only to show he'd heard me. "This way, sir," he said, and had me and Bill walk in front of him to where Cliffy was standing trying not to spit. When he saw me, his eyebrows butted together and his face hardened around his fleshy nose. Sergeant Robinson looked as relaxed as ever, with his left hand in the pocket of his overcoat.

"You know," Cliffy said, "somehow I knew you'd show up. I guess we can't have a side-show crime in this town without you."

"Thanks," Bill said.

"Bots," Cliffy said contemptuously and looked around. I waited for Robinson to pull a spitoon from his pocket, but he didn't. Cliffy glanced at the policeman who'd escorted me and Bill, and said, "I'll take care of these two now, Mathews. Thanks."

Mathews nodded and took his flare away.

Cliffy put his fists on his hips while he narrowed his eyes at Bill and me. He said, "What are you doing here?"

"My bot gets the police calls. When he told me about the truck, I thought I'd come over and have a look for myself."

"They ought to outlaw them things," Cliffy said, almost to himself.

I grumbled back, "When radios are outlawed, only outlaws will have radios."

Cliffy meditated on that for a moment, looking none too happy. He said, "There's the truck. Now, move along before I run you in as an accessory." It was almost a snarl, but not quite.

He actually succeeded in surprising me. I said, "Make me worry."

He held up his fat fingers and ticked them off. "One, you're there with that hat on the beach. Not illegal in itself, but very interesting when you hook it up with number two, you're there when the truck full of spines is hijacked. Now, wonder of wonders, you're here again when the hijacked truck is found."

"What has the hat got to do with this?" I said, thinking of Avoirdupois.

"It's just peculiar, that's all. Ain't it peculiar, Robinson?"

"Peculiar," Robinson said.

I waved a hand in front of my nose and said, "Before the accusations get too thick out here, maybe you can tell me what's in the truck."

"What's it to you?"

"That seems to be the question, doesn't it? The fact is that the spines are part of a case I'm working on."

"Too bad."

"Maybe Harry will tell me." Before Cliffy or Robinson could do anything, I turned and called out, "What's new, Harry?"

Harry said something angrily to Hilda, and marched over to us while Hilda watched with soft, worried eyes. By the time Harry got to us, he was smiling and had his hand out. I shook it. "Well," he said, "it looks as if the police were a little more efficient than you thought."

"Hah," said Cliffy, and even Robinson smiled.

"They're good, all right. Maybe they're so good they can tell you why somebody bothered to borrow a truck full of plastic blowfish spine necklaces and then give them back."

Cliffy and Harry frowned at each other.

I said, "The truck *is* still full of necklaces, isn't it?"

"You're mighty smart for a guy who just got here," Cliffy said, prodding me with the words as if they were his stubby fingers.

"I'm not smart, I just pay attention. Harry and anybody else with an opinion has told me that the necklaces are all the same. Whoever's been stealing these necklaces all over town is finding that out the hard way. When the Polynesians who stole the truck found out that these necklaces were just like all the others, they had no reason to keep them. Or is the truck empty after all?"

Cliffy puffed himself up and said, "All of that's pretty obvious, isn't it?" He spit quickly, pretending nobody had seen.

"Of course it is," said Harry. "All the spine necklaces are the same."

"Maybe none of these geeks," Cliffy's eyes swerved at me and he went on, "know that."

Robinson shook a finger slowly in Cliffy's direction and spoke as if he'd had an idea. "Or maybe they know it, but are thinking wishfully."

"Thinking wishfully?" Cliffy said as if he were making sure he'd gotten the punchline of a joke. He smiled at me and said, "What about you? You think anything wishfully?"

"Just about dinner," I said.

"Tough guy," Cliffy grumbled. "What do you know about this?" He nodded to Sergeant Robinson, who pulled a folded sheet of pink paper from his righthand coat pocket. I unfolded it and read, "Happy day! Medium Rare loves you!"

Suddenly I was as cold as Hilda looked. I'd be seeing Medium Rare for the first time the next day at the Aquaricon. But she cast a long shadow before her. I felt as if I'd already seen her, as if I already knew the rank smell of her breath as it blew down my neck. I said, "Some geek gave me one of these when he tried to buy the spine necklace a friend of mine brought back from Hawaii."

"Talk about your geeks," Cliffy said and shared a chuckle with Harry and Robinson. "Did you sell it to him?"

"No. I'm kind of sentimental for a geek."

"Please don't take offense," Robinson said.

"No offense taken. After toxic waste and nose drops, it would take more than one bad rib to exercise me. Does this have anything to do with the truck?"

Cliffy snapped the paper with a finger and said nastily, "These flyers are showing up all over town, usually in the company of somebody who wants to purchase one of these blowfish spine necklaces. If the owner doesn't want to sell, he usually wakes up with a bump on the head and short one necklace. Sometimes there is some money missing, too, but more often, not."

"You figure Medium Rare is somehow tied up with the dynamic duo that borrowed the truck?"

"I don't like tidy coincidences. What do you figure?"

"Nothing, at the moment. I'm just watching the master at work."

Harry began to laugh but was cut short by a petrifying glance from Cliffy. Cliffy looked at me, but his face was different, tired. It was a face that wanted to go home to the wife and kids, and think about nothing more taxing than how to work the pop-top on a can of beer. The mouth in that face said, "If you're mixed up in this, we'll find out eventually. You'd better have something good up your nose or we'll nail you to the wall." Robinson shook his head.

"I can't say I haven't been warned." I nodded at each of them and walked away through the crowd with Bill.

16

A Brisk Business in Hoo-Doo

It was a long, dark ride back to Malibu. Clues, such as they were, swirled through my head, not sticking one to the other. It was obvious that the Polynesians—one of whom might be named Pele—were after something very special. They might have found it and returned the truck and the rest of the spines out of courtesy. I didn't know if Harry kept a close enough inventory to tell if only one were missing. Was Medium Rare looking for the same special spine, or was she looking for some other spine entirely?

Thinking tended to run in circular ruts and throw off more questions than answers—threadbare, slightly shabby questions. I was so tired that at least once when I saw a red light, I knew that something ought to be done about stopping the car but it didn't occur to me till Bill yelped that the something should be done by me.

When I got the Belvedere into the garage at last, I turned off the engine and just sat there listening to the silence that gathered around my ears and the occasional hiss of a car going by on Pacific Coast Highway. It wasn't long before hunger drove me into the house.

If you didn't count the rabbits, what I found in the living room was the usual scene. The sound was too loud on a car chase careering around the TV screen. The surfers had paired off but were still watching the action while they stroked each other and the rabbits, pretty much at random. Well, it was early yet. Bowls of yoyogurt were within easy reaching distance.

"What's shaking?" I called out, barely able to hear myself.

"You look really dogged," Hanger cried from her seat on Mustard's lap.

"Dogged, drilled, and wiped out. Is there any food?"

"Leftover pizza," Thumper shouted. He frowned. "Captain Hook didn't eat much. He just did magic with the pepperoni. Pulled it out of the air." Thumper reached into the air as if he were pulling a book down from a shelf.

"I was getting tired of rabbits, anyway." I said.

Stepping over rabbits and their byproducts, I went to hang up my trench coat and found Whipper Will and Bingo leaning on pillows and each other while they read books.

Bingo looked up at me and said, "What's happening, Holmes?"

"Confusion, small mayhem, large doubts. The usual."

"Sounds as if we're getting our money's worth," Whipper Will said without looking up.

"I hope so," I said. "I wouldn't want to be doing this for nothing."

Bill followed me into the kitchen, where two slices of pizza waited on a round sheet of cardboard. Next to it was a pile of pepperoni slices. Evidently there was still some magic in them, because as I watched, one of them kind of burped and pulled itself into two slices, each the same size as the original. Bill sat down and began to move the slices around like checkers.

I was too hungry to worry about the magic being infectious, so I picked up a slice of pizza and took a large bite. It had been sitting there a long time. Room temperature had congealed the cheese into something you might use to re-sole your shoes. The tomato sauce was cold. The disks of pepperoni were stiff. The pizza was delicious. I even sampled some of the in-credible pepperoni. It was just so much ground meat.

The first slice of pizza was gone almost be-fore I knew it. I took up the remaining one and began to munch as I looked out the window. The surf was a little rougher than it had been when I'd left Busy Backson's apartment, and the foam was luminescent as it curled toward the beach.

Blocking my view of the ocean was a shadow vaguely in the shape of a hat. Orange lights on the sawhorses that surrounded it winked at me. The fact that the hat was still there told me that the two Polynesians had not yet found what they were looking for. Which meant I still had a chance to find them and somehow get them to cure Captain Hook. It would also be OK if they told me why they wanted the blow-fish spine necklaces.

Under a light out on the public walkway, Captain Hook—at the moment the Great Hook-ini—was waving a couple of torches around for an admiring crowd of strangers. I gathered his friends could no longer stand him.

He threw a torch high into the air, caught it, stuck the burning end into his mouth, pulled the naked torch out, and blew fire back onto it. I watched him while I finished my pizza. He was pretty gnarly, actually, but he didn't look

happy. He was just going through the motions.
Captain Hook was still inside the Great Hookini somewhere, and he'd be in a killer mood
when he was freed at last.

Still, it had to be done. Captain Hook was
who he was. It wasn't right for him to be somebody else. Especially if that somebody else
might set the place on fire. And he'd have more
fun being unhappy if he could choose his subjects.

The nutrition in the pizza hit my system, and
I felt as if I were a balloon being inflated, but
I was punchy from lack of sleep—as shown by
the length of homey philosophy I was capable
of spinning out. I told Bill I was going to bed.
As I stumbled off, he was climbing up onto a
chair so that he could watch the Great Hookini
through the kitchen window.

The next morning, I awoke to find myself
alone in the bedroom with some sunshine that
looked much brighter than I felt. In the
kitchen, I looked out the window and saw that
Whipper Will and Bingo were out running their
surf-bots with the other surfers. Bill was sitting on a countertop, plugged into an outlet. I
ate breakfast without disturbing him, then I
unplugged him. His eyes snapped open.

"Airport Stanton Hotel," I said.

He leaped from the counter and said, "Right
this way, Boss."

When we got into the Belvedere, I just sat
there for a minute with my hands in my lap.
Bill waited as patiently as the car. I said, "I
feel as if last night didn't exist, as if I've never
been away from behind this wheel."

Bill said, "Is that good?"

"Better than doing magic all night, I suppose." I started the engine and carefully
backed onto PCH.

The day was clear and as bright as the sunshine in Whipper Will's bedroom promised. Cars moved along easily, nobody in much of a hurry. It wasn't a holiday, but the usual holiday crowds strolled with their bots and their boards and their blankets. The ocean was blue, but it had more character than the sky, which seemed a little garish for a sky. Out on the ocean, the white cream of waves seemed to leap like big fish.

I drove up the hill at Colorado and rolled through Santa Monica on Lincoln, a hodgepodge of small businesses with big signs. Traffic thickened for no good reason and stayed thick until I was below Marina del Rey. Maybe everybody was going to visit his yacht. Lincoln swept past the airport, not much concerned with the big silver bananas that seemed about to sit on the center divider until they landed with a screech of wheels and rolled off on business of their own. Lincoln joined Sepulveda and went down to Century Boulevard where a line of hotels, looking as if they were lengths of runway that had been stood on end, shot up on either side of the street.

Bill got me to the Airport Stanton all right, but he had no particular ideas where I could park without spending my life savings. We gave up looking on the street and parked under the hotel. I had the satisfaction of nicking a rear fender all by myself.

On the elevator from the parking levels up into the hotel lobby, Bill and I rode with two well-dressed women who crowded themselves as far away from us as they could get. Each of them wore a crisp print dress in a fruity color, and had a chunk of transparent rock hanging around her neck on a chain. They held thick booklets to their nicely rounded chests while they talked excitedly about their latest experience in a former life. As far as I could tell, they'd both been a lot more interesting before they were born.

The lobby was a cavern with a brightly flowered carpet. Right now the carpeting had a lot of competition from the crowds of people, each as trim and neat as a billiard ball. Every one of them carried one of those thick booklets, and most of them had managed to work rocks into what they were wearing. One way or another, they all had the sort of unfocused enthusiasm and faraway eyes that made Gone-out Backson look like a candidate for a long rest in a place where they'd *make* you rest and no back talk.

I walked through the lobby, feeling a little out of place wearing brown, but people either smiled at me as if they knew me, or they ignored me. In a conspicuous place was a long table next to a placard that said, AQUARICON REGISTRATION HERE.

Registering cost me ten bucks, and all it bought me was the right to go into the dealers' room, where I would have the opportunity to spend more money. They wanted to charge me for Bill, too, but I talked them out of it. Sometimes, when I'm feeling chipper, I'm able to do things like that.

The dealers' room was really a number of rooms, none of them smaller than an airplane hangar, and all of them cold enough to hang meat. In a smaller room, the pattern of big, bilious flowers on the walls would give you a headache. Here, it just crossed your eyes. Tables were set up around the walls and in two aisles down the center of the room. Some of the tables held crystals, others held electronic gizmos with too many antennas, and still others held things that looked like board games but probably weren't. Men and women stood behind the tables, doing a brisk business in hoo-doo.

"This is great," Bill said.

"You can be excited for both of us," I said as I began to tour the room. The place was very quiet for a zoo, all reasonable explanations and low scientific discussions about electromagnetic cleansing of the aura, debirthing, crystal therapy, astrology.

The things that looked like board games would tell you what you and your friends were really like and what you could expect from the future. Your money fully refunded if you weren't satisfied and if you could find the guy who'd sold it to you after he'd changed his name and his sex and moved to a higher plane of existence, or maybe just to a different state.

One guy, dressed in crushed purple velvet and enough rings for four hands, was selling tapes and sheet music that had been dictated to him by Bach. Bach had been better at composition when he was alive. The tape this guy was playing sounded as if he'd recorded an air conditioner in a bowling alley.

A round, ruddy woman with a cloud of white hair was laughing a lot and selling mementos of DEMETRIUS, THE DOG FROM ATLANTIS. The backs of photos of a primitive-looking glass statue of something with four legs and a snout explained that Demetrius had been carved by the simple native craftsmen of the Lost Continent of Atlantis. Why it was lost was never explained, but the woman had evidently found it in her backyard out in Pomona. The original dog was not molded from glass, but carved from mystic crystal. The dog, she said, was still alive after ten thousand years.

I picked up one of the glass dogs she had for sale and said, "They don't look very lively to me."

I was a very silly boy. She laughed as if I'd complimented her chocolate cake and said, "These are just glass replicas."

"Does your original move much?"

"No. But then, what do you expect from a crystal dog?"

"Depends on what I paid for him. For what you're charging, I'd expect him to do windows and speak French. At the very least."

The laughter bubbled away from her, leaving an old, dry, predatory woman who said, "You'll never get anywhere with an attitude like that." I didn't even have a chance to grunt and walk away before she reignited the smile on her face for the next guy who strolled by.

There was a lot more. I could have had my palm read either by eye or by machine, I could have had my handwriting analyzed, I could have had my past lives charted, or signed up to have my nodes retuned, or made an appointment to have my chakras detoxed. None of it was any crazier than three ice cubes on a hot griddle, but then, the dealers' room was a big place, and I'd probably missed the really good stuff.

I hadn't seen Gone-out Backson in the dealers' room, so I dragged Bill back out into the lobby where a guy stuck a sheet of paper into my hand and walked on. The paper told me that for only one hundred fifty dollars, I could attend a lecture on how we could encourage people from space to help change the Earth. At the top of the paper was a very dark, fuzzy picture of something with a big head and glowing eyes. It could as easily have been a picture of me or the front end of a Chevrolet.

At the moment, I had bigger problems than how to change the Earth, and I needed a little help myself. Then I saw a pale-blue suit. It brought out the blue of Gone-out Backson's eyes. Something glinted on his tie. Even from across the room I knew what it was, but I walked in his direction anyway.

17

Like Circles That Cross in the Night

Bill and I weaved our way among members of a big crowd that had gathered near the escalator. In the center of it, Gone-out Backson stood about arm's length from a perfectly normal-looking woman, aiming an electronic gadget at her. A corkscrew thing on the front of the gadget seemed mighty disappointed about something, because its stiff length pointed at her toes.

Gone-out spoke loudly, but otherwise as if he were a doctor, and he and the woman were alone. He said, "You see, you are tired because your aura is diffuse. You must learn to concentrate it," he clutched his hand at his chest, "and allow it to fill your body with energy. Try this." He pulled a crystal necklace from his pocket and hung it around the woman's neck. He backed off a few yards, then approached the woman again, his corkscrew still sagging. He was a lot farther away than arm's length when the corkscrew suddenly rose until it was parallel with the floor. The audience moaned as if Gone-out had just done a triple back somersault.

"You see," he said. "The crystal acts as a lens to focus your energy."

The woman's eyes were moist with tears. She wiped some of them away with the back of a hand. "I feel wonderful," she said as she fondled the crystal. "I need this crystal."

"Of course you do," Gone-out said. "Please keep it with my compliments." He looked around and raised his voice. "If I can be of service to anyone else, I will be in the dealers' room at table 703."

Most of the people moved away, but some of them crowded around Gone-out and began to ask him questions about which kinds of rocks would be good for which parts of their bodies. As Gone-out spoke of quartz, carnelian, and topaz, my breakfast began to back up on me. Bill nodded at what Gone-out was saying and announced, "It must be true. I'm full of semiconducting silicon."

Gone-out's head snapped in our direction, and those pale blue eyes took us in. He wasn't surprised to see us, or even very interested, but those blue eyes knew everything about us there was to know. Despite this, he didn't look any less like a lizard than he had the day before. He said, "That's all for now, my friends. I'll see you in the dealers' room at table 703."

As the hard cases drifted away, Gone-out walked to us, the honk on his tie picking up a lot of light. He said, "You haven't found Medium Rare."

"No. But I've met a lot of her friends."

Maybe he didn't like my tone, because he sneered as he said, "For a man from beyond, you are a very poor believer."

"I've been working on it," I said, "but nothing seems to help."

Gone-out smiled coolly and said, "As the reincarnation of Raymond Chandler, I appreciate your bold wit. Let's go into the bar and await Medium Rare's arrival."

"What about your customers?"

"They'll wait," Gone-out said.

"And like it, I suppose."

"I suppose," Gone-out said, as if it were no concern of his.

He was stopped by fans not more than a dozen times as we walked to a corner of the lobby littered with couches and overstuffed chairs. They were done in the same flowered pattern as the walls and the carpeting. The hotel management had probably paid somebody a lot of money to think of doing that.

Gone-out Backson sat on a couch near enough the flow of traffic to keep an eye on it, yet far enough away that we had an illusion of privacy. Our order was taken by a thin, well-used blonde in a green outfit that showed her legs went all the way up. She came back a minute later with Gone-out's brandy and my beer, then waited to see who would be the sport. Gone-out said, "If you are running true to form, your bank balance is trying to walk under a duck."

I nodded, and he grandly paid the bill as if he were buying me an artificial kidney. The blonde took the money without a word, and Gone-out watched across the top of his brandy glass as she walked away.

We sat in polite, friendly silence sipping our various brewskis. Gone-out was thinking about something beyond that room. Either that, or he really enjoyed his brandy.

Men and women strolled by with determination, or involved in animated conversation, or with no more on their minds than Demetrius, the Dog from Atlantis, had on his. They were all neat and clean, and from the looks of things could afford the time and money to indulge in a little low-grade metaphysics. They might even have had enough time and money that they could afford to believe in it. If Gone-out wanted to browse in other people's wallets, he'd chosen the right wallets.

Gone-out said, "I can't tell if you don't approve of me, or if you just talk like that because you're preoccupied with Chandler."

"If I'm really not of this Earth, as you say, then I have a right to either one."

Gone-out nodded long enough that I was sure he was thinking about something else. Suddenly, he almost slipped onto one knee and pleaded, "Teach me. You are wiser than I. Teach me."

"Sure, " I said. "Everybody wants a bank account that's able to walk under a duck. Lesson one is 'Don't whine.' "

"I wasn't—"

He was interrupted by the arrival of a large white shape whose voice boomed from the bottom of a deep, nasty well: "Ah. Here we all are, then." He bowed to each of us. "Good to see you again, Gone-out." Avoirdupois took Gone-out's hand in both of his and shook it. Without letting go of Gone-out, he went on, "And you too, Mr. Marlowe. I warned you that our paths might cross again." He chuckled down in his warm inside cupboards as if the crossing of our paths pleased him very much. "Though I must admit I am surprised you know each other." He smiled. "I would not have expected the two of you to run in the same circles."

"Circles cross," I said. "Just like paths," I said.

More deep, dark laughter. "Right you are, Mr. Marlowe. Right you are. It was certain to happen sooner or later." He leaned close to me, his eyes big and round and said, "Have you made any progress with the small matter we discussed earlier?"

"What matter was that?"

His laughter gathered like rocks rolling down hill. "You are a caution, sir, that is certain. But perhaps you are right. This is no place to speak of such things."

Gone-out was smiling politely at us, following the conversation, waiting for someone to tell him what was going on. Avoirdupois harrumphed. As he sat down, he put his hand on Gone-out's knee and said, "It is of no consequence, Gone-out, I assure you. How have you been, my dear boy?"

"I've been fine."

Avoirdupois grunted and said, "No need to be circumspect with me, sir. No, indeed not. If I know you, you are still wasting your time with Medium Rare."

Gone-out pressed his lips together.

"You mistake me, sir. Your life is your own. I only observe that a woman like Medium Rare, whose methods were old when the Dark Ages were but a twinkle in the eye of Time, if I may describe them in so metaphorical a fashion, has no place at a modern, scientific New Age–type convention such as this. And, if I may say so, someone with your talents might do better following another master."

"Medium Rare sees all, knows all, tells all. She is the beginning and the end. She is—"

"—at the very least the Serpent of Time biting its own tail? You disappoint me, sir. Really you do. Quoting such rubbish." Avoirdupois laughed until I thought something inside his rotund body had shaken loose. But he suddenly became serious and shrugged.

"Your jokes are not welcome here," Gone-out said.

"One may sometimes say things in jest that one would not dare to say any other way. But,

I will admit, that is neither here nor there. The fact of the matter is that Mr. Marlowe can find out for himself which of us is correct. Even as we speak, Medium Rare is erecting her tent in a questionable neighborhood of the dealers' room—space 1204."

Gone-out snapped his fingers and said, "That was the disturbance in the ether I felt."

"To be sure, my boy. To be sure. Shall we leave Mr. Marlowe to his work?"

Tersely, Gone-out said,"You seem very eager to have Mr. Marlowe visit Medium Rare."

Avoirdupois surprised me. He laughed and shrugged, both at once. "While there is no sport in a sure thing, it can sometimes have its uses."

I stood up and said, "I'll bet you guys would be even more interesting if you actually had a subject to talk about."

Avoirdupois laughed and said, "You are a corker, sir, and make no mistake."

Gone-out just winked at me broadly.

As I walked back into the dealer's room, I felt as if I'd been wrapped up with a big red bow, and it had been done by experts.

18

I Paint What I See

The dealer's room was busier than it had been before, but the people walking through it were just as interested in form without substance. Bill was fascinated by everything he saw. I tried not to get caught up in the idea that maybe all these people with their crystals and organic color generators and electronic spirit cleaners knew something that I didn't.

I could have told them I was not of this Earth. Maybe they would have let me in for free and set me up with my own lecture. Maybe. But maybe too much reality would not be good for business; facts are more convenient if you just make them up. Maybe hope just came in strange packages. We didn't know everything, not even on T'toom.

I found Medium Rare's traveling show set up in a room I had not yet visited. Traffic was light. Avoirdupois had been right about the neighborhood, anyway.

On one side of Medium Rare's tent was a woman who claimed that in past lives she had been every one of the monarchs of England.

The woman was selling her book as a public service to set the record straight. On the other side of the tent was a slim old party dressed all in white, even down to his white pencil of a beard. He was demonstrating what he described as a magic wand. It looked like the finger of a crystalline skeleton. He said it could sweep the bad vibrations out of your house.

Medium Rare's tent was something to see. It was worth the drive to the airport. Just sitting there staked to the carpet, it swooped like a bird on the wing. It was a violent pattern of red, yellow, and blue that actually made the pattern of flowers in the carpet look restful.

Long tables pulled the eye back to the door flap of the tent. On the tables stood paintings of various sizes, some not much bigger than my hand, others big enough to surf on, and many sizes in between. The paintings were of places not of this Earth, or not of anyplace on Earth that I had ever seen or heard of. One showed twin blue moons without a hair out of place looking down on a landscape of such intense red desolation as to be terrifying. Another showed green land that rolled away to cliffs of hulking, breastlike shapes. In the foreground were small yellow huts. A third showed spiders with big eyes and hands crawling over a silver object that might have been a machine; either that or an egg laid by a toaster. All the paintings were like that: lyrical and colorful, and full of images so alien they made you uneasy even when you didn't know what you were looking at.

I recognized two of the paintings. But the one that frightened me the most, oddly enough, was the most familiar. It was very familiar, indeed. Medium Rare and I would have to talk about that picture. Yes, we would.

Between the place where the long tables met, just in front of the door flap of the tent, sat a woman. When I first saw her, she was gaping at me as if I were something long lost that had surprised her with a visit. A glass ball stood on a golden tripod on the card table before her. She wore a long blue dress that looked as if it had been riveted together from old jeans. Her white blouse puffed and billowed as if she had not so much put it on as sprayed it from a whipped cream can. Around her shiny golden head was a scarf that matched the tent. Peeking under the scarf was a headband. Medium Rare was a robot. A Surfing Samurai Robot.

"Wow," said Bill as he tried to crawl into one of the paintings.

Meanwhile, I walked up to Medium Rare. She peered at me so hard I imagined her little robotic eyeballs were bulging, though I was probably wrong about that. She was still catching flies with her mouth.

"Medium Rare?" I said.

She nodded.

"I'm Zoot Marlowe, a private detective. I'd like to ask you a few questions."

"You are not of this Earth," Medium Rare said. Her voice was musical and had the lilt of someplace far from Southern California, but not as far away as the subjects of those paintings, not nearly that far. It was a lilt I'd heard in old black-and-white horror movies.

"That seems to be the consensus among the livelier element." Not funny, but quick. About right for the circumstances.

Medium Rare said, "Have we met?"

It was a funny question, considering what I'd been through lately. I said, "Not exactly, but I feel as if I already know you."

"Yes," she said. "I should have foreseen this."

"You mean extrapolate?" Bill said.

"No," she said calmly. "I should have predicted this meeting using my psychic powers."

"Robots don't have psychic powers."

"I'm a robot. I have psychic powers. Therefore robots have psychic powers."

The logic of Medium Rare's answer seemed to bother Bill. "Erk!" he said. "Erk!" His legs shot up inside him like a window shade, and he sat there vibrating on his shiny round bottom.

"Sit," Medium Rare said, indicating a folding chair with a sweep of her hand. I found that Medium Rare swept her hands a great deal when she talked. They dramatically blocked out words and pictures in the air. Tying her hands behind her back would probably have been as good as applying a muzzle.

I sat. People drifted past, barely glancing at the paintings. Some of them seemed embarrassed to be seen in their vicinity. I had Medium Rare to myself, and she had me.

"Tell me about the paintings," I said. I hadn't planned to start with that request, but I hadn't planned on being that shaken, either.

She said, "I have a spirit guide named Rupee Begonia."

Bill said, "Robots don't have spirit guides."

"You really upset him," I said. "Or what looks like upset, anyway."

"He is a simple robot," Medium Rare said. "He will assimilate the data eventually and no longer be upset."

"Erk!" Bill said.

I waited. A little girl stopped and looked at a painting, and her mother dragged her away.

Medium Rare said, "Over the years, Rupee Begonia has led me to many planets not yet known to the beings of this sphere. I paint what I see. One of the planets is inhabited by creatures like you."

I nodded. The familiar picture had been of a slaberingeo grazing in an abo forest on T'toom.

If she was a fake, she was damned good and would do till the real thing came along.

"The fools don't believe me. They say I am old-fashioned. I say they are fakes, with their machines and their science. Not everything in the Universe can be explained by science as the beings of this sphere understand it. 'The science of any sufficiently advanced race is indistinguishable from magic.' "

"So I've heard."

"It is common enough wisdom if you know where to look." She smiled wistfully, as if remembering when she was young, when she was just a can opener, maybe. "Most people don't bother. They are too busy figuring up their next scam." She shrugged. "It is of no consequence, except to those who lose their shirts paying off charlatans." All those lost shirts made her sad.

"OK," I said. "So you're the only one in the place who's on the level. That still doesn't explain your interest in blowfish spine necklaces."

She closed her eyes, making her look like a golden statue. Her smile was a thousand years old. She said, "You have been approached by my people."

"I was nearly murdered by one of them."

Medium Rare sighed and said, "Even I must take what I can get, and only the Ultimate is perfect. What are the necklaces to you?"

"Ask Avoirdupois."

"Avoirdupois is a fool, but he is tenacious."

"That isn't all. He has connected the spines to a certain top hat on the beach at Malibu and hooked them both to a certain blond Polynesian."

"And you?"

"I have a client and an aching head."

"Perhaps we can be of use to each other." I waited while she squeezed the bridge of her nose between her eyes. I didn't know what

good a nervous twitch like that would do a robot, even one equipped with a psychic sense
and a spirit guide. She was still mangling her
nose when she said, "But not here. The con-
flicting auras at the Aquaricon disturb the
ether. You must visit me at my home, and all
will be made clear to you."

"If you're good enough to do that, it'll be the
first time."

She smiled and said, "Awaken your bot and
bring him to me."

"Bill," I called.

"Erk," he said.

"Bill, come on over here."

Bill extended his feet a short way; they
sprang back into his body, then slowly extended to their usual length. He walked to Medium Rare, saying, "A psychic robot, gee."

"Interface," Medium Rare ordered. A cable
snaked out from somewhere under her dress
and met a similar cable that snaked out from
Bill's belly. At the tip of each was a disk covered with bumps and holes. The disks touched
with a spark, and a second later, it was all over.
"Got it," Bill said as he reeled in his cable.

"Tomorrow," Medium Rare said.

"I could have predicted that," I said.

19

Cruise Patrol

The afternoon was young when I drove back to Malibu with nothing much to do except think about things. That didn't get me anywhere, and wouldn't till I saw Medium Rare the next day, so I parked the Belvedere across the front of the garage and went into the house.

Thumper was in the living room, looking at the mess as if it had disappointed him in some way. But he had his hands in the pockets of his chinos, so he wasn't in danger of doing any work. I said, "Where are all the rabbits?"

"Captain Hook figured out how to stuff them back into things." He pulled open a pocket of his pants and twisted his head to look into it. He said, "He even stuffed a few in here. They're gone now."

I said, "As long as they're gone. Anybody know how to wash a car?"

"I know," Bill said.

"Then you can be in charge," I said. "What about you?"

Thumper said, "Sure. Better that than cleaning up the living room."

"Where's everybody else?"

"Around," Thumper said without concern.

We collected some old plastic pails and loaded them with soap and polish, and some rags that had been pretty aggro T-shirts once. I put on Will's short johns again and followed Thumper outside, where we slopped around a lot of soapy water and got very silly with the hose. Bill pointed out spots on the car we'd missed. All in all, it was a wet, slippery afternoon with a clean car at the end of it.

Thumper, Bill, and I looked at the gleaming car. That was part of the job, too, the part you wait for. Water beaded up on Bill and rolled off, but both Thumper and I needed some dry clothes. Instead of putting them on, we went out back and lay down on the sand in the sun.

A lot of robots were surfing. I could see Mustard and a few of the girls running up and down the shore with their control boxes. Nobody got close to the top hat.

Captain Hook dropped onto the sand next to me and said, "This is positively the most amazing—"

"We don't want to hear about it," Thumper said.

"Observe," said Captain Hook. He manipulated the air as if it were a deck of cards, then offered the imaginary deck to me and asked me to pick a card, any card. Bill took a card. After a little more show biz, Captain Hook told Bill what the card had been. Even Thumper was impressed when the captain got it right. But the captain still wasn't happy. He said, "I need a vacation."

"I'm working on it," I said.

That seemed to surprise him. He watched my legs dry, then got up and walked down the beach, throwing clouds of doves into the air. He gave the hat a wide berth and stood watch-

ing the water slide up to his toes, then back
into the foam.

We had Chinese for dinner and a Gino and
Darlene movie for dessert. It wasn't the evening I would have chosen if I'd had a choice,
but at least nobody tried to ream out my vibes
with a hunk of rock.

The next morning, Whipper Will announced
that he and Bingo were going grocery shopping. I was in the kitchen with Bill, listening
to them bang around in their bedroom, getting
ready to go. I drained my coffee cup and was
rinsing it when I said, "You have Medium
Rare's address?"

"Right here in the old bubble memory," Bill
said.

"Let's get to it, then."

I expected him to leap off the chair with a
reassuring exclamation, but he didn't move. He
said, "I don't know where it is."

I don't know what kind of look I had on my
face, but Bill could have astonished me less if
he'd grown a nose from his forehead.

"What about the old bubble memory?"

"I got L.A. County in here, Boss. Changehorses is not in L.A. County."

"Where is it?"

He wanted to shrug but he didn't have any
shoulders, so he made a small mechanical
noise back in his machinery. The front door
slamming brought me out of my trance, and I
ran through the house to swing it open. "Will,"
I cried as loudly as I could.

Will and Bingo were half way across PCH,
but they heard me and came back, looking surprised and curious. I waited for them. Will
said, "What?"

"I need a map that shows a town called
Changehorses, probably in California."

His eyebrows went up.

"I seem to have found the edge of Bill's bubble memory."

"Can it wait?"

"Can Captain Hook wait?"

"All right," Will said. We all went back into the house. Will pulled heaps of maps out of the bottom drawer of his dresser and threw them onto the floor, where Bingo sorted them. Bingo found what she was looking for and handed it to Will.

He spread a map of California on the bed. He looked up something on a list, turned the map over, and looked closely at it. If his nose had been a match, he'd have set the map on fire. "Here it is, above Newhall. You might be able to find it by yourself but having a guide with his stuff wired might save you a few hours."

"Want to apply?"

"There's the groceries."

"And the sun and the sand and the surf. I guess the Malibu Chamber of Commerce is going to repossess all of that tonight."

"Right you are, dude. How often can I score an adventure? Want to come, Bingo?"

She shook her head. "Somebody around here has to keep their stuff wired. You guys go on cruise patrol. I'm going to get groceries." She walked from the room, singeing the air.

"One aggro mama," said Will appreciatively.

We all seemed to get very busy then, though not much needed to be done before we got into the Belvedere and headed toward Topanga Canyon.

Bill was sitting in the back seat, seeming to enjoy the ride, but I worried about him. Finding one of his limitations must have been as tough for him as it would be for anybody. Can robots hurt? Maybe he had an overloaded silicon semiconductor. Or maybe I'd just had too

much coffee. I was the only one who seemed to
be bothered.

I drove us among the trees and the rugged-
looking cliffs. Prickly puffs of faded green
scrub hung off high hills when it wasn't too
difficult and gave off a sweet, spicy scent that
almost had me hanging out the window. Whipper Will got us from there through a business
district that thought it was quaint but couldn't
quite hide the cheap come-on, and from there
onto a freeway. We went east, then north.

For a while we drove between high cinder-
block walls, behind which I could see the roofs
of houses that all looked the same. We passed
enormous, weedy lots, and the freeway widened. The lots gave way to hills that rolled in
like tidal waves, then kept their distance as if
they were afraid of playing in traffic. A lot of
big trucks shouldered their way around us,
grumbling and puffing black smoke as they
climbed a grade with all the effort of toe-
dancing elephants.

After leaving the freeway, we drove through
a nice residential area with houses somewhat
larger than shacks, and a lot of tall spindly ev-
ergreen trees and well-manicured lawns that
swept like velvet to the street.

Once out of the residential area, we rolled
without noticeable transition into a wild forest
that grew right to the edge of the road, making
it seem to be a length of white masking tape
that had been laid down over the trees and
brush. We drove through the shade and pine
smell like a submarine through water.

The road gave us our money's worth of hair-
pin turns and views that made you wonder why
people even bothered with art. In the middle
of a fairly straight stretch stood a blue sign
that said GAS—FOOD—LODGING—SPIRITUAL AD-
VICE, 5 MILES.

20

Like Something Out of Poe

There wasn't much to Changehorses but a gas station called "Spirit Gas," a combination grocery store, restaurant, and post office called "Medium Rare's Emporium," a bar called "Medium Rare's Changehorses and Dance," and a few houses that looked as if they'd been left in the bushes to die. The name of the gas station must have been a misprint.

Bill had the address of Medium Rare's house, but on Whipper Will's map, the town was barely a freckle. There was no way to know where in town the house was.

I pulled into a spot in front of the emporium and got out of the car. The air smelled of syrup and pine dust and was much colder than the air in Malibu. I was glad, for once, that I had my trench coat and hat.

A couple of rustic types—all plaid flannel and beards—were sitting on metal chairs near the front door. I shivered, thinking how cold that metal must be. But they were real he-men, complete with frozen bottoms. I guess they didn't see many strangers in Changehorses, because every eye that wasn't nailed down was all over me. I nodded to the rustics as I walked into the emporium. Whipper Will nodded. Even Bill nodded. They nodded back, but I think it was just reflex.

Inside, the emporium was warm enough that I couldn't see my breath, but that didn't mean it was warm. The air was heavy with the brown smell of cheap restaurant cooking, and I decided I could wait a while longer for lunch.

We passed counter after counter of absolute junk—bumper stickers, key chains, candy, coffee cups, glow-in-the-dark skulls—things that the Here Today—Gone to Maui Souvenir Company would have been embarrassed to carry. Something called "The Legend of Change-horses" had been shellacked to slabs of tree trunk. Everything was priced high so the faithful wouldn't have too much money to get into trouble with.

Every piece had Medium Rare's name or likeness on it, sometimes both if they wanted the piece to move. Bill seemed particularly fascinated by the eyes jumping in a three-D portrait of Medium Rare staring raptly into her glass ball. On almost every counter top was a stack of flyers that said, HAPPY DAY! MEDIUM RARE LOVES YOU! As far as I could tell, the flyers were free.

Business was slow that day, and we got the entire attention of a balding, middle-aged man whose taste in shirts seemed to run to fringe. A bar on his shirt pocket said, MERLE. We caught him prowling behind the counter with a small feather duster that he occasionally used to tickle the merchandise. He smiled and, in a melodious drawl, asked how he might help us.

I was about to ask for directions to Medium Rare's place when Whipper Will said, "Elvis? Is that you?"

I heard the wood in the handle of the duster crack as Merle gripped it hard. He licked the smile off his lips and glared at Will, daring him to say anything else. "Name's Merle," he said and jabbed at the bar on his chest. Signals flashed between him and Will as surely as if they'd been talking on the telephone, though neither one of them spoke or moved.

At last Will said, "Right," as if he'd come to a decision. Merle nodded, as if satisfied. The smile returned, but it went no deeper than his teeth. I asked for directions, and Will repeated the directions back to Merle to make sure he had them right.

"She'll help you, I'm sure," Merle said and clucked meaningfully at my nose.

"I'm sure she will. And when she's done, we'll come back for a key chain and a coffee cup to remember the experience by."

"You do that," Merle said. "We got a sale on Medium Rare tea sets."

Will and Merle said good-bye to each other and wished each other luck. They both seemed to understand that the words were hiding more than they were telling.

We managed to get past the display cases without buying anything and walked back out into the cold, sweet air where the old men hadn't moved. Only their eyes followed us as we got back into the car, revved the heater, and drove up the hill.

I said, "What was that all about?"

"I just thought I knew him, that's all."

I nodded and waited for more. It never came. Will was as silent and brooding as the tall trees on either side of the road.

Merle's directions were simple and finely polished by many retellings. Finding Medium Rare's place was easy. We turned right at the stop sign, a big landmark in Changehorses, and continued up the hill till we came to a gravel side road, nearly a path. We bounced up that till it widened into a circular drive at the top of the mountain.

Without much grace, the drive swept by the front of a big old house that had once been some dark color, but the paint had peeled and faded until the house gave the appearance of a thundercloud with some light showing through. Thin trees taller than the house stood around like mourners waiting for somebody to die.

Something was in the air up here. It filtered the sun's light, darkened colors, made the world seem slightly more real than it had been below, which, of course, made it look not quite real at all.

I pulled up behind an ancient station wagon and turned off the engine. Wind sighed through the trees. None of us felt much like getting out.

Whipper Will said, "It's like something out of Poe."

"What's Poe?" I said.

"I'll show you when we get back. Some bright afternoon when you can stand it."

I had no idea what Whipper Will was talking about, so I grunted and got out of the car. Something was watching us. It might have been the house itself for all I knew. Maybe it was just Medium Rare peeking through a key-hole.

Nobody would ever take Medium Rare by surprise. The steps up to her wide front ve-randa squeaked as if I were pinching the tails of mice. The veranda itself was a big sound box. You might tiptoe across it, but every step you took would boom like cannon fire. Will and Bill crept up behind me, quiet as two guys playing bass drums. Still nothing from the house.

I looked for a bell to ring and found none, so

I knocked on the door. At first I thought the knock was echoing around inside the big house, but the sound got louder. Somebody was coming a long way across hardwood floors to answer my knock. Whipper Will licked his lips. Mine were dry, too, but they always were. I waited for the door to open.

When it opened, it opened on a very crisp-looking young man. Even in that cold, he wore a T-shirt and jeans. The jeans had a sharp crease, and I think the T-shirt had been pressed too. On the front of it was a picture of Medium Rare and the same greeting as was on the flyer. His shoes were black and shiny as canned olives. Above his thin white face and wire-rimmed glasses was hair the color of dust, slicked back into very thin daggers that hung down his neck.

"I am Edgar Allan," he said as if announcing that dinner was served.

Will laughed.

I said, "Sorry. He probably thinks you're something out of Poe."

Will laughed again, then pulled the flat of his hand down over his face, composing himself, keeping his laughter in a cage that was none too sturdy. Edgar Allan made a smile a little smaller than the smallest smile imaginable.

I said, "I'm Zoot Marlowe. These are my friends, Whipper Will and Bill. Medium Rare should be expecting us."

Edgar Allan nodded and stepped back so that we might enter.

The room was high, long and narrow, and made entirely of darkly polished wood. Nothing was on the walls but small electric sconces and, possibly, flowers carved into each corner. In that special, mysterious, yellow light they were using, it was difficult to tell. Chairs of the same wood stood at intervals, but they were almost frivolous in a room that was otherwise so stark. It looked like a coffin for a giant who had lived well and now was going to be buried well. I knew it was not a coffin, though, because there was a hallway at the far end.

Behind one wall an excited voice muttered, then more excited voices joined the first. But nobody was angry, they were just excited. Edgar Allan fitted his fingers into something invisible, and pulled the wall across from the muttering into two sliding doors that rumbled on their rollers like faraway thunder. Beyond the door was the bottom of a spiral staircase that twisted upward.

We followed Edgar Allan up the cold stone steps, listening to the echoes gather into what sounded like an army of demons. Durf was the only demon on T'toom, but if he had friends, they'd sound like we did mounting that staircase.

The top of the staircase was at the end of a long, wide hallway. Edgar Allan began to walk along the black velvet runner in the center of the floor, and Bill started to follow him. I grabbed him. I didn't have to grab Whipper Will.

A horse, muscles gleaming like moonlight on water, leaped through the wall at the end of the hallway and ran toward us, its hooves galloping in midair. It made no noise but a high, thin wailing, not loud enough to awaken anybody in the dead of night, but pretty unnerving if you were just on your way back from the bathroom. Edgar Allan waited patiently while the horse raced up to him, leaped higher into the air, and was gone, leaving only a smell of horse hockey and two very frightened beings.

Edgar Allan began to walk again, but before I moved, I said, "What was that?"

"One of the changed horses."

I made an interrogative noise. Maybe I was just clearing my throat.

"Medium Rare will tell you about it, if you like," Edgar Allan said.

I walked down the black velvet runner, listening to Whipper Will's breath rasp in quick gasps, knowing mine sounded the same. I wondered if Medium Rare always welcomed her guests with the same little wildwest show. Just because she somehow had seen a corner of T'toom didn't mean I could trust everything she did or said. It might mean I could not trust her at all.

We came to the wall through which the horse had first jumped, and Edgar Allan slid it open as he had the wall downstairs. He stood aside and bowed. I thought of a fat white bot who made similar gestures. I led the way into an octagonal room hung with more velvet. In the center of the room was a white octagonal table. On either side of the table was an octagonal stool. The table and the stools glowed with their own milky light. On top of the table was a glass ball on a golden tripod. The glass ball also glowed, but with smoky shadows that almost became things and then decided not to. I had never been in that room, but it was familiar.

I looked back. The door was closed and gone as if it had never been. I chuckled, just to keep up my courage. Whipper Will looked as if he needed a chuckle himself. Bill said, "I thought there would be more horses in here."

I was going to suggest Bill shut up when all the light in the room went away. Two gasps. I fumbled for Whipper Will in the absolute blackness and tripped over Bill. When the light came back on, I was on the floor blinking up at Medium Rare, who was sitting on the octagonal stool across the table from us. Her wrists were resting on the table. The milky light made her face look like a single nugget of gold. She might have been sitting there since the trees outside were saplings.

"Amthor," I said.

Medium Rare said, "Is that a greeting where you come from?" It was as if a stone were speaking.

Will said, "Amthor is the phony mentalist in *Farewell, My Lovely*. He had a place just like this. I knew it looked familiar."

Medium Rare frowned. "Mentalist? Phony mentalist?"

I stood up, feeling better, and said, "You shouldn't have let Gone-out Backson help you design this place. He's too much of a Chandler fan."

"You know Gone-out?" Medium Rare said with surprise.

"We've met. He's a big fan of yours as well as Chandler's."

Medium Rare nodded, a statue nodding. "He suggested I read this Chandler. It appears I should have done as he suggested for my own protection."

"We all need protection from guys like Gone-out." I glanced at Will and guessed what he was thinking. I said, "Speaking of needing protection, we ran into some of your stock."

"What stock is that?"

"Edgar Allan called it one of the changed horses."

Medium Rare laughed too loudly for that small room. The velvet drapes absorbed some of it, but the raucous sound banged around like a tractor in a toll booth. She laughed alone, and so did not keep it up for long. Still smiling, she said, "This place is called Changehorses because this is where the stagecoach line used to change their tired horses for fresh ones. It was also land that was sacred to the local Indians, so there was a disagreement. When the owners of the stagecoach line would not see reason, the Indians felt it necessary to curse the land. After that, the horses that came through here still changed."

She paused long enough for me to assume she had finished the story. I was about to say something clever and ignorant when she said, "But now, they changed into frogs."

I guess the three of us looked stupid because she said, "The horses changed into frogs. Not all horses. Not all the time. But just enough. The Indians were subtle. The apparition you saw is the spirit of a horse that lived out its life as a frog."

Will tried not to laugh, but the laughter burst out of him. Medium Rare was not pleased by it, but she waited for him to stop before she said, "This story is of more than passing interest to me. It is the reason I came here. This is still sacred land. One can do things here, spiritual things, that one can do at few other places."

"Things with blowfish spine necklaces?" I said.

"Perhaps. Please sit."

"There doesn't seem to be room for all of us."

"It wasn't meant that there should be. Gone-out got that right, anyway. I will consult with only one of you."

"You're the detective," Whipper Will said.

"That's what I keep telling people." I sat across the table from Medium Rare. She didn't do anything, but the door behind me opened, showing the length of hallway and Edgar Allan waiting motionless in the center of it.

Whipper Will said, "If anybody wants us, we'll be downstairs watching the car go by."

"Hey, Boss," Bill cried.

"Go with Whipper Will. That's an order."

Bill followed Whipper Will out, and the door closed on a room that looked like one where bad things had once happened to a guy named Marlowe.

21

I Ain't Got No Body

Medium Rare said, "Suppose I were to tell you I am interested in blowfish spine necklaces only as a collector?"

"I guess I'd ask to see your collection."

"I am not required to show it to you."

"Look," I said, "we can play Ask Me Another all day long, but you didn't invite me up here for that, and I didn't drive all this way for that."

"Why did you drive all this way?"

"Because every time I turn around, somebody connected with you is showing an unhealthy interest in blowfish spines. First it was a very delicate and tentative kind of guy in a dive bar in Malibu. He had one of your flyers and said he worked for you. Then it was a clerk at a souvenir distributor. He actually went so far as to knock me cold for my spine necklace, even though a shipment of hundreds of similar necklaces would be coming in soon."

"What has this second gentleman to do with me?"

"He was wearing a honk."

"I see. I suppose it would do me no good to tell you that many people wear honks, and that some of them have nothing at all to do with me."

"No good at all. It seems to me that somebody who was collecting blowfish spine necklaces would be collecting real ones, not fakes, no matter how good the fakes were. It seems to me that somebody so interested in blowfish spine necklaces is probably interested in one particular one that looks a lot like all the others, but is different enough that she would know it when she saw it. Do I interest you at all?"

"Slightly. How do you become involved in this?"

I leaned on the table, and the smoke in the glass ball seemed to gather on my side like a school of fish hoping for food. I said, "I figure if I find the necklace for you, I'll have a little peace. That, plus a hundred a day and expenses."

"You are not very convincing as a detective."

"You don't read enough Chandler." I smiled and said, "Besides, I found you."

Medium Rare nodded and studied the smoke swirling inside her globe. To me it was just smoke. She concentrated as if she were reading the morning paper. The room contained no noise but the sound of my own breathing, and no smell but the light machine oil inside Medium Rare. Time did not exist. I could have been waiting for minutes or hours.

At last Medium Rare said, "Very well. I will pay you a retainer of two hundred dollars. You can pick it up at the emporium down the hill."

I nodded, and said, "I told you my interest in blowfish spine necklaces. What's yours?" I assumed she would tell me the same kind of quarter-truth I'd told her. Still, her story would be entertaining.

"I'll show you," she said and began to make rubbing motions over her glass ball without actually touching it. Music came from somewhere, the same three-note figure over and over again; it was not as interesting as what the surfers generally listened to, not as interesting as trucks changing gears. Medium Rare said, "The music will lull you to sleep. Please do not fight it."

The music was boring, but sleep seemed miles and centuries away. There was a hiss that was not part of the music. The smell of an orchard full of oranges came to me. I did not quite feel my nose hitting the table.

And then suddenly, I wasn't asleep any more. I was wide awake, and very tall. Then I saw I wasn't tall, but floating like a kid's balloon near the ceiling of Medium Rare's consultation chamber. Very far away, very thin bells tinkled in a breeze from another world.

Below me, Medium Rare sat motionless across the table from somebody who looked a lot like me, except his head was resting on his nose, which looked a little crushed and wrinkled. I wanted to reach down and make him comfortable, but I was having a little trouble with my own body just then, having no more control than a baby who'd just discovered his fingers. The more I looked at this guy, the more I was convinced it *was* me. I was in two places at once. Of course, Malibu and Hermosa Beach are in two places at once, and nobody thinks anything of it.

"Do not be afraid," Medium Rare said. Her voice didn't come from the body on the stool, but from a point near me, near the ceiling. It sounded tinny, as if it were broadcast from a great distance through an old lo-fi radio. I would find that all voices sounded that way here. I managed to turn my head, and saw another Medium Rare. This one was floating next to a woman I'd never seen before. They were transparent, no more than smoky suggestions of being. I wasn't all there myself.

The new woman was chunky and wore practical shoes just right for hiking. Her matching coat and skirt could have been a uniform. A ruffle of white no bigger than a hand hid the top button of her blouse. Hanging around her neck below the ruffle was a string of pearls that, at the moment, she was twisting around the fingers of one hand. Her tongue searched her lips, which moved in and out as if she were constantly about to say something but hadn't yet chosen her words. Her eyes moved quickly, looking at nothing and everything, as if she were a little bewildered.

"This is Rupee Begonia," Medium Rare said.

"Charmed, I'm sure," Rupee Begonia said in a voice that was none too sure of itself. She never stopped playing with the necklace.

"Rupee Begonia is my spirit guide. She will take us to Pele and Lono."

I had enough control over my new body now that I didn't stiffen or jump when Medium Rare mentioned Pele. But Pele's name made me more interested in whatever was going on.

"Take my hand," Rupee Begonia said. We rose through the ceiling of the room, through dusty attics full of ancient trunks and clothing, through wooden beams, through rats' nests, through termite colonies, through genuine lath and plaster, and at last hovered over Medium Rare's house. Her roof needed fixing.

We lingered there for a moment. Except for the tinkling of the tiny bells, all was quiet. I could see the Belvedere and the side road and a few lights below that must have been Changehorses. I didn't see Bill or Whipper Will, but they may have been under the roof of the veranda or under the trees.

Then, without effort, Rupee Begonia was

pulling us through the air. There was no cold, no wind, though we flew fast enough to smudge details on the ground as we rushed over them. Soon we were nowhere near Los Angeles, not on any map at all.

We were flying over patterns of torch fire, then hundreds of camp fires, then a smooth blue ocean whose ripples glowed with light coming from the penguins who played in the water. We were not interested in any of these things. The ocean became smoother yet, smooth enough to reflect the three of us. The universe was a funhouse full of mirrors. I caught glimpses of myself pinched in two, with legs like a couple of Vienna sausages, with no nose at all. Not soon enough, the mirrors were obscured by scarfs of color that swirled around us. But we were not interested. Beyond the scarfs, an array of black holes stood before us like a wall that extended to infinity in all directions. Rupee Begonia drew us down into one of them, and suddenly we were not moving at all, but hanging near the ceiling of a room.

It was a nice room, if a little old-fashioned. I'd seen ones like it in old Westerns. The wallpaper was green, flocked in a sedate floral pattern. Brass lamps hung from the wall, and enormous ceiling fans turned above round tables where people in evening clothes sat drinking, talking and doing magic at each other. Out through the window, I could see the lights of a great city. Nothing told me which city it was, which time zone it was, which planet it was.

Two Polynesians were sitting alone at one side of the room, drinking from coconut shells. The man wore a black tuxedo. The woman wore a white gown that started at the top of her boobs, then swept to the floor like a theatrical curtain. Her creamy bronze skin made the white gown seem to be made of neon, and the white of the gown made her smooth, dry skin seem mysterious and in need of touching. She was a blonde, a blonde Polynesian. Scarcer than hen's teeth, Busy Backson had said.

I had no doubt that they were the ones who had stolen the Pantages truck from Harry's loading dock. A similar pair had been seen on the beach near the top hat. Another pair had taken a taxi to Kilroy's. I tried hard to believe that there were three pairs of crazy Polynesians in the Los Angeles area, each pair containing one blonde woman. I tried, and failed. It was easier to believe that there was only one pair of crazy Polynesians around.

I had an idea. At the moment it was a small, weak thing, barely able to crawl, let alone stand. But it was an idea worth having.

"There they are," Rupee Begonia said with relief.

"Can they hear us?" I said.

"If you want them to."

"Not just yet. Where are we?"

Medium Rare looked at Rupee Begonia, who swallowed and blinked a few times. Her hand was back at her necklace. She said, "Well, you know, there seems to be some question about that." She explored a cheek with one finger. She was as cute as a paper flower. "I can find my way here through the spirit plane, but I really have no idea where we are in the mortal plane."

"Our mundane location is of no consequence," Medium Rare said. "You asked me what my interest in blowfish spine necklaces was. Here it is. I am looking for them on behalf of these spirits."

I have never been good at reading the faces of bots, not even ones as sophisticated as Medium Rare. Was she lying? Was it possible for her to lie? Asking seemed pointless. I didn't know why she might want that special spine necklace herself.

"Introduce me," I said.

Medium Rare closed her eyes for a moment and spoke as if she were addressing a group: her voice was not really different in volume or even tone, but in a thing I can describe only as focus. She said, "Good evening, Pele and Lono."

The two Polynesians looked up at us. A few of the other people in the room looked up, too, saw nothing, and decided not to get involved. Pele and Lono smiled, using all their big, square teeth. Pele said, "Have you found it?" Her voice bent the English a little, but the result had a lot of charm.

"No. But I brought someone who claims he can."

I waved. Pele and Lono looked in my direction, but a little high and to the right. I wondered what they were seeing. I said, "I'm Zoot Marlowe. I'm a detective." They heard me. Focus is everything.

"You will find our spine for us?" Lono said. It was a voice deep as one of Pele's portable holes.

I said, "I'd be kidding both of us if I promised something like that. But it would be helpful to know why this blowfish spine necklace is different from all other blowfish spine necklaces."

Lono glanced at Pele before he said, "It floats."

"It is a spirit necklace," Medium Rare said.

Pele said, "We won't go home without it."

My idea was a little stronger now, kind of wobbling around on its own. Focusing like mad, I said, "Won't or can't?"

Pele got a little hot then. Color rose in her cheeks, and her hair actually seemed to take on a reddish glow. Calmly, Lono said, "A detective who can ask questions like that can think up his own answers." His eyes bored into me, wanting me to understand. Maybe he was being vague because he didn't want Medium Rare and Rupee Begonia to know any more than they had to. Maybe he just enjoyed playing games. He wasn't vague enough for me.

"I believe I can," I said. My idea had hair on its chest now. It could bellow from the tops of mountains.

"You are very good at understanding the knowledge of the spirits," Medium Rare said. "I would not have expected it."

I focused on Medium Rare and said, "I can also pick my nose with either hand."

"Your patter is offensive."

"Absolutely." I focused on Pele and Lono and said, "I have a little problem of my own that you might be able to help me with."

Grimly, Medium Rare said, "You are not here to make deals with them. Only to gather information."

I said, "What difference does it make as long as I help them?"

She bit her lip in a spot where there was already a tooth mark.

"What is your problem to us?" Pele said.

"I thought we might work a trade. If I find the spine necklace you want, maybe you can see your way clear to curing my friend of being a magician."

That surprised them. Lono leaned across the table to whisper into Pele's ear. She didn't like what she heard. To me, she said, "We are sorry about your friend. The barrier works automatically. Still, your idea of a trade is a good one. You find the proper necklace, and we will speak further. Until then, whoever has the necklace will have bad luck."

"Fair enough," I said. "Where are you two at the moment?"

Medium Rare moaned. Suddenly, as if we were at the end of a stretched rubber band, we were snapped through a confusion of lights and sounds into the place with the colored scarfs. Medium Rare, Rupee Begonia, and I hung at the edge of a green rift as the scarfs crawled like high clouds from nowhere to nowhere. I was a little dizzy.

"What happened?" I said.

"I don't quite know—" Rupee Begonia began.

Medium Rare said, "The interview was at an end. I severed the connection."

"Mighty thoughtful, but the detective normally does that. It's all part of the service. The detective or the client. Or are *you* the client?"

"Your interest in finding the proper spine necklace seems to be neither academic nor even financial. I don't trust you. I don't want to see Pele and Lono hurt."

"How would I hurt them?"

"You'd keep the necklace for yourself."

"And what would I do with it?"

"Lono seemed to think you'd know." Medium Rare turned to Rupee Begonia—a neat trick, hanging there at the tattered end of a green scarf—and said, "Take us back to my consultation room."

Rupee Begonia closed her eyes. If she was trying to concentrate, her nervous mouth and hands hadn't heard about it. Then she grabbed each of us and dragged us back through the funhouse, back across the ocean with the glowing penguins, back across the field of campfires and torches, and suddenly we were hanging near the ceiling of Medium Rare's octagonal room. The glass ball was empty. Medium Rare and the geek were still sitting there. The geek still had his nose mashed into the octagonal table.

Then the floating Medium Rare was gone,

and the one at the table began to move. She yawned up at me. She said, "Thank you, Rupee Begonia." Suddenly, Rupee Begonia was gone and the glass ball was full of smoke again. Medium Rare stood up, and the door to the long hall slid open. Edgar Allan was standing there, waiting.

Feeling a little queasy, I said, "What about me?"

"You?" Medium Rare said. She smiled and said, "You ain't got no body. And nobody cares for you."

22

Not a Bad Way to Spend Eternity

Medium Rare made big conjuring gestures with both hands as she said, "You will toss forever on the spirit winds, never again knowing flesh." She nodded to Edgar Allan, who came into the room and lifted my body over one shoulder. I felt violated, used, as if I'd been cracked open against my will and filled with sewage.

Medium Rare mused, nearly to herself, "It is not a bad way to spend eternity. You will know neither hunger nor thirst nor fatigue. More importantly, without a spirit guide such as Rupee Begonia, you will not visit the same place twice. Anyone who sees you or hears you will think only that you are an hallucination, a bad dream, something to fear and forget." She nodded again to Edgar Allan, and he took steps toward the door.

I dived for my body with all the control of a paper airplane. Edgar Allan had not taken two steps before I was on it, and trying to get my foot in the door. Behind me, Medium Rare was laughing. I don't know what she was doing,

but there was no more way into my body than
there was into a walnut.

Focusing as hard as I could, I cried, "Will!"
Would he and Bill hear me downstairs? If they
could hear me, could they get up here in time?

Then, against all logic, Will and Bill were
standing in the doorway. "Grab me and run,"
I cried.

"What?" Will said, looking from my body to
me—or slightly too high and to the right of me.

"Do it."

"Look out," Medium Rare cried.

Will made a grab at my body but missed because Edgar Allan took a step back as he half-
turned to look at her. He tripped over Medium
Rare, who was trying to prevent Bill from
pushing the backs of Edgar Allan's knees. Will
grabbed my body as Edgar Allan and Medium
Rare hit the floor. Bill squeaked clear and hustled after Whipper Will down the hall.

"Get them," Medium Rare shouted.

I floated after Will, Bill, and my body. I said,
"Quick. Changehorses."

"You got it," Bill said, and began to whinny
like a horse.

"Ribbit!" Will said loudly, a big frog in a little pond. "Ribbit!"

I could hear the hubbub of a gathering crowd
at the bottom of the corkscrew stairs. Making
all that noise themselves, they'd never hear the
animal sounds Bill and Will were making. Medium Rare and Edgar Allan were certainly
close behind us. We were trapped. I floated
past Bill and Will, and hovered at the foot of
the stairs.

A crowd was congealing in the giant's coffin,
but no leader had yet emerged to lead a charge
up the stairs. It was a mixed crowd of men and
women, the likes of which you could see on
any street corner. The one thing they had in

common were lost and empty eyes that
searched for things this world did not contain.

I focused so they could see me. Hoping the
name would have the same effect on this crew
as it had on Merle back in Changehorses, I
spread my arms and intoned, "I am Elvis."

That got their attention, which was all I
wanted. They stared at me dumbfounded and
quiet—quiet enough to hear a horse's whinny
and the night call of a frog. That frightened
them, and they backed away from the entrance
to the stairwell, the crowd knotting like the
smoke in Medium Rare's glass ball.

Will hit the bottom of the stairs at a run and
kept running. They'd been expecting a horse
with moonglow on his muscles, but they got
one old surfer and a small ducky robot; they
stepped back just the same. Not being too polite about it, Will was able to push through the
surprised crowd. The front rank fell back on
the true believers behind them, leaving enough
confusion to slow Medium Rare and Edgar Allan when they got to the bottom of the stairs.

A moment later, Will was behind the wheel
of the Belvedere. He shot down the mountain,
hauling Bill and the short body of a big-nosed
alien in the back seat. The part of me that
wasn't in the back seat led the car along the
twisting road.

A big, invisible hand pushed me off course,
and a universe of ugly green bubbles spurted
at me from a point deep in the western sky. I
cried out and tried to hug the spire of a pine
tree, but my hands went right through. No
hunger, no thirst, no fatigue, but fear. Plenty
of fear in the spirit plane.

Using the last of my concentration, I focused
on getting my consciousness down into my
body. Maybe without Medium Rare blocking
me, I could manage it. I fought against the
spirit winds like a hummingbird in a hurri-

cane. Green bubbles were all around me. Inside each one was a clutch of eyes and tentacles. I fought harder and slipped through the roof of the car. Bill had my head in his lap. The green eyes watched as I turned to match the position of my body. I don't know if they were angry or sad or just bored with the spirit winds, but those eyes were the last thing I saw before I slid into my body the way a hand slides into a glove, and I retreated to an infinity point of my own.

I awoke to a vibration and a hum that had been part of the dream I'd been having. I opened my eyes. At first I thought I hadn't made it back to the physical plane, that the green eyes were still looking at me, but then I blinked and the eyes became friendly. They were Bill's. I sat up next to him on the back seat of the Belvedere, and saw that we were on a freeway, speeding through pregnant yellow hills. I rubbed my nose. It was still sore from where it had hit the table. Strangely enough, it was the only part of me that hurt.

To the back of Whipper Will's head, I said, "Where are we?"

"Are you cool, dude?"

"All in one piece, anyway. Where are we?"

"Not far from Castaic."

"Anybody after us?"

"No way, ho-zay. I cruised north instead of south."

"I hope that's tricky enough."

The hills slid by us. I wanted to think, needed to think, but my mind was a solid brick of clay. Bill was watching me. I told him I was fine. He said, "You bet," but he kept watching me.

I said, "I thought you guys went outside."

"Colder outside than a brass bathing suit," Whipper Will said. "Bill and I decided to wait in the hallway."

"In the hallway, it was warmer than a brass bathing suit," Bill said.

"Great patter, Bill," I said.

"You got it, Boss."

A few miles later, Whipper Will said, "What happened in there?"

"I don't know myself. Maybe it was all a dream." I rubbed my nose. I told him most of the story, leaving out only the deal I had made with Pele and Lono. No point getting Will's hopes up about Captain Hook.

"Astral projection," said Will as if he were impressed.

"The screwball's answer to the old reliable one-way trip to the bottom of Santa Monica Bay."

Whipper Will took us farther north. Occasionally, I turned to look out the back window, but if anybody was following us, he kept changing cars to do it. At the Castaic off-ramp, Will turned the car around and we headed south, back toward Los Angeles.

The country was pretty, if monotonous, just the thing for a guy who was trying to dig his brain out of a landslide. Whipper Will drove smoothly while he hummed what may have been a tune. Bill looked out the window, saying nothing. We soon passed the Changehorses off-ramp. I felt better when I saw that no marching band was waiting for us. We continued to drift south.

Medium Rare was wrong about Pele and Lono. They were not spirits. They were also no more Polynesian than I am, despite their current appearance. Even before I knew their names or had seen them for the first time, I'd known they were not of this Earth. The top hat, of course, had given them away.

Pele and Lono were from Yewpitz, a planet we Toomlers had had dealings with long before the AW-OL guys intercepted the first broadcast from Earth. The Yewpitzkitziten were a strange and not very reliable race, but not without their charm—kind of like the surfers in Whipper Will's house. The ones I'd seen looked more like eggbeaters than Polynesians. Why they chose to design one of their ships to look like a top hat was anybody's guess, but I knew for a fact it had been done before.

As a race, the Yewpitzkitziten were intrigued with tricks and trickery: the gnarly old philosopher may have been thinking about them in particular when he wrote about the science of a sufficiently advanced race.

None of which explained why they were interested enough in blowfish spine necklaces to steal Harry's truck. Except that blowfish spines coincidentally looked a lot like slaberingeo spines, and slaberingeo spines are what make the Standard Hyperspace Interstellar Propulsion unit work. If they'd somehow lost their spine, the SHIP unit wouldn't work, and it would take centuries for them to get home, or to anywhere else in the galaxy. They'd look hard for their spine, or for a replacement. Yes, they would.

No matter what their motive, they'd illegally parked their hat on the beach and stolen a truck and who knows what else? I should turn them in to the police at my earliest opportunity. Three things prevented me.

The first was that I didn't know where they were, though I assumed the place where I'd spoken to them was not located any deeper in the spirit plane than was the San Fernando Valley. The second was that an unhappy Yewpitzkitziten could start a lot more trouble than the police or anybody else on Earth were ready for. Portable volcanos and instant thorn bushes were only the beginning. The third was that I knew what it was like to be a very strange stranger. I'd give them any slack I could.

None of which meant that I wouldn't look for the spine they wanted. As far as I could tell, nobody would be hurt if I found it. Not Captain Hook. Not Pele and Lono. Maybe not even the person who had it at the moment.

I had an idea about that. The airplane Whipper Will and Bingo took back from Hawaii had been wrapped up in a strange fog that hadn't bothered any other plane. Maybe it was just bad luck. More likely, somebody aboard that plane was carrying an unbalanced slaberingeo spine. If they still had it, they might not mind my finding them.

A green car roared up beside us and kept level. It was small and feisty, with lines so streamlined, the bodywork looked as if it had melted into that shape. There was nothing so odd about the car or its actions. But the driver was a circus all by himself. He glanced at me through round glasses whose frames hung from his face a little crookedly and with no more confidence than a man on rubber stilts. His white beard fell in finger waves from his nose and looked as natural as suspenders on a goose. Then he lifted one long hand and pointed a pistol at me.

I cried, "Drop back, quick!"

While Whipper Will said, "What?" the person in the green car squeezed off a shot. His car swerved at that moment, and the bullet went somewhere other than into my head. The shot sounded frail and far away against the road noise. The green car pulled ahead of us and kept going. I'd have gotten the license number, but it had conveniently been splashed with enough mud to plant petunias in.

"Follow that car," I cried.

"What?" Will said again.

"That green car. Catch it."

Will said nothing more but hunched over the wheel. The Belvedere chugged as Will tried to accelerate too fast, caught itself like a drunk regaining his balance and then steadily picked up speed.

"What's going on?" Will said.

"The driver of that car took a shot at me."

"I thought some gravel hit us."

I didn't know what to say to that, so I concentrated on making the car go faster. Sitting in the back seat as I was, my efforts did all the good you might expect. We closed the space between us and the green car, but couldn't go fast enough to actually catch it. I was about to ask Bill to get out and push when I heard a siren and saw lights flash behind us.

Whipper Will saw them, too, and grumbled, "Pigs." Over his shoulder, he yelled, "I thought you were driving. I didn't bring my license." I passed him my temporary license. He was a little taller than the description said I was, but there was no comment about noses, so maybe he'd be able to fake it.

Will slowed the Belvedere and pulled onto the shoulder. In the distance, the green car was a bug scurrying along the highway. It went over a rise and dipped out of sight. A few seconds later, it reappeared much farther away.

The highway patrolman strolled over to us, getting out his book. His partner watched us through the windshield while he spoke into a handset. After that, there was a lot of very polite dialogue concerning safe driving habits, with particular reference to the speed limit. The patrolman took my temporary license from Will and studied it gravely. He copied some information off it, then walked back to the patrol car. A few minutes later he came back, handed the license to Will and said, "Remember, traffic laws are there for your safety."

"Yes, sir," Whipper Will said, as if admitting it had been he who'd put the overalls in Mrs. Murphy's chowder.

The patrolman gave Will his ticket and walked back to the patrol car. Will stuffed the ticket into his pocket, started the Belvedere's engine and accelerated till he was driving enough under the speed limit to be comfortable. A few seconds later, the highway patrol car roared past us, crossed three lanes without signaling, and got off at the next off-ramp.

By this time, the green car was long gone.

23

The Big Broadcast

By the time we got back to Malibu, the afternoon was almost gone, and a lot of the western sky had been plated with gold. It had been a good day. I'd astrally projected for the first time, and had not quite been trapped in fairyland. On the way home, somebody had taken a shot at me, but that was OK because they'd missed. Whipper Will had chased them, netting me nothing but a ticket for speeding. He had been right. You didn't need a license to drive, only to get caught. Oh, and yes, the guy who'd taken a shot at me had gotten away without revealing his license number.

Though it was early enough for the surfers to still be bickering about dinner, I felt no livelier than twenty pounds of French fries. Captain Hook was in Will and Bingo's bedroom, making dirty clothes circle through the air like floppy, misshapen vultures. I complimented him on the trick and asked him to get out. I was not very polite. It had been a good day. Good and long, and I was ready for some rest.

* * *

The rest ended with somebody shaking me. Sleep receded, allowing me to open my eyes. It was light in the room, meaning I'd slept through the night. I no longer felt like French fries, but I was still twenty pounds of potatoes.

"Wha . . ." I said, waving Whipper Will away from my arm.

"Somebody on the Ameche." His voice seemingly came through layers of cloth.

"Huh?"

"The blower. The phone."

I struggled to my feet and made it to the kitchen without bumping into more than a couple of walls. Bill had the phone to the side of his head, listening intently.

"Interesting conversation?" I said as I took the receiver away from him.

"I don't know. They didn't say anything."

"Hello?" I said into the phone.

"Zoot? This is Busy."

"Right both times. What's up?"

"Somebody's been here. They went through my blowfish spine collection."

A chilly wind blew through the kitchen. I may have imagined it. I said, "Have you called the police?"

"Of course, silly."

"Why call me?"

"You're a detective. I thought you might be able to help. You seemed awfully interested in blowfish spines the other day."

"Well, everybody's after blowfish spines. It's the latest thing. Haven't you heard?"

"You sound drunk."

"The result of hard work and clean living." I turned away from the phone and cleared my throat, surprising Bill so that he jumped and looked at me. Into the mouthpiece, I said, "Anything missing?"

"Not that I can tell."

"Who knew about your collection?"

Busy Backson's end became quiet. Her breath was soft and even, and so peaceful she might have been sleeping. She said, "It wasn't exactly a secret."

"I see. Then all we have for suspects is the immediate world. Anybody hear about your collection just recently?"

"Not from me."

"What about Gone-out?"

"Wait a minute," she said. There was the clatter of the receiver dropping on the floor. While I waited for her to come back, I used one hand to pour myself a cup of the coffee left in a Pyrex pot. It was tepid, bitter stuff, but I felt a little sharper for drinking it. In the phone I heard shouting, a man's voice and a woman's voice. It could have been Gone-out and Busy. It could have been the Man in the Moon and one of his moonbeams.

I had choked down three sips of coffee when Busy came back on the line. "He says he told a guy named Avoirdupois." She was angry now. She sounded as if every square inch of skin on her body itched, and it was all she could do not to scratch. I knew that any minute now, I'd start to itch too.

I said, "Uh huh. What, exactly, did you want done?"

"Breaking and entering is still a crime, isn't it?"

"Sounds like a crime to me," I said. What did I know?

"When they get here, I'll ask the police for a professional opinion. Will you help me?"

I said, "Look, Busy, I don't know what I can do for you that the police can't, but I'll try."

"Gone-out's a dope," she said, "but try to keep him out of it." She hung up without saying good-bye.

I sat down in a chair to look at Bill. I wondered if I were still a little groggy from sleep and from my astral projection, or if I had suddenly turned stupid. I should have been going to the airport. Instead, I said, "Can you manage to get me to the *Interstate Eyeball* office?"

"Sure," said Bill proudly. "It's in L.A. County."

I ate some jam and toast just to keep my stomach from doing gymnastics, showered, dressed, and a half-hour later, Bill and I were eastbound on the Santa Monica Freeway. It was a nice day if you were in the mood.

Bill had me drive up Fairfax through tangles of stop-and-go traffic on a street lined with small shops and restaurants. We turned right at Wilshire and found that the address I wanted was a building faced in white marble. It was short for the neighborhood, being only ten stories tall, and had a shoe store taking up the first floor.

Finding a place to park on the street took a better detective than me, and I had to park in the building's lot. I could have bought a pair of shoes for what parking cost me. Inside, the building was old but well-kept, with tan carpeting that still held patterns where somebody had run a vacuum cleaner over it. Bill and I waited for the elevator, then climbed the stairs to the fourth floor. Each floor had a small porthole in one wall that looked out on a view that must have been really something before they put in the chrome monster next door. We went in at a door that said INTERSTATE EYEBALL— ENTER.

It was a bright, airy office with big windows and white paint that smelled fresh. Traffic noise growled up from below as from a pit full of bears. Sound that was more static than music leaked through a common wall.

Behind a counter dividing the room was a Teletype machine that stood in one corner chuckling softly to itself as it typed the latest

news. In another corner was a small TV set
with its antenna thrust out the window. Along
one wall were piles of yellowing papers, probably back issues of the *Eyeball*. In the middle
of the area behind the counter was a desk with
a computer on it. Avoirdupois sat behind it,
very involved with whatever was on the screen.
His hands rested on the desk on either side of
the machine. Black cables snaked across the
floor like jungle vines.

There was no coffee pot, no water bottle,
nothing a man would need to make his office
more like home. Avoirdupois was a Surfing
Samurai Robot and wouldn't need them.

"I will be with you in a moment," Avoirdupois said without looking up.

"Big story?" I said. "Two-headed baby,
maybe?"

Avoirdupois' head jerked in my direction,
and his eyes seemed to take a moment to focus.
When he saw who it was, he smiled. It wasn't
a good smile. The SSR people would have to
work on it. He said, "Very good, sir. I'm delighted to see you. Truly I am. And, if I may be
so bold as to notice, this is the second time I've
seen you not wearing your necklace. The first
time I thought nothing of it, sir, concluding you
had judged, as I had, that the Aquaricon was
no place to be attracting attention to yourself.
But to be without the necklace twice is too un-
usual to be mere coincidence. Might I venture
to guess that you have had the good fortune to
sell the necklace to someone not of this
Earth?"

"No such luck. I'm here on another matter."
Bill was standing as close as he could to the
Teletype without being behind the counter. He
was chuckling back to it.

"Well, well, sir. Delighted to see you in any
case, I'm sure." He pushed back from the desk,
and an enormous silver plug studded with hun-

dreds of silver pins drew up under his white vest. "I've just been composing my report on the Aquaricon. Interesting business, sir, and no mistake. If I may ask, how did you make out with Medium Rare?"

"We didn't get along. She thought I was too inquisitive."

He shrugged. "An odd complaint for one in the business of answering questions, is it not? Well, no matter, sir. There are plenty of other fish in the sea." He laughed in that cute way he had, like two blotters making love. "Now, sir. How may I be of assistance?"

"Gone-out Backson's sister had her place ransacked today."

Avoirdupois shook his head. "These are terrible times we live in, make no mistake."

"Not interested?"

He laughed and opened his hands wide. "It is hardly the kind of news the *Eyeball* normally concerns itself with."

"I thought you might take a more personal interest."

"I don't follow."

"Gone-out told his sister that he'd told you about her blowfish spine collection. You're the only one I've talked to lately who both knew about her collection and would be interested enough in it to want a private look."

He laughed as if I'd just told an off-color story. He said, "You are a pip, sir, make no mistake." More seriously he said, "But if you are accusing me of burglary, sir, I'm afraid you make the effort for nothing. I've been here all afternoon."

"Witnesses?"

"If I may say so, sir, you are not the police, and I would be within my rights not to answer your questions. However, it suits me to show my good faith in that other little matter by proving my innocence in this one. If you will step around here, sir, I will show you the *Eyeball* uplink log. I have been writing and transmitting since noon."

"Logs can be faked."

"So they can, sir. So they can. But you may also speak with my neighbor down the hall," he cocked his head at the music, "and confirm that my equipment has been interfering with his radio reception since that time." He folded his fingers across his stomach and looked pleased with himself.

It was all wrong. Avoirdupois hadn't had any more to do with ransacking Busy's apartment than I had. Either that, or he had an acting attachment in that great, bloated body of his. So it was the long shot, after all. Sometimes they pay off, but you never know when.

I said, "Then whoever did the deed has what they want, or they don't. If they do, the affair is over as far as they're concerned. If they don't, they'll be making more trouble. I suspected you of taking the special blowfish spine from Busy's apartment. They would know you hadn't done that, but they might still think you had the spine. You might meet aliens before I do. And you might not like it."

"I am gratified by your concern, sir." He leaned toward me against the desk and said in a low voice, "Tell me, sir. Who do you suspect?"

"It's a puzzle, isn't it?"

"Jigsaw or crossword?" Bill said. We both ignored him. Fuzzy music continued to come through the wall. Avoirdupois switched off his computer. A hum I hadn't even been aware of died, and suddenly the music was much louder and clearer. The volume went down. Almost at the same moment, the door opened, letting in Detective Cliffy and his playmate Robinson.

Cliffy gaped at me as if I'd already offended him just by being there. Robinson was as emotional as usual. Cliffy said, "I should have known you'd be here."

"You guessed, but you wanted to surprise yourself."

Cliffy shot a look at Avoirdupois and said, "This guy been bothering you?"

"Not at all, sir. Mr. Marlowe and I are great friends."

Nastily, Cliffy said, "Robinson and I want to be your friends, too. That's why we want you to answer a few questions."

"Ah," said Avoirdupois. "No doubt Busy Backson mentioned my name."

Cliffy's mouth twisted as if his lips were trying to escape. He said to me, "You just have to go and muddy up the waters, don't you?"

I just looked at him. Suddenly static buzzed through the room again, only this time it didn't come through the wall. It came from the TV set. Nobody had been within ten feet of the TV set. Till this moment, nobody had had any interest in it. Now it was on. Horizontal lines jumped through confetti, then the picture cleared. On the screen were two people I knew. The last time I'd seen them, I hadn't quite been myself.

Pele and Lono were sitting behind a desk. Behind them was darkness. They could have been at a local TV station, or aboard their ship, or in a studio they'd used their superscience to put together for the occasion. They looked composed and confident, as if they were on TV all the time. Pele said. "Greetings, people of Earth." Her voice echoed, booming in through the windows and from the walls around us. Anybody with a radio or a TV was getting the broadcast. I wondered how the guy next door was taking it.

Pele went on: "Something of ours has been stolen by one of you. We want it back." She grew angrier as she spoke. "We want it back *now*. We warn you, it will bring its possesser bad luck. If you have what is ours, put an advertisement into the personals of *The Interstate Eyeball*. We will see it and contact you. False advertisements will not be tolerated. If what is ours is not returned to us within a week, we will destroy Los Angeles. The Hollywood Hills will erupt in primordial fire such as has not been seen since the age of the dinosaurs. If you doubt us, speak with Harry at the Sue Veneer Novelty Company."

Harry would like that. The publicity would be good for business. I, on the other hand, did not like it much. Everything was out in the open now, and the clock was running.

24

A Pineapple With My Name on It

Cliffy was on the phone to headquarters when Bill and I left. I didn't envy Avoirdupois the afternoon he was about to have, but there was nothing I could do for him. Even doing something for Captain Hook seemed unlikely. Saving Los Angeles seemed out of the question.

I could go home to T'toom, and nobody would know the difference. I tried to make that a paying proposition, but I couldn't shake the feeling saving Los Angeles was my business, just like trouble. Maybe it's because Los Angeles was where Philip Marlowe did all his best work. It was his monument, a little gaudy and lacking refinement, but he wouldn't mind; the carnival atmosphere would only give him an opportunity to exercise his patter.

We got down to the Belvedere and drove south, toward Los Angeles International Airport. The sun shone as brightly as before, and the traffic had clotted no more than usual. The few people walking had worried expressions, and they kept looking toward the Hollywood

Hills. But maybe they always looked worried. Maybe the rest of it was my imagination.

Bill, also curious about the Hollywood Hills, kept looking at them out the back window of the car. I was too busy driving to do anything but drive. I was confident that if the Hollywood Hills exploded, Bill would not keep the fact to himself.

On La Cienega Boulevard, I said, "Let's have some radio. See if the mayor has announced yet that he doesn't like threats." I leaned forward to turn the knob when Bill said, "Listen to this, Boss."

Bill opened his mouth, and classical music came out of it. The effect was eerie, like finding out that under certain conditions rain and corn flakes are the same thing. The music was nice, but it wasn't what I wanted at the moment. I said, "News." Bill rolled his eyes up into his head until a man's voice spoke from Bill's mouth. Bill's eyes came back. The effect was still eerie.

A man with a voice like polished ebony was talking about the threat Pele and Lono had made. He began to interview somebody with a wisp of a voice who was speaking over a telephone. The guy with the wispy voice was Doctor Somebody-or-Other from Pasadena Tech, an expert on the local geology. He spoke earnestly, as if he were trying to convince himself as well as the listeners: "The Hollywood Hills are actually part of the Santa Monica Mountains. They are in no way volcanic, but are the result of a subduction, or wrinkling, of the surface of the earth."

The interviewing voice said, "So the chances of anyone forcing the Hollywood Hills into volcanic activity are slim."

"Absolutely. Once upon a time, there *was* volcanic activity in the Los Angeles area. But since the creation of the San Andreas Fault, there has been none. That is, there has been no volcanic activity near Los Angeles in the past fifteen million years. That's a long time. Even for a geologist." He favored his audience with a wispy laugh.

"So, in your opinion, the two were just bluffing."

"That's my opinion. There is no way for anyone to do what they have threatened."

"Thank you, Doctor."

Another voice came on and told me how this had been a special report, and that the mayor would be along in a moment with a statement. I told Bill I'd heard enough. He closed his yap, and the voice went away.

I hoped that doctor was happy with his small mind. He was one of those guys who thought that if he couldn't do something, then nobody could. Harry at the Sue Veneer Novelty Company might have some news for him. So might Captain Hook.

We were driving through bare, rolling hills dotted with oil pumps—big mechanical insects nodding at the ground. Behind us, there was a boom, as if somebody had struck a muffled bass drum once. The boom echoed from the hills, making it sound important.

"Wow," Bill said.

I guessed what the excitement was, but I wanted to make sure, so I pulled over and stopped. There was a lot of room on the shoulder along that stretch of road, and a lot of other cars were pulling over, too.

I cracked my door and took in the smell of petroleum and of water that had stood in one place too long. I looked back the way I'd come and saw smoke drifting upward without a care from the Hollywood Hills to hang over it like a wreath. There was another boom, and sparks flashed up through the smoke and went out as they rose. A few people screamed, and others swore. That doctor from Pasadena Tech would have a lot of explaining to do. Film at eleven. Me? I got back into my car and drove south.

The airport was not as crowded with departing citizens as I would have expected after Pele's gentle reminder. Maybe they didn't have their tickets yet. I found the Sandwich Airlines terminal and parked where nobody would tow my car as long as I kept feeding quarters to the meter. Bill did his meter trick, and gave me two hours of grace. I walked through the concrete structure and took a big, slow-moving elevator to the bottom. A plane thundered over, shrieking as it tore the air to shreds.

The Sandwich Airlines terminal was too bright to be friendly and too big to be intimate, but it contained a carefully calculated artificial air of excitement that would be good for business. The decor was similar to what it was at Kilroy's, but on a much larger scale. A necklace hanging from the ceiling and made of big plastic butterflies turned lazily in the air conditioning. A picture of a woman who, but for the shiny black hair, looked a lot like Pele, held up a sign that said: HAWAII'S ORIGINAL AIRLINE WITH THE ORIGINAL NAME.

People with suitcases were lined up to buy tickets and get their seating assignments. The men and women behind the counter looked the way clerks always looked when they're worked too hard by the public. I wouldn't get answers out of them.

I walked past the counter and into a crowded open area with a magazine stand on one side and a coffee shop on the other. Nothing leaped out at me. I said, "Bill, I need to find somebody who knows dirt about this airline and won't be afraid to talk about it."

"Follow me, Boss," Bill said brightly and waddled down a wide corridor. I followed him into another room, this one with a row of big wheels down one side.

"What's this?" I said.

"Baggage carousels. Luggage comes through the hole in the wall and falls onto the circular conveyer. People gather round and pick up their suitcases and stuff."

There were no people in the room. I said, "We're going to talk to a baggage carousel?"

"No way," Bill said, shocked at my suggestion, and toddled over to one of several robots that was mostly luggage cart. The robot part was nearly new and wore a Surfing Samurai Robot rag around his head. His face was wide and pleasant, but not overly bright. The luggage cart part was banged-up and blotchy green, and looked as if it had been dropped out of an airplane. Maybe more than once.

As we approached, the cart smiled and said, "Afternoon, folks. Help you with your bags?"

"No bags," I said.

The cart said, "Thank you, sir," and the lights went off behind his eyes.

"Watch my dust, Boss," Bill said. He looked up at the cart's face and said, "We got bags."

The cart's eyes lit up again and the smile came back. He said, "Afternoon, folks. Help you with your bags?"

Out of the corner of my mouth, I said, "This isn't going to work."

To the cart, Bill said, "How are the old hetrodynes hanging, dude?"

"OK, I guess."

"What happened to your cart?"

"This is a loaner. Mine's in the shop."

"Tough," Bill said, meaning it. I watched, fascinated.

The cart said, "Afternoon, folks. Help you wi—?"

I cut in, saying, "Our bags came in three days

ago on the Sandwich Airlines flight from Hawaii."

"Which flight was that, sir?"

I didn't know the flight number. I said, "It was the only one that day that landed in fog."

His face didn't curl up. I don't think he was built for it, but his lip twitched. He was thinking, or whatever robots did instead. "I remember. A long time ago."

"A little short on memory," Bill whispered to me.

"Sure," I said. "Three days. A long time ago."

The cart said, "Bad luck."

Hoping I wasn't going too fast for him, I took a chance by saying, "Bad luck with the luggage."

"Yeah. I heard. Bad luck. Was supposed to come to LAX. It went to Rio de Janeiro. It went to Nome. It went to Bangkok."

"What happened to it?"

"They found it. It just flew in from Bangkok."

"And, boy, are its arms tired," Bill said and yocked.

"Huh?" the cart said.

Ignoring Bill's joke, I said, "I want my luggage."

"Yes, sir. It'll be just a moment."

Bill asked after the cart's components again, and the two robots seemed to be getting along pretty well, when one of the baggage carousels began to turn. A couple of black-and-white checked suitcases came through the hole, slid down a ramp, and began to go around the carousel. They stopped in front of me. The baggage tags were business cards that said BORIS OT—OT'S POTS. They gave a Century City address and phone number.

I reached for the bags. The cart grabbed my wrist—not hard, just so I couldn't move it any more than if my hand had been buried in stone.

The cart said, "I'll need to see some identification, sir."

As I pulled away, he let go of me. I snapped my fingers and said, "It's in my other pants. Come on, Bill. We'll go get it."

"Sure, Boss," Bill said and reached up to shake hands with the cart.

"Thank you, sir," the cart said.

The carousel began to turn again as I rushed out of there looking for a pay phone. I found one, dropped a quarter into it, and dialed a number.

"Ot's Pots," a voice on the other end said. It was the cheery voice of an old man.

"Mr. Ot, please," I said.

"Speaking."

"Mr. Ot, this is Mr. Cart at Sandwich Airlines. We found your luggage."

"That's nice of you, young man, but somebody already called about that. I told him we'd be down tomorrow, when our clerk will be in."

"Just double checking, Mr. Ot. Oh, and by the way, have you had anything stolen lately? Something you brought back from Hawaii?"

"I sure did." Suddenly suspicious, he said, "Say, who is this, anyway?"

"Just a guy who wishes you nothing but good luck. It was a blowfish spine necklace, wasn't it?"

At the other end there was raspy, old man's breathing. Mr. Ot said, "You know a lot for just some guy."

"You wouldn't happen to remember who gave it to you, would you?"

"I don't know you," Mr. Ot said. "I don't know anything about you." He hung up the phone. I listened to emptiness and stared at the keypad because it was in front of me. I hung up the receiver, but otherwise, I didn't move.

In Hawaii, Mr. Ot had been given a slaberingeo spine necklace because somebody wanted it transported back to L.A., never mind why. If he thought about it at all, Mr. Ot probably thought it was one of Harry's authentic reproductions of a blowfish spine necklace. It wasn't the plane that had bad luck. It was Mr. Ot and his necklace. That's why he'd lost his luggage.

Now the luggage was back. That meant he no longer had the spine necklace and the bad luck that went with it. If he hadn't thrown it away or lost it, it had to have been stolen, probably by the person who'd given it to him in the first place, or an agent of that person. If I didn't find that person soon, Pele would destroy Los Angeles with impossible volcanoes, and Captain Hook might never again have a chance to be his normal, nasty self.

Following the signs, I got out of the airport and headed up Sepulveda. According to Bill, there was no easy way to get to Malibu from the airport, but taking La Tijera to La Cienega would help.

At the corner of Sepulveda and La Tijera, a ratty-looking guy was roaming the center divider with a pineapple in each hand. More were piled against the stoplight pole. When I stopped for the light, he rapped on my window with his knuckles, and I rolled it down. He handed me a pineapple, and before I could ask him what was going on, the light changed and the guy behind me honked. I handed the pineapple to Bill, and turned right onto La Tijera.

"Usually those guys sell oranges," Bill said.

"Yeah," I said. "And most of them don't look like Lono."

I swung the car along a side street and came out on Sepulveda again. When I got up to the corner, nobody was there but a tall, handsome black guy selling roses. I honked, and he ran

through traffic to my car. While giving him a
buck and randomly chosing a pink rosebud, I
said, "Where'd the Hawaiian guy go?"

"What Hawaiian guy?"

"He was on this corner selling pineapples."

"I'm here for three hours, Holmes, and I
don't see him."

The light changed and I drove up La Tijera
again, feeling something crawling across the
back of my neck. Bill still held the pineapple
in his hands. I said, "I think this pineapple has
our name on it."

25

The Show in the Oahu Room

Bill was right. Getting to Malibu was a matter of a lot of backing and forthing, but the sun had not yet set when I pulled into the garage and shut the door. In the living room, Captain Hook, the Great Hookini, was sawing Flopsie (or was it Mopsie?) in half. The rest of the surfers watched closely and occasionally let loose a bubble of nervous laughter.

Whipper Will and Bingo followed Bill and me into the kitchen, where I handed Bingo the rosebud. She took it, smiling as if she were about to cry, and sniffed it as if breathing too hard would break it. She punched Will gently in the arm and said, "*You* don't bring me flowers."

"He will now," I said.

Will turned his gaze to me and held it there. I smiled. He smiled back and said, "This part of the case?"

"I guess so. Buying it bought me some information."

"Anything to get cranked about?"

"Not yet." I had Bill set the pineapple down on the table and said, "I think this is a clue."

"Gnarly," Will said.

The pineapple sat there, not much less mysterious than the Sphinx. I hefted it and turned it over in my hands. It was just a pineapple.

"Nobody gives away pineapples for no reason," Bingo said.

"Yeah," I said. "I had the same clever thought."

We could look at the pineapple for the rest of the day. It could decay before our eyes. We still wouldn't know anything. I found a big knife in one of the drawers and laid the pineapple on its side. Juice spurted as I carefully sliced the pineapple into wheels. I sliced it again, and again. Up toward the middle, I hit something hard—two flat wooden disks.

I carefully worked the point of the knife between the pineapple pulp and the disks, and finally dug out a small wooden statue of a guy with very big eyes and a tongue down to his belly button—a tiki. The wooden disks turned out to be the bottoms of his feet. Shoved into a space between an arm and one side was a small roll of paper.

"How'd that get in there?" Bill said.

"The science of any sufficiently advanced race?" Bingo said.

"Could be," Will said. "It looks enough like magic."

I grunted and put down the knife in the puddle of pineapple juice that had spread on the table. Not surprisingly, the paper I pulled from under the tiki's arm was damp and sticky. I unrolled it and found a message handwritten in fancy script:

Zoot Marlowe:
Be in Kilroy's Oahu Room tonight at 7:30

*for more information about our missing
property. Ignore this order at your peril.*
                                     Pele & Lono

Will blew a long, low whistle. I'd have done
it myself if my nose hadn't been in the way.
My hand was shaking. I rested it on the table
to make it stop.

I didn't mind the Yewpitzkitziten stealing
trucks and using portable volcanoes and quick-
growing thorn bushes. It bothered me only
marginally that they had threatened to destroy
Los Angeles with some prehistoric fireworks
and could evidently make good their threat.
But the insult was now personal. They'd somehow gotten a message inside an undefiled pineapple—maybe they grew it that way—and had
known where to deliver it. All to invite me by
name to a private party.

I wondered how many other guys in the city
were sitting at a kitchen table full of pineapple
juice and thinking dark thoughts. Polite applause came from the other room.

Bingo said, "Pretty cool. Are you going?"

I said, "If I don't, it seems an awful waste of
a good pineapple."

I left Bill home. Call me sentimental, but I
had started to think of him as alive, and I didn't
want him to get hurt, if there was to be any
hurting done that night. Besides, I didn't need
him. I knew where Kilroy's was.

When I drove into Kilroy's parking lot, I was
stopped by a kid wearing a short red jacket so
tight it pulled at its buttons, a matching bow
tie attached with an elastic strap, and a per-
petual leer. When I stopped, he leaned in and
said, "Private party tonight, bub."

"It must be nice to be so tough on a cold
night like this."

He smiled, which didn't improve his leer, and he said, "You'll do, bub. Got any I.D. ?"

I showed him the tiki. He nodded once and said, "Good luck finding a parking space, bub. We're busy tonight." He waved me through.

He was right about the lot. It was full. I had to park halfway up a dark alley and walk back. I rounded a corner of the restaurant, and as I walked through a patch of black, I heard a mote of gravel moving behind me. I had it in mind to turn around, but before I could, someone had slipped a cord around my neck and was trying to take my head off as if it were a slice of cheese.

I squeezed my fingers between the cord and my neck, and we tussled for a bit, breathing hard and grunting, but neither of us in the mood to talk. I was about to sag into his arms, hoping to put him off his guard, when suddenly the cord began to stretch like a string of well-chewed bubble gum. I broke through the cord and turned just in time to see somebody dressed all in black run around the fateful corner. I ran after him, but he was gone. I didn't even hear footsteps. He could have been three feet away from me, standing still as death in a shadow, and I never would have seen him.

"Anything wrong?" asked a strong, manicured voice at my elbow.

I glanced to my left, and for a moment thought this was the guy I was looking for. He wore a long black cloak and an enormous slouch hat that shaded his eyes. His lips were red, and his small teeth glistened like that of a wild animal. He evidently moved like one, too. But he was too tall for my man. And I would have remembered the get-up, as dark as it was. I said, "I thought I heard something."

"Someone tried to kill you just now, didn't they?"

"Sure. That's why I come here. For the excitement."

His laugh was low, throaty, and more than a little nasty. " 'The weed of crime bears bitter fruit.' I fear we will harvest some of it this evening." He walked quickly toward the front entrance. His black clothes made him seem to be in shadow, even when he walked through pools of light. I followed closely, but when I got inside the door, he was gone. His nasty laugh rolled through the dim hallway like the last fragments of a bad dream.

Puffy Tootsweet stood behind the display case, idly shuffling menus. Nothing was flying through the air. Nothing was singing. Somebody was putting on a show in the Oahu Room, and they didn't want anybody to be distracted.

When she saw me, Puffy said, "I thought I might be seeing you tonight. Every other shamus in town is here. And some from out of town too. The Oahu Room's upstairs."

I nodded, and said, "Anybody just go by here?"

"I didn't see anybody."

"That's not what I asked you."

Puffy shrugged her big shoulders. "I felt a wind. You tell me if somebody went by."

"I guess he can cloud women's minds too."

"As long as he pays his bar bill," Puffy said and laughed.

I found a stairway hung with old fishnetting and went up it to a big room that had not been decorated quite so aggressively as the restaurant and bar downstairs. Subdued light escaped from behind man-size tikis in the corners. Here and there, glowing colored balls dangled from the ceiling in nets. Each of the round tables had its own little flame in a red glass jar. At one end of the room, a bar seemingly made of yellow wooden poles was doing a brisk business. A low, carpeted stage was pushed against one wall. I did not see my overly dramatic friend from downstairs, but he was probably skulking there somewhere. He wouldn't be able to help it.

The room was crowded with people who had nothing in common but a foxy look around the eyes. Evidently the desire to be a detective was a disease that was no respecter of sex, age or money.

There was a big guy in a wheelchair speaking with a guy who could have been his twin brother. Nearby, a guy wearing shorts, a Hawaiian shirt, a baseball cap, and a number of tanned muscles was showing an ancient lady wearing tweeds to a chair next to a greasy-looking guy who had on a suit a size-and-a-half too small but who was growing a very large and imposing mustache. The greasy guy immediately began to talk and wave his hands at the tweedy woman, while she smiled politely and began to work on the knitting she pulled from an enormous purse.

At another table, an Oriental gentleman dressed in a white suit sat lightly tapping together his steepled fingers while he watched everything. He was smiling gently through mustaches no thicker than spaghetti that dripped along his upper lip and down either side of his mouth.

At the bar, a nicely barbered man and a woman in evening clothes made comments to each other while they smoked and drank. At their feet was a small, short-haired dog looking very bored but who perked up enough to yap at the ankles of a wiry guy, also in evening clothes, who had half a pair of glasses screwed into one eye and slicked-back blond hair. He seemed to know the two with the dog.

I began to sidle over to two guys standing in the corner. They were as tweedy as the old lady but seemed to be dressed for some other time or place. One of them was thin and clean-shaven, and puffed on an enormous pipe. The other one had explosions of hair down the sides of his face.

The one with the pipe shot a look at me. But it wasn't just a look. It was a stare, an analytical examination that could see inside me, that knew everything about me. It sucked at me like that for a few seconds, catalogued me, filed me and put me away. The man favored me with a tiny nod. He knew. I didn't know what he knew, but he knew. I was glad when the eyes went back to other business. I stopped my sidling and studied the room again.

In the far corner, near the bar, but not so near as to be contaminated by the woman and two men in evening clothes, was a line of tall, rangy gentlemen wearing the uniform: trench coat, fedora, honest, world-weary expression. Each of them occasionally sipped something brown from a short, wide glass. They did not talk to each other. Each of them could have been alone in a hard-boiled universe with his hard-boiled thoughts. I sauntered across the room in their direction.

I passed a table where a middle-aged woman with short blonde hair and a perky manner said to a dark man in a very nicely tailored suit, "I certainly admire your calm, sir. Back in Cabot Cove, if we'd been threatened with volcanoes, the exodus would have already started."

The dark man touched the knot of his tie and shrugged with one shoulder. When he spoke, it was with a reedy English accent and with his hands in motion. He said, "Ah, well, you must understand the psychology of the average Angeleno. They are used to earthquakes, you know. A volcano must be a nice change because you can actually see the lava coming. 'I love L.A.,' and all that." He punctuated his pat-

ter with a smile which did nothing to increase
its sincerity.

As I approached the line of guys in trench
coats, my hearts began to beat faster. I had
never met a real gumshoe before, and I didn't
know how I would stack up. Was the hat OK?
Was the trench coat properly worn? Was the
patter clever enough? I walked up to a guy at
random. The guy smiled a little when he saw
me, but it was not a pretty thing. "Marlowe?"
I said.

"Nix," he said. "Spade."

"Seen the black bird lately?" I asked.

"What black bird?"

"You'll find out."

I moved down the line to a guy who'd been
watching us. He said, "My name's not Marlowe
either. It's Archer."

"Miles?" I said.

"Lew."

There were a few more guys I could have
tried, but before I had a chance, something
happened on the little stage. Grass thrust up
through the pile of the pale carpeting and grew
almost to the ceiling before a cloud of hot, sul-
phurous smoke exploded next to it and made
it wither into limp brown threads, revealing
Lono wearing his tuxedo. Next to him, unboth-
ered by the heat and evil-smelling smoke, stood
Pele in her white gown, looking like a dream
of all things forbidden and wonderful.

They didn't have to ask for everybody's attention. They had it, and they used it. Pele said,
"We are impatient. The broadcast was a mistake. The one we seek would not respond to
threats. Now we try something else." She
turned her head, seemingly meeting each pair
of eyes in the room. She wasn't as good as the
guy smoking the pipe, but she was good
enough. She went on, "You are all detectives.
Some of you are professionals. Some of you

are talented amateurs. You are all famous, your exploits told in song and story. We want you to find what is missing. The successful one will be well rewarded."

The man with the pipe-smoking gentlemen stepped forward and said, "Excuse me, madam, but perhaps you'd be good enough to reveal what you wish us to find."

"Jolly good, Watson," said the man with the pipe and patted him on the shoulder.

Lono said, "We search for something that looks like a blowfish spine but is not. It floats in the air."

The blond man at the bar said, "Did'ya say a blowfish spine that floats in the air?" He pulled the glass thing from his eye and blinked at them.

Momentary fire flared up around Pele. Angrily, she said, "You are a fool. It looks like this spine of yours, but it is not."

Near me, a short guy in a very dirty and rumpled trench coat waved one hand, writing something in the air with cigar smoke. With the embarrassment of a slow kid who knew he was slow, he said, "Excuse me, miss, but if it wouldn't be too much trouble, if it isn't a blowfish spine, what exactly is it?" His voice had the charm of a gate with a rusty hinge.

Pele raised her chin a little and narrowed her eyes. Lono opened his mouth but whatever he had intended to say was interrupted by a shrill whistle. Somebody yelled, "Raid!" and suddenly, the room was full of policemen.

26

A Night Too Full of Policemen

The maniac who owned the whistle kept blowing it while policemen streamed into the room like a dark blue fluid, waving guns around and ordering us to keep calm. I was calm. As far as I could tell, everybody else in the room also had seen a policeman before. The only one who wasn't calm was the guy with the whistle. Pele and Lono didn't stay around to find out what was going on. In a hot flash and a cool green burst, they were gone.

Cliffy and Robinson strode into the room as if they were taking an enemy position. Cliffy looked around, disgusted for no particular reason by what he saw. He slapped Robinson on the chest with the back of his hand, and Robinson stopped whistling. The air still rang. Hustling up behind them was Puffy Tootsweet, angry enough to fry butter on her scalp. She grabbed Cliffy by the arm, spun him around and said, "What's this raid shit?"

"Hands off, grandma. We're the police. This is a raid. Is that simple enough for you?"

"There's nothing illegal going on here."

"So you say."

Robinson leaned toward Puffy a little and said quietly, "Cliffy doesn't have a chance to yell 'raid' very often."

Cliffy impaled him with a glance and said, "If you're done with the exposé, maybe you could round these geeks up and move 'em out. We'll be at it all night as it is."

One of the gumshoes, Spade, I think it was, said, "The lady has a point. What's your beef?"

Cliffy said, "You're in for questioning."

"On what grounds?" Spade said.

"You'll hear about grounds till they're coming out of your ears," Cliffy said. Robinson leaned over and whispered something to him. Cliffy almost bit off his own lip, but he said, "Look, the city's in big trouble. The mayor isn't pulling any punches when it comes to saving it. We think you nice people know what's going on. We'd appreciate your cooperation." It really hurt him to say that. He was happier calling out, "All right. Move 'em out." He pointed meaningfully toward the door.

Puffy watched us, angry as if Cliffy'd taken away her liquor license. I waved at her, but she only nodded in return. She liked policemen fine, I guess, but only to say hello to.

They packed us into a big black-and-white bus that had little amenities like bars on the windows and convenient places where you could attach handcuffs. A strong smell of disinfectant was very loud and emphatic about cleanliness. The police didn't cuff us, but they didn't take down the bars either. The engine grumbled to life and took us across town.

At night, Los Angeles looked no less sedate or more trashy than any other big city. North of us, the Hollywood Hills glowed with an unholy red light that washed the city with blood. Smoke, lit from below, rose and knotted and changed like a devil creature looking for a properly hideous form. Occasionally, sparks jumped through the smoke, trying to get away. They got away and died almost in the same instant.

It was cold in the bus, and the fact we would spend the night inside a police station didn't make us feel any warmer. Lights played against windows and were reflected back at angles so bizarre, they seemed to have come from nowhere. A few of the riders leaned toward seatmates and shared secrets in a tone not much different from the laboring of the bus's engine. Behind me, a woman laughed occasionally, but for the most part there was nothing to listen to except traffic noise and sometimes the anguished cry of a faraway siren. It was a big city, and this night there was nothing in it for me but policemen.

I was sitting next to the guy with the pipe and the piercing eyes. His friend was right behind him, next to the guy in the rumpled trenchcoat. The guy took his pipe from his mouth and said, "You know more about this than you are telling." He had a nice English accent, but you could listen to that voice for a long time without knowing the thoughts behind it.

I said, "That would be easy. I haven't told anybody anything yet." It would be a long bus ride. There was plenty of time for conversation.

"Ah, but you have," he said. "You are not of this Earth, but you are presently living in Malibu."

I allowed my eyebrows to lift the brim of my hat slightly. I said, "It just so happens, I am of this Earth. As a matter of fact, I am of this Bay City. Early in life I had a run in with toxic waste and nose drops. As for where I live now, there's no way for you to know."

"But it's elementary, sir. There is a grain of

sand on the collar of your coat. I have been studying it for the previous ten minutes, while you have been busy watching the city as it passed. It is a grain of a size and kind that is to be found only on the beach at Malibu. Your shoes are well scuffed on the sides, as if you often walked through sand, not the shoes of a mere visitor. The conclusion, while not absolutely certain, was distinctly probable."

"Amazing," the guy's friend whispered as if the guy with the pipe had picked three winning Lotto numbers in a row.

"As for your origin," the man said, "it is as plain as the nose on your face." He wanted to smile, but his lips were too tight.

I said, "You should have been here last week when I hadn't heard that gag."

He shrugged and put his pipe back into his mouth. We were passing a Mexican restaurant with a crowd of people in front waiting to get in. They were wearing clothes I'd seen advertised just that week in the paper, so they had probably paid too much for them. I moved my head and could now see a reflection of the guy next to me. His eyes were half closed, but I don't think he was sleeping. He would never sleep while there was something going on that he could observe and analyze.

I said, "How do you figure it?"

"I beg your pardon?"

"Those two with the stage show. Where are they now, for instance?"

"I have no idea," he said around the stem of his pipe.

"Imagine that," I said. "A guy like you without an idea."

He liked that enough to smile, but not enough to open his eyes any wider.

I settled back in the hard seat and attempted to prove to myself that the guy with the pipe didn't have the only brain on the bus: I didn't know how Pele and Lono got the tiki into the pineapple, but chances were good that hadn't been their toughest problem. Once they decided to have a meeting, they had to decide what to say to the multitudes. Can't assemble multitudes and then not tell them anything.

But they couldn't tell the multitudes everything. Pele and Lono wanted their hideout kept secret. They wanted the fact that they were aliens kept secret. They wanted the real use of that slaberingeo spine kept secret. They had a lot of secrets, yet they needed help. I'd been walking a tightrope just like it since I first met the surfers. A tickle in the wrong direction, and you're on exhibit at Pasadena Tech—if you're lucky.

Somebody had told the police about the big meeting because that somebody wanted to discourage all the high-priced talent from looking for the right blowfish spine necklace. That somebody was probably the same somebody who currently had possession of it. Why they wanted it, I still didn't know. Except as a novelty, it wouldn't be of any use to anybody but Pele and Lono. How this certain somebody got it was an interesting question too, but not so important.

If that was the case, knowing who tipped off the police would probably solve my problem. I wouldn't have to find Pele and Lono. Once I had the necklace, I wouldn't have to do more than peep, and they'd come after me. And in a big hurry.

A lot of people knew about the meeting. Just for the record, Pele and Lono knew. Puffy knew. Some of her staff certainly knew. The detectives who'd been invited knew. Unless Puffy, or one of her people, or one of the detectives had the necklace, nobody who knew had a motive. Of course, the answer was that somebody else knew. Which put me right back where I'd started. Maybe I didn't have a brain after all. Or maybe I just needed to find Pele and Lono.

* * *

Downtown was deserted when the bus rolled through it. There was a lot of glitter and swank up near the Music Center, and an occasional bum moved quickly on the bone-white sidewalk, but mostly we had the streets to ourselves. The bus circled the old Hall of Justice, a square cement building with ornamental gargoyles at each corner of the narrow ledge, below the windows of each floor. Some lights were on in rooms where cleaning people were mopping up that day's heartache. Either that, or policemen were sorting out more of it. I'd be in one of those lit rooms soon. The bus came to a driveway and dived into a garage under the building.

The garage was a great closed space tightly packed with official vehicles and the stink of ancient oil and exhaust fumes. Cliffy and his coppers took shifts riding us up in a big freight elevator that somehow managed to have scuff marks on the ceiling as well as the walls and floor.

We were taken along wide marble halls to a big room that was pleasantly warm. It was paneled in nice old wood that newer public buildings only dream about. Over the years, people with itchy fingers and not much to do had carved names, dates, phone numbers, and obscene suggestions as high as a tall human could reach. Light beat down from a line of white globes onto rows of metal folding chairs with scabs of paint still on them. There were no shadows anywhere. My friend with the dramatic black clothing slouched in a corner with his arms folded.

The hard guys sank into chairs, pulled out crushed packs of cigarettes, and smoked slowly, letting the smoke go up into their nostrils. From the glum looks on their faces, they got no pleasure from it. Real men didn't, I guess. The three in evening clothes sat in a cor-

ner and yakked as if they were at the produc-
er's house and each was about to get the big
part. The dog curled up under the woman's
chair and went to sleep.

We were left alone for a while. Sure, no
hurry once the cattle were in the pen. Then a
uniformed policeman took away the guy with
the pipe. His friend wanted to go, too, but the
policeman made it clear that Detective Cliffy
would be talking to one person at a time.

The night dragged by like a sledge full of an-
vils through glue. There didn't seem to be any
pattern to who came next. No one who was
taken away came back. The thing the tweedy
lady was knitting grew longer. Cigarette smoke
was just something to look through while it dissolved your lungs. It wasn't long before everybody looked up when the cop came into the
room, hoping to be the next victim. I went to
sleep.

I awoke thinking at first that no time had
passed, but I had a crick in my neck and was
alone in the room except for the dramatic guy.
He was staring in my direction but I didn't
have to be there. He was just staring.

"It just doesn't add up," he said.

"What doesn't?"

He was startled. Evidently, he'd been talking
to himself. Louder now, he said, "They want
us to find their necklace, but they won't tell us
anything about it or even who they are." He
laughed, but it was a poor, weak thing. "And
I'd like to know how they put the tiki into the
pineapple, and how they come and go."

"I'll bet you would."

"You needn't use that sarcastic tone. When
you've clouded one man's mind, you've clouded
them all. Something new would be of great
benefit to my sanity."

I nodded, encouraging him.

"And it's not always easy knowing what evil lurks in the hearts of men."

"It's never pleasant going through other people's garbage."

While he was agreeing with me, the cop came back and took him away. I sat by myself, but I wasn't good company. I had too many questions and not enough answers. Besides, I'm always grumpy after four in the morning.

After a while, tentative light came through the big, pebbled glass windows on one side of the room. At first it just filled the room with a sort of general glow, but after a while it made a definite white patch on the floor that crawled toward the opposite wall so slowly you couldn't be sure it was moving until you forgot about it, then looked back later.

The cop came back and said, "You." I pointed at myself and looked around, surprised. He waited at the door, not amused. He'd been there all night, too. He took me to the end of the marble hallway, then down a flight of wide stairs. Only echoes were at home.

He took me to an office one floor down. It was a big old room, but not as nice as the one above. In the rising sunlight, the green paint on the walls—as much a part of civil service as the post office—looked nearly new. The room smelled as if too many worried people had sweated in it.

There were three desks in the room, far apart and lonely on the worn green linoleum. Behind one of the end ones, Cliffy sat with his head in his hands. Robinson was at the middle desk, fiddling with a small tape recorder. He had a lot of tapes in a stack to one side.

"Here's the last of 'em, sir," the policeman said.

"Thanks," Cliffy said without looking up.

I sat down in a wooden armchair across from Cliffy, and waited for the policeman's footsteps to get to the door and fade along the hallway.

Cliffy looked up suddenly and pursed his lips. He'd put on twenty years since I'd seen him last. "I don't like you," he said. That didn't seem to call for an answer, so I waited. "I don't like you or anything about you. I don't like this job, or the night just past, or a couple of clever geeks who come and go in puffs of smoke."

"I get it," I said. "You're an unhappy guy."

"Yeah, I'm unhappy. That's why I save the best for last." He took a deep breath, nodded at Robinson, who started his tape machine, scratched the side of his head, and said to me, "Go ahead. Be brilliant."

"What do you want to know?"

"How do I stop those hills from fizzing and popping?"

I shook my head. "I guess I'm just tired."

"Yeah," Cliffy said. He opened his hands to me and said, "Look, do you have a line on those two who called the meeting?"

"I don't know where they are, if that's what you mean."

He ticked off items on his hand: "First, you're there on the beach with the hat. Second, you're there when the truck of gimcracks gets stolen. Third, you show up when we find it. Fourth, you're one step ahead of us when that Backson broad has her apartment rattled. Fifth, somebody thinks you're enough of a detective to be on the guest list of the most exclusive party of the year. Do you see a pattern emerging here?"

"I might. If I was looking for patterns."

He put his head in his hands again and spoke to the desk. "We'll let it slide. Now, is there anything at all you'd care to tell us? Any little thing at all?"

"I don't know how there could be," I said. "I'm just one guy. You have an entire force behind you, not to mention computer links to every law enforcement outfit in the world."

He looked up and pondered me, but I almost

didn't know him. All the nastiness was gone from his face. He was just a very tired guy trying to do his job. Maybe that's all he'd ever been. He said, "In the world, yeah." He shook his head. "There's too much magic in this case. I ought to interrogate some of those wand jockies up at the Magic Palace."

"Tomorrow," I said.

"It's tomorrow already," he said and rubbed his face as if his hand were a washcloth. He looked at his watch and smiled emptily. "I gotta be at work in two hours." He shook his head and said, "Turn off your Judas, Robinson. Let's go home."

"Can I ask you one question first?"

He was facing me with nothing behind his eyes. I didn't want to push him but I needed to ask. I owed myself that.

"Sure," he said. "We never close."

"Just this: Who told you about the meeting?"

Cliffy's face didn't change. He didn't turn his head, but he said, "What do you think, Robinson? Is it any of his goddam business?"

For answer, Robinson popped open his tape machine and carefully removed the tape.

Cliffy said, "Robinson says it's none of your goddam business, but I'll tell you anyway because it won't do you a damn bit of good no matter what your game is. The tip was anonymous. Came into the switchboard about a quarter after seven. I didn't even hear the voice."

After that, Cliffy had a police car drive me through Los Angeles' morning traffic, said by those who didn't live in Los Angeles to be the worst traffic in the world. I wouldn't know. I'm afraid I nodded off a couple of times.

Kilroy's was shut up tight when I arrived, and my Belvedere was the only car around. All the hubcaps were still there. I got into the car and delicately drove it back to Malibu.

27

Magic Words

Malibu was far away, farther than T'toom. I almost fell asleep more than once, and another time the guy on my tail awakened me with his horn when the light changed to green. At last I turned into the garage and stopped, not quite hitting the back wall. I turned off the engine and listened to the traffic behind me swishing by. People who had not been up all night were awake and doing. I sat, feeling as if my bones were wax and sagging badly. But I didn't want to sleep in the car. I'd already slept too long sitting up.

The house was quiet, and I didn't disturb it. I got into Will and Bingo's bedroom. They were sleeping straight as a couple of logs, just touching heads. They were snoring, Will the alto, and Bingo the bass. I took off my trench coat and hung it carefully over the back of a chair. I collapsed onto my nest of dirty clothes. The snoring didn't bother me.

It was afternoon when I awoke with an idea. I'd slept too long or not long enough, because my brain felt as if it were full of warm soapy water—heavy, slippery and not much good for thinking. The idea floated in the soapy water like a shiny new sailboat. I stumbled through the empty house to the kitchen where Bill sat, swinging his legs. He was exactly the companion I was looking for. He didn't want anything from me.

On the beach, the surfers were working their surf-bots pretty hard, but they managed to avoid the hat—which by this time had white stains dripping down its sides. A couple of kids were playing near it, just outside the sawhorse barrier, while some adult leaned against a wooden backrest reading a magazine. The hat had been there so long, it had become just another piece of junk on the beach.

Captain Hook sat on the brick wall fronting the tiny brick patio, looking out to sea while he opened his fist time and time again and released butterflies into the air.

Later, after three eggs, half a package of bacon, and enough coffee to refloat the Titanic, I got a phone number from Bill and called it. While I waited for someone to answer, I became aware that I was wearing last night's clothes. It was like being buried up to my neck in manure.

"Magic Palace," said a cheery female voice at the other end of the line.

Trying to speak with the rolling tones of my friend in the black slouch hat, I said, "Yes. I'd like to make a reservation for this evening."

"Fine, I'll just need your membership number."

"Membership number?"

"Yes, sir. This is a private club. Only members and their guests are allowed in."

"Fine. Fine. How does one become a member?"

"You need to be a magician and to be recommended by someone who is already a member."

"That's all?"

"Well, there's the dress code. Gentlemen must wear coats and ties. No blue jeans are allowed."

"The dress code. I see. Thank you very much."

I hung up and went outside, where I sat on the wall next to Captain Hook. He'd stopped doing butterflies and was doing pigeons—tiny pigeons no bigger than hummingbirds. They strutted on the public walkway, pecking at specks in the blacktop.

The day was fine and the sun was warm on my face, a face that lately had seen too much darkness. I enjoyed it all for a moment before I said, "What's happening, Hookini?"

He smiled and said excitedly, "This is positively the most . . ." His voice trailed away with his smile, and he said, "You want to see a trick?"

"That's a good one with the pigeons. Ever been to the Magic Palace?"

"What's that?"

"It's where all the magicians hang out."

"Wow," he said, imagining the place.

"Want to go?"

"Sure."

"You'll have to wear a suit and tie."

"OK." He didn't sound certain. He probably hadn't worn an outfit like that since graduating from high school.

I walked out onto the beach, further scuffing my shoes on both sides with that special sand they have in Malibu, and watched Whipper Will give his surf-bot a long, wild ride. When the self-congratulatory shouting was over, I said, "I'll need a suit and tie for Captain Hook. We're going to the Magic Palace."

For a moment, he looked at the top hat. Then

he turned back to me and said, "I guess you know what you're doing, dude. But they only take members."

"We'll work something out."

He handed his control box to Bingo and walked with me to the house. We took Captain Hook into the master bedroom, and Bill came in to watch. Will excavated deeper and deeper into his chest while Captain Hook stood there smiling and, thank Durf, not making any more pigeons.

At last Will pulled three white shirts out and threw them onto the bed. Even in that room, thick with the musk of humans, those shirts smelled like something special—a little like dust, a little like wet laundry, and a little like advancing age.

As if he were doing a magic trick himself, Will flourished a plastic bag up off a gray and white pinstripe suit and told Captain Hook to put on the coat. Smiling like a goof, the captain did as he was told and stood there in the suit coat and noisy Hawaiian shirt, looking like a half-painted wall. Will pulled the coat straight, touched the shoulders, and stood back to get some perspective on the problem. "It'll do. He'll look like a gorilla at the opera, but it'll do."

Captain Hook wore his new clothes all afternoon, kind of awed by them, acting as if they were made of gold. I showered and changed, ate some more and slept some more, and after a while actually stopped feeling as if I'd been crumpled and thrown, and had missed the wastebasket. Just for the fun of it, I even did a little thinking.

It was a long shot that Pele and Lono were at the Magic Palace, just as it had been a long shot that they were the ones to search Busy Backson's apartment. But during my flight

with Medium Rare and Rupee Begonia, I had
seen Pele and Lono dressed in fancy clothes,
sitting in a room full of people drinking and
doing magic at round tables. I had never been
inside the Magic Palace, had never heard of it
before Detective Cliffy mentioned it, but imagining the place had a room just like that would
not be difficult.

Besides, Pele might wear that white number
because she knew how good she looked in it,
but Lono was not the type to wear a tie unless
he was forced to. They'd both arrived in Malibu dressed more for a backyard barbecue
than an audience with the queen. But you
needed a coat and tie to satisfy the Magic Palace dress code. No blue jeans allowed.

The sun sank into the Pacific, doing a lot of
fancy decorating with the clouds. With the
darkness and the stars, a wind came up. It was
warm and came in gusts, as if someone were
opening and closing an oven door. Red wind,
Chandler had called it, a wind that makes
strange things happen.

When it was fashionably late, I loaded Bill
and the captain into the car, the captain riding in Bill's usual shotgun position, and Bill in
the back seat. The going home traffic had
mostly gone home, but the air was wild that
night, and you had to drive for all the half-
bright boys with expensive cars as well as for
yourself.

We went out PCH to the Santa Monica Freeway and got off at La Brea. Then north along
the S-curves that had probably been a cow path
when Los Angeles was young, curves that nobody had taken the trouble to straighten out.
On the other side of the running sore Hollywood had become, Bill told me to turn right at
Franklin, a street that was too narrow for the
weight of traffic it normally carried; but that
didn't keep the half-bright boys from racing

from red light to red light, stopping at each
one with an angry squeal of brakes.

I was not the most popular guy in town when
I waited to turn left. My opportunity came,
and I gunned the car up a steep driveway that
led to a covered drive where very clean-looking
young men were parking cars. I traded the Belvedere for a square of cardboard, then walked
out from under the small roof and stood there
with Bill and Captain Hook, looking up at the
Magic Palace.

The wind was strong up here, making the
trees thrash with crashing noises and playing
catch with whatever was loose, which included
my hat, Captain Hook's hair, and smoke from
some very unlikely volcanoes. The perfume of
night flowers fought hard against a harsh,
boisterous smell from the center of the Earth,
and lost.

In the warm air, the Magic Palace rose above
us, all spires and gables and fancy bric-a-brac.
It may have once been a private residence, or
it may have just been built to look that way.
Well-placed lights sprayed up the sides in narrow fans, making the dark places look mysterious, as if they hid secrets that might pounce
on you when your back was turned. Above the
Magic Palace were the dancing fires of the Hollywood Hills, adding a sinister, shimmering
quality to the lights and shadows that even a
clever decorator had not been able to create.

Far away in the other direction, the lights of
the city were a spill of glass beads that ended
suddenly at the blackness of the ocean.

"Are we going in?" said Captain Hook.

We went in. The lobby was small, lined with
books, and very quiet after the furious activity
of the air outside. In one corner, a very pretty
woman wearing a blue dress made of clouds
sat behind a small wooden desk. You could
have read by the shine of her bright red lip-

stick. Her dark hair was piled high and had a stick through it to keep it together. She smiled and gave us her full attention.

I said, "We're not members, but the Great Hookini, here, is a visiting magician."

Captain Hook grinned, and poured pencils from a small can he took from her desk. He reached into it, and pulled out a brown-and-white rabbit three times its size. He put the rabbit on the floor, where it hopped to a corner and wiggled its nose at us.

The receptionist applauded politely, but I got the impression she had seen better. She said, "Does the Great Hookini know any of our members?"

"He knows Pele and Lono."

The perfectly formed curves of her eyebrows went up. They stayed up while she watched us and spoke softly into a telephone. A moment later, she put her hand over the receiver and said, "Lono says he never heard of the Great Hookini."

"Great kidder, that Lono," I said, and took the phone from her. "Lono?" I said into it.

"Who is this, please?"

"We met once. Medium Rare introduced us."

Through the receiver I heard music and laughter and the clink of glasses. Lono said, "Who is this Medium Rare?" His voice was cautious as a man peeking around a corner.

"I guess folks from Yewpitz have short memories."

A sharp intake of breath might have been static on the line. He said, "Ah, yes. Hookini. My old friend. Please let me speak to the girl again."

I handed the telephone back to the receptionist. A moment later, she relieved me of thirty bucks—ten bucks apiece, even for Bill—and said, "Walk over to the wall, say the magic words, and you can get into the club."

"What magic words?"

"A guy like you should never be without magic words." They didn't need to pay for electricity if they had her smile. Bill and the captain and I went to the wall. "Go ahead, Bill," I said. "Say magic words."

Bill saluted, gathered himself together as if he were going to blow the wall down, and said, "Open sesame." The wall of books swung open.

28

The Troubles of a Sufficiently Advanced Race

The Magic Palace was trickier than a lawyer's promise. On one wall was a mirror that didn't reflect anything but the room behind you. A small chamber to one side held an invisible string quartet playing Mozart on very visible instruments. Farther on, on a table, inside a glass globe, a shriveled head made of green smoke was singing requests. At the moment, it was rendering "Ah, Sweet Mystery of Life." Captain Hook wanted to make studying each thing his life's work. It was unfair for me to keep him moving. I was unfair. Each room was done in a different color of flocked wallpaper. I was looking for the green room.

It was through a dark hallway in which green, glowing bats swooped at you and some crazy guy laughed. It was along some stairs that looked square and true, but weren't. You thought you were walking down, but were really walking up. It was through a doorway so low, it might have been built just for me.

The green room had a bar that looked as if it had been carved out of a single tree trunk bigger than a two bedroom house. Smiling devils were carved on the front. Along one wall of the room, picture windows looked down the hill onto the lights of Los Angeles. Fans hanging from the ceiling wound up cigarette smoke as if it were gray yarn and tore it into nothingness. There was still plenty of smoke in the air. I could stand the smoke as long as I had to. All the tables were crowded, and the noise was no louder than you might expect from a roomful of people being charged too much for having a good time.

In one corner, Pele and Lono sat drinking from coconut bowls. They watched us come, and neither one of them stood up when we arrived. They were not happy to see us, but curiosity was there, keeping their eyes steady and their mouths a little slack. I made introductions. They nodded, and Lono said, "Is one of you really a magician?"

As if somebody had dropped a quarter into him, Captain Hook said, "This is positively the most amazing display of magic ever to be seen by mortal man. Observe my empty hand. Observe again." He opened his hand a second time, and bats swarmed from it, beating their wings against the air with a noise like muffled applause. They flew up through the ceiling and were gone. Nobody else in the room paid much attention. In a place like this, what was another bat more or less?

I said, "Hookini is good all right, especially considering that last week he was just some guy with a surf-bot and a nasty disposition. Then he met a hat on the beach."

Pele took a casual drink from her coconut shell. For a moment, Lono drummed his fingers on the table. He didn't stop when he said, "Please sit down."

There were only two empty chairs. Bill stood between me and Pele, trying to see what was in her bowl. It seemed to bother her, so I let him. When we were all cozy, I said, "About that hat—"

Lono interrupted me by saying, "The hat never attacks first."

"It didn't have to attack at all. You could drop an atomic bomb on that hat and not hurt it. The captain, here, just threw an old bottle."

"His disrespect must be punished," Pele said, not quite managing to clench her teeth while she spoke.

I said, "We can sit here telling each other what time it is until we look like that singing head in the other room, but that isn't curing Captain Hook—the Great Hookini to you."

Pele patted Bill in the beak and ran one finger around the top edge of her coconut shell. She was trying to be cute, but she had too much character for that. Beauty was all she'd ever have, no matter how coy she was with her fingers. Danger radiated from her. She said, "He might be cured if. . . ." She let the word dangle like an unplugged electric cord.

Lono said, "Maybe Hookini would like to see a show?"

"Show?" Captain Hook said as if somebody had mentioned dinner.

"The Magic Palace has magic shows all evening long—closeup, stage, new talent. All you have to do is get in line."

"I'm new talent," the captain said. He stood up, ready to bolt.

"Go on," I said. "Have a good time. I'll be back for you later."

It wasn't magic, but just the same, I blinked and he was gone.

Pele said, "What about the bot?"

"He's with me," I said.

"Tell him to sit down before I melt him into a little puddle."

"Sit down, Bill." I patted the chair the captain had just vacated. Bill was getting settled when a young lady wearing enough green satin to upholster the inside of an egg cup asked me if I wanted a drink. I told her I didn't, and she went away.

Pele licked her lips and swallowed. She threw a glance at Lono, and he tossed it back. She said, "How did you know we are from Yewpitz?"

"You're not the only ones in the room who are not of this Earth." I tapped the side of my nose. "I recognized your ship the first time I saw a picture of it in *The Interstate Eyeball.*"

"I told you we came in too low," Pele said and socked Lono in the arm.

Lono ignored her. "Can you help us find our blowfish spine necklace?"

I smiled and said, "You've been playing out that line too long. We both know your problem has nothing to do with blowfish. You're looking for the slaberingeo spine that goes into your SHIP unit."

"All right. Yes. Can you help us?"

"Can you cure Captain Hook?"

Lono nodded.

"All right, then," I said, and leaned at them across the table. "Tell me all about it."

"About what?" Pele said. Her hair would begin to glow any minute.

I shook my head, stood up and said, "If that's the way it is, I guess I'll be going. Come on, Bill. Let's go find the captain." I moved away, but slowly. Behind me, the two of them were having a hurried conversation in a language that sounded like a tape being played sideways.

Something whizzed by my head, and seconds later a hardy-looking thorn hedge was growing up in front of me. There was scattered applause. I stopped and, still slowly, looked back at them. Pele was drinking, and Lono was beckoning to me. I wandered back to the table in no particular hurry and sat down. Bill clambered onto the chair next to me and began to swing his legs. I put my elbows onto the table and waited.

Lono said, "You're right, of course. We come from Yewpitz. Our ships have been coming to Earth for centuries."

I nodded. "Some guys are making a good career saying they know you."

"It's possible some of them do. We pick up a lot of test subjects. We do physical and mental examinations on them and let them go. That's usually the end of it."

"Usually?"

Lono leaned into me and said, "We picked up a female near Hilo and gave her the usual treatment. She was as excited as some we pick up, but not nearly as frightened. When we put her down a few hours later, we discovered that she'd stolen our slaberingeo spine." He took a long drink, and when he put down the coconut bowl, his hand was shaking. He said, "You wouldn't happen to have a spare?"

"Not that'll fit your ship, no. I have a sneeve."

"Ah." He and Pele both nodded.

Lono went on, "By the time we found out what had happened, she was long gone. We knew we couldn't get home without the slab spine, so we began to look for her. We were staying at a hotel in Hilo when she called us." He took another drink. There wasn't enough liquid in there for him to do that. Then the bowls were magic, too. I wondered if they were somehow siphoning brewski out of a bottle behind the bar.

Pele said, "She had the nerve to offer us a trade." The thought of it made her growl. Steam rose from her as she spoke. That wasn't just patter. It was real steam, hot enough to roast chicken.

Lono said, "She would give us back our sla-beringeo spine if we would come and speak to a convention of her flying-saucer friends. You know flying saucer?"

I said I did.

"We refused to do it," Pele said. "It would taint the experiment, spoil everything the Yew-pitzkitziten race has been doing for hundreds of years."

"Also," said Lono, "if we made a deal with her, someone would surely find out, and there would be no point in our going home."

Pele growled again. A soft blue flame was coming out of each ear, nearly invisible against the green wallpaper.

"How do *you* manage?" Lono said.

"Manage what?"

"You look like a Toomler, yet you walk around with no cares."

"No cares may be overstating the situation just a little. But the truth is, I manage because I tell them my mother took drugs in the Six-ties. Or that I had an early run-in with toxic waste and nose drops."

"They believe you?" Lono said.

"Those who don't have kept their lips but-toned so far."

"Stupid beings," Pele said.

"Smart enough to find you in Hilo. So you traced her to Los Angeles and ransacked her apartment. If I were a stooge, I might think the police on Yewpitz would be interested in hear-ing about that."

That stopped Lono with his coconut bowl halfway to his lips. Pele glared at me, but what else was new? Lono put down the bowl and said, "How would we find her to do that? We never knew her name."

"No?" I said, using polite interest to jack up my eyebrows.

"You might as well believe me. It's true. We never know their names. This one we called Lulu."

"Why?"

Lono looked surprised. "I don't know. She looked like a Lulu, I suppose."

"Go on, then."

"There's nothing to go on with. We knew she lived in Los Angeles, so we came here hoping to find the slaberingeo spine. So far we have not."

"You knew what city she lived in, but not her name?"

Pele's hair was definitely red now and wavered like fire. She shouted, "Our studies are extensive, but we had no interest in her name! Forget the name."

Her voice had fallen into a hole of silence. People were looking at us. She looked back at them. I tried to be invisible. Soon the party continued.

"Even so," I said calmly, "nobody I know makes suspects as good as you two."

"What makes us such good suspects?" Lono said in a voice as calm as my own.

If I'd had a cigarette to light, I would have done it then. I said, "You stole that Pantages truck from the loading dock at the Sue Veneer Novelty company."

Pele shrank into her chair and clutched her coconut bowl as if it were her dolly. Lono just looked grim.

I said, "You stole the truck and went through the spines and didn't find the one you were looking for. But what you did find was a Certificate of Authenticity attached to each fake. Each certificate was signed by Busy Backson and showed her picture. You now knew that

Lulu's Earth name was Busy Backson. How am I doing?"

"You are most entertaining," Pele said around gritted teeth.

"It gets better. After you knew Lulu's real name, you looked her up in the phone book and found her phone number listed, but not her address. A lot of women are listed that way. You called her the same way you called the Big Orange Taxi Company from the Sparkle Room bar, and not quite knowing why, she showed up at the location from which you called. She looked around, saw nothing of interest to her, and drove home. You followed her in the truck. After you found out where she lived, you drove the truck a few blocks and ditched it."

I was making all this up, but it sounded good, and it must have been close to the way it happened because I could see by the looks on their faces that they bought the whole package, right down to its brand-new white sidewall tires.

Almost too softly to hear, Lono said, "But we didn't find what we were looking for."

"I could see that by the all-points bulletin you two put out, and by the meeting at Kilroy's, later. Did you know that a lot of us spent the night in the Hall of Justice downtown because of your little gathering?"

"Certainly you can't blame us for that," Pele said.

"No. I can't blame you for that, but your getting hauled in too, would have been a nice touch, good for morale."

Pele said nastily, "We may be stupid. We may be as guilty as you say. But you must help us or your friend will remain a magician forever."

"I guess it's the *threats* part of the evening," I said.

Lono said, "Will you help us get home?"

What could I do? I nodded and smiled. I said, "Come on. I'll take you to it."

"You know where the slaberingeo spine is?" Pele said.

"Isn't that why you're doing business with me?" I said, hoping I sounded more confident than I felt.

"Must you answer a question with a question?"

"Why not?"

Lono smiled and put a hand on Pele's arm. He said, "We haven't gone out since the meeting and not much before."

"I'll take you to the spine," I said.

The two of them spoke in that sideways language again and decided they would chance it. I don't know what the big deal was. If things began to go sour, they could use their private exploding escape route.

We got ready to go. The thorn bush had evaporated into nothing, just as had the thorn wall out by Harry's loading dock. I found Captain Hook and told him I'd be gone for a while, and would he like to stay here. He would. Boy, would he.

On the way out, I let Pele and Lono go before me, and I stopped to speak to the receptionist. I said, "You know, those two are the ones who threatened to destroy Los Angeles."

She nodded and smiled as if I'd just announced a cure for the common cold. She said, "Absolutely. It'll be a wonderful effect."

"Effect?"

"Absolutely. Turning the Hollywood Hills into volcanoes is the most spectacular trick ever done by a member of the Magic Palace." She seemed really pleased about that. "None of our other members would dream of spoiling it."

"Is that what Pele and Lono told you? That it's a trick?"

"Well, sure. Isn't it true?" Doubt scampered across her face, leaving no mark.

I leaned with one elbow on her table and told her a secret. I said, "You know, sometimes the science of a sufficiently advanced race looks just like magic."

Confusion leaped onto her face and stayed. I nodded and wished her a good night. Bill and I followed Pele and Lono out into the warm gusting wind.

29

Fair Game for the Wind

I paid to get my car out of hock, and we rode down the hill, Pele and Lono in the back as if I were their chauffeur. The wind shuddered against the windows of the car, trying to get inside. Trash was caught up into whirlygigs that danced along the street. Anything not tied down was fair game for the wind that night.

Above us, the Hollywood Hills still fulminated. Apparently Pele and Lono did not quite trust me. Which was just as well. I could have been guessing wrong.

Pele and Lono watched me drive along Franklin, then up Highland to the Hollywood Freeway. Petulantly, as if I'd broken a promise, Pele asked "Where, exactly, are you taking us?"

"Changehorses," I said, seeing how they liked it.

"What's that?" Pele asked.

"A townlet just north of L.A. County. Medium Rare lives there."

A lot of heavy breathing came from the back seat, but it wasn't young love, nothing Gino and

Darlene would have been familiar with. Lono
said, "How would she get the spine?"

"Busy Backson's brother, Gone-out, is a
friend of hers."

"Gone-out Backson must have a lot of
friends," Pele said, her voice colder than the
marble walls in the Hall of Justice.

"But only one who could possibly have
known about the big meeting. It was a private
gig, with invitations going only to people who
were professionals at keeping secrets. But you
can't keep a secret long from somebody who
knows astral projection. The call tipping the
police went in to the switchboard about seven-
fifteen, before the meeting started, but not so
long before that the clan hadn't already begun
to gather. Hanging there like a ghost, Medium
Rare saw what was going on. Or Rupee Begonia or one of their friends on the astral plane
saw it and reported it to her. Either way, Medium Rare called the news in to the police, in-
timating these folks, being detectives, might
know something about the Hollywood Hills
volcanoes."

"What would the meeting be to Medium
Rare?" Lono said.

"If she had the spine, she wouldn't want anybody looking for it. Especially not anybody
who might find it."

"She didn't know what those detectives were
there for. The detectives didn't know, themselves."

"No. She was taking a chance, but not much
of one. If she was wrong, she wouldn't lose
anything. If she was right, she'd get what she
wanted, which was time."

"Time for what?" Lono said.

I imagined Pele sitting next to him, emotions
on a low boil, face grim but on the edge of wild
anger. I said, "Time to use the spine. I don't
know what for."

Pele's laugh was a glass shattering against a cement floor. It sounded a little hysterical. More breathing was done in the back seat. Lono said, "So the spine wasn't even at Busy Backson's apartment when we looked for it."

"I don't know. I guess it doesn't matter. You didn't find it."

Pele and Lono sat in the back seat, silent and unmoving as two sacks of grain. The wind picked up as the Hollywood Freeway hooked into I-Five and headed north through a tunnel of darkness. It made blustery noises as it rocked the Belvedere. I rolled down the window, letting in wind that smelled strongly of dry, spicy plants and bounced through the car like a loose bundle of laundry fresh from the dryer. I closed the window and said, "Can you handle the slab spine?"

"What?" said Lono as if he'd been thinking about something else.

"The slaberingeo spine is obviously unbalanced. Can you handle it without it attracting flower pots that drop onto your head from twelfth-story windows?"

"We have a hyper-spanner."

"Good enough."

I took the Changehorses turnoff and drove up into the mountains. If anything, the wind was stronger here. Tall trees scratched at the sky, trying to get a handhold, and bent from side to side far enough that they looked about ready to break off. Brush and twigs flew at us, and once I thought I saw a branch the size of a man's arm blow past. Through the crack between the top of the window and the body molding came a strong, dusty smell of pine. Straight ahead, where the road cut through the trees, I could see the sky. Stars gathered in huge crowds, as clear and bright as headlights. I thought of Avoirdupois and what he could do with that: "Headlights of the Gods!?"

The road widened, and we were in Change-horses. No light showed anywhere, not even on the coffee shop or the bar. Pieces of tree leaped like deer across the cement apron between the pump islands of the gas station. I kept driving. I made the Belvedere climb the hill, and then climb harder when it turned onto the gravel side road. At the top, I almost ran into Merle.

A lot of people joined Merle, and they crowded around us. I shouted to Bill to lock his door, and I locked mine. I didn't have time to notice whether everybody in the crowd had that distant look all Medium Rare's followers have, but they seemed determined to stop us without being actually angry. Some of them had sticks, but most of them pounded on the body and top of the car with their fists. I drove slowly through them, as if I were making head-way through a herd of cows, and stopped in front of the main house.

I felt silly just sitting there trying to see ev-erything at once. Bill was crouching under the dashboard. I felt hot breath on my neck, and Lono whispered to me, "She knew we were coming. She doesn't want us here."

"Yeah," I growled. My eye caught on two somethings hanging in the sky among the snap-ping treetops. Despite all the wind, they were hanging there as steady as the stars I could see through them. They were gauzy somethings in the shape of women. One might have been Ru-pee Begonia. The other might have been Me-dium Rare. I couldn't hear what Medium Rare was saying. Even if I was outside the car and in still air I probably wouldn't have been able to hear her unless she focused properly, but I could see her waving her arms around, order-ing her troops to gang up on us. They began to rock the car.

We could have sat in the car all night, or waited for Merle and his friends to break the windows and drag us out, or we could have just gone home. Going home would have been the smartest thing to do. I said, "Can you do to those clowns what you did to Captain Hook?"

"Make them magicians? But why?" Lono's breath came in hot gusts on my neck. Except for the crowd, I might as well have been outside.

"Can you do it?"

"We can do it," Pele said.

I turned to look at them. Each of them pressed a forefinger against the ceiling of the car. They watched their fingers, concentrating hard. I heard a buzz that got angrier and higher as I listened. The body of the car began to glow, and the crowd leaped away from it. The buzz went so fast it became a shriek. When it seemingly couldn't go any higher, it went higher, and the car threw off a flash. Red lightning like snakes crawled over the people outside the car. They collapsed, and the red lightning crawled into the ground.

Up in the sky, Medium Rare's arms hung limp.

We waited for the people to get up. Bill nearly crawled into my lap, watching. We were all breathing at the same time, as if our lungs were harnessed together.

A tall guy in a business suit stood up, looked around, frowned for a moment, then smiled as if he wanted to make sure we saw his back teeth. Merle got up. Then a woman dressed for the office. In ones and twos and threes, people stood up, all smiling at each other.

Merle was closest to me, and, as he pulled handkerchief after handkerchief from his fist, he began to sing in a low mournful voice, "You ain't nothin' but a hound dog. . . ." The guy next to him—a fat old man with a round, shiny head—ignored him. He was making change appear from the ear of another guy, who was busy wrapping his wrist watch in a dirty rag.

Rabbits and lit cigarettes began to appear from nowhere. When the magic act was in full swing, I cracked my door and waited. Nobody noticed. I opened my door, stepped out, and gestured to the others in the car. We got out and ran up the stairs to the house.

The door wasn't locked. I guess Medium Rare never expected us to get that far. Hoping that Edgar Allan was outside doing tricks, I crossed the giant's coffin and pulled open the sliding doors. Bill and Pele and Lono followed me up the spiral stairs to the second floor hallway. No horses came at us. I opened the second pair of sliding doors and stepped into Medium Rare's octagonal spirit chamber.

30

Cockeyed Opportunists

The black room had to be bigger than it looked. Gone-out Backson was standing behind Medium Rare, who was sitting on her milky, octagonal stool at her milky, octagonal table. Her eyes were shut. Gone-out was wearing a nice dark suit, which the black velvet hangings made to look as if it were powdered with chalk dust. Next to the table was a cardboard box big enough to hold a washing machine. It was filled with blowfish spine necklaces. One of them had probably been stolen from me in the parking lot of the Here Today—Gone to Maui Souvenir Company. One of them might have been a slaberingeo spine necklace, but I doubted it, because draped over the glass ball on the tripod was another spine necklace. A teardrop of lead was tied with string to one of the spines. That would be the ringer.

Pele thought so, too. Hissing through her teeth, she took a step forward, but I put a hand on her arm. She looked at me, angry enough to spit hot lava in my face. I nodded in Gone-out's direction. He was pointing a pistol at us. Before anybody could do anything I'd regret, I told him, "The guy with that spine necklace always has bad luck, and you're standing close enough to get burned. If you fire that pistol, chances are it will jam or misfire. Or you could just blow your hand off."

"Shall we try the experiment?" It was the same polished voice sifted through the same lizard lips, but it had gone bad and turned nasty.

I sighed and went on, "You may not believe this, Gone-out, but you didn't get any taller or put on any muscle when you picked up that pistol."

He grinned confidently at me.

Pele didn't like any of this. She swung up her arm and aimed her open hand at Gone-out. He didn't have time to duck out of the way and didn't have the presence of mind to fire his pistol. The sparkly stream of water hit him right in the chest. It was a weak stream, like the spurt from a nickel squirt gun. Gone-out looked down at the wet spot. Pele looked at the palm of her hand.

Lono pointed. A flash of green at Gone-out's feet left behind a single perfect red rose.

"It's the spine," I said. "It's unbalanced."

I thought it was Gone-out's play, but he licked his lips and glanced at Medium Rare, and said nothing. I said, "Ain't the waxworks grand? So lifelike."

Gone-out's gun wavered, but not enough.

Pele and Lono watched us carefully, but made no move to get involved. Without their magic, they were just two tourists waiting for the Auto Club to arrive.

Gone-out said, "You are too clever by half. But Medium Rare is the one who has the necklace."

As if on cue—she may have actually been waiting for her name to be mentioned—

Medium Rare's eyes fluttered open, and she looked at us calmly. She put her hands on the octagonal table, on either side of the glass globe, and said, "Thank you for bringing Pele and Lono here, Mr. Marlowe. You may leave now. We have business to discuss."

"Then the welcoming committee outside was just for me."

"Too clever," Gone-out said.

"Indeed," Medium Rare said. "He is very clever to have discovered that I had the spine."

"Not clever. Just observant. You made a lot of mistakes."

"Hah," said Medium Rare.

"Think about it. You take the trouble to get me up here, strip me down to my soul, and introduce me to these two spirit friends of yours, Pele and Lono. You tell me you want to help them find their special spine necklace. But then you won't let me tell them about my friend the magician, or ask them where they are. What does that suggest to you?"

"I'm sure you'll tell me," Medium Rare said around a smile no warmer or more appealing than an old slice of toast.

"It suggests that you wanted me to find the necklace, but for yourself, not for them. You were afraid that if I found it and was able to give it to Pele and Lono, I would do it and not cut you in at all. How am I doing?"

Medium Rare said nothing. She wasn't smiling now.

I forged ahead. "If that wasn't enough, somebody called the police and told them there was a big party in the Oahu Room at Kilroy's. Could you be that somebody?"

She said more of nothing.

"But this is the best part. Without any help from you, I find these two that you say you want to help. Then, instead of your just giving them their necklace and wishing them good luck, you set it out like a piece of merchandise and say you have business to discuss."

"Are you quite finished?"

"No. There's one more thing. You weren't surprised when Pele and Lono walked in here, solid as bricks and as transparent as an elephant's rear end. I think you knew all along that they weren't any more spirits than I am."

Medium Rare's fingers moved on the table. Behind her, Gone-out was looking at her, waiting to see what she would say. His gun, forgotten, was pointing at a corner of the room. I wasn't worried about him anymore, but I wasn't leaving, either. Not just yet.

Medium Rare was not a criminal, not in the sense that she made her living at it. She was just a cockeyed opportunist. Therefore, when she did something wrong, and you caught her at it, she had to justify herself. That's what I was waiting for. I was waiting to hear what her game was.

The silence was as dark and deep as the black velvet on the walls. Medium Rare stopped moving her fingers, but she didn't look at me. She looked into the glass ball full of smoke. She said, "I know the wisdom of the ages."

I could have been clever then, but I nodded instead.

Medium Rare went on, "Being wise in this time, in this place, in this plane, is not easy. There is a con artist behind every crystal, a clever faker behind every out-of-body experience, a wishful thinker behind every story of reincarnation."

"The woods are full of them. And you, all alone in the open with a clear view of the sky."

"A clear view of the sky. Well-put for an unbeliever. With the world so full of jackanapes, I need proof that I am not just one more."

Quietly, as if to himself, Gone-out said, "She is the beginning and the end. She is the Serpent of Time biting its own tail. She sees all, knows all, tells all."

As if Gone-out had said nothing, Medium Rare went on: "When I first met them, I knew Pele and Lono were not spirits. Spirits have no interest in earthly things like necklaces. Yet, they were not of this Earth either. The conclusion was obvious. They were from space. They had been in body where I had been only in spirit."

I said, "And you wanted them to tell everybody that the pictures you'd painted were true and accurate representations of other worlds. And if they wouldn't do that for you, they'd never get their spine."

Pele sat down on the vacant octagonal bench and looked volcanic eruptions at Medium Rare. Medium Rare didn't notice. She was still involved with her glass globe. Lono leaned against the wall with his arms crossed. Nobody seemed happy.

Medium Rare looked up at Pele. She said, "I was tired of being the butt of New Age jokes. I wanted the respect I deserve. Are these things so terrible?"

"Not so terrible," said a new voice. "Just wildly overblown." Busy Backson followed a pistol into the room. She was wearing tennis shoes now, and a thin, off-white jacket with a lot more pockets than anybody needed, but otherwise, she was dressed much as she had been in her apartment. She said, "You know, I just want them to speak at my club. *You* want them to get up in front of everybody and tell them how swell you are. Hello, Gone-out, you predictable creep. Hello, Zoot. Thanks for all your help." She reached for the necklace.

"Uh, uh, ah," Gone-out said motioning with his own pistol.

Busy froze, but she did not move away.

I shook my head and said, "I suppose if

you're going to shoot somebody, you might as well keep it in the family."

"You shouldn't have followed me, Busy. Medium Rare's need is greater than yours."

Busy unfroze, but she was still tense. "Yeah, yeah. Sure, sure. I didn't have to follow you. I knew you'd be here. I haven't asked you in weeks to clean the fish tank, but you had to finally get around to it, didn't you? Creep."

"The spine was in the tank?" I said, surprised.

"Yeah. Rubber-banded to a fake fish. Anyway, Gone-out was gone. The spine was gone. Who else would he take it to?"

"Be glad you're rid of it. It's bad medicine."

"Oh, it's movie Indians now, is it?" She sounded chipper, but her pistol seemed to be getting a little heavy.

"Bad medicine. It twice stopped you from killing me."

Not looking nearly puzzled enough, she said, "Why would I try to kill you?"

"For the obvious reason. I was looking for the spine, and you were afraid I'd find it."

"What makes you think I had it?"

I gestured at Pele and Lono and said, "When we get together we don't just talk about the weather."

That got me a very small, "Oh," from Busy.

I shrugged. "When the guy with the beard took a shot at me, and his car swerved just at the right moment, I thought I was pretty lucky. Then, when some guy tried to strangle me with a cord in the parking lot of Kilroy's, and the cord broke, I thought that was too much luck. I wasn't having good luck. Yours was just bad. Because of the spine."

"I didn't have anything personal against you. As a matter of fact, I think you're kind of cute. But I had a higher cause than cute to worry about."

I said, "UFO nuts," and made an impolite noise.

Lono said, "Will you let me know when you've decided who's going to blackmail us?" He walked out of the room, went slowly along the hallway, and sat down on the top step of the spiral staircase.

Gone-out said, "Go home, Busy." He was a little less casual with the gun. It looked like a stand-off.

Suddenly three things happened at once. Busy dived for the necklace; her brother took a shot at her; Pele saw my control of the situation fading fast, so she took a chance and dived at the necklace herself. Gone-out's gun only clicked, giving Busy time to accidentally knock the necklace to a corner of the room when she tried to sweep it from Pele's grasp. An eyeblink later, panels in the ceiling fell onto Busy and Gone-out, knocking the guns from their hands and pulling enough velvet loose from a wall to wrap around Pele. She fell back into the mountainous velvet with a squeal, and more of it dropped on top of her.

Gone-out and Busy had staggered back against walls, their hands to their heads, and were slouching there, a little confused. I picked up the guns, and put one in my waistband. Two-gun Zoot, the Scourge of the Spaceways. I was about to help Pele when Lono walked into the room with his hands up. Behind him, with his own pistol, was Avoirdupois, looking very pleased indeed.

"All the suspects are here now," I said. "We can serve dinner."

Avoirdupois laughed his laugh and said, "You are a pip, sir, and that is certain. And I must thank you most sincerely for leading me to some authentic aliens. Good evening, madam." He bowed a little at Medium Rare. She refused to look at him.

"Which are those?" I said.

He laughed, and it seemed to get away from him. His entire body shook, and his pistol made figure eights behind Lono's back. I wanted to jump him, but I was standing nearest the slaberingeo spine and didn't want to chance taking an unscheduled express drop to the ground floor.

Pele threw a sheet of velvet off her and glared at us. She said something in her sideways language that sounded like someone clearing their throat and spitting the result into a pail full of sand.

"Ah, there you are, my dear. I'm delighted that you could join us. I always say that two aliens are better than one, and that's a fact." Avoirdupois' eyes rolled around in his head like loose marbles, then lit on the spine on the floor. "This certainly must be the article that all the fuss is about." Still aiming the pistol at Lono, he took his other hand from a pocket. The hand was wearing a paisley oven mitten. With the protected hand, Avoirdupois bent to pick up the necklace. Just to be fair, I said, "Nix. Bad news."

Gone-out grumbled, "You can say that again." He was feeling over his head as if it were a cantaloupe he was testing for ripeness. Busy had collapsed onto the velvet.

"So you say, sir. So you say. So might all of you say. But, knowing as I do that every last one of you has a stake in this little trinket, you will forgive me if *I* only thank you for your concern, and tell you that this mitten immunizes me against the effects of the curse." He held up the mittened hand and chuckled like a big truck changing low gears. "It does, and that's a fact. Perhaps you will not be amazed when I tell you that I found it in the classified ads of *The Interstate Eyeball*."

"Curse?" Medium Rare said.

Avoirdupois bowed as if Medium Rare had asked him to dance. He said, "Curse. Indeed, curse. You would not believe me if I told you half of what I know. I hardly believe it myself. But you can read as much as you care to about the Curse of the Slaberingeo Spine Necklace. It's all in back numbers of the *Eyeball*."

He bent quickly, as a man that size never could, but as a well-designed robot might, and snatched up the necklace with his protected hand, laughter gurgling in him the whole time like water through an open pipe. He said, "And now, my dear aliens, if you want this trinket, you will have to deal with me, make no mistake of it. Just one short interview. Just a few photographs." There was a mechanical whine, and a camera rose from under Avoirdupois' hat.

I looked at Lono. Lono looked at me. I walked across the room and helped Pele to her feet. Her hands were warm and smooth and dry. She didn't say thank you, but she didn't scream at me, either.

"You'd better go with him," I said in a low, grim voice that frightened even me.

Gone-out said, "The real Marlowe would be disgusted."

Busy and Medium Rare just looked at me like a couple of snakes.

Avoirdupois pushed Pele and Lono out with his gun. I watched them carefully and followed silently, but not too closely. About one quarter of the way to the door, Avoirdupois tripped over the nap in the carpet, and while catching himself, dropped both the pistol and the necklace. I kicked the necklace to Lono, and dived for the pistol. I came up with it pointing at Avoirdupois.

Avoirdupois backed into the wall hard enough to jiggle the pictures and cried, "I've been swindled!" Angrily, he pulled off the mitten, and with contempt, threw it to the floor. His lower lip came out, and his eyes got big. He had the look of the baby it was easy to take candy from. He saw the pistol in my hand and slowly raised his arms.

Lono reached for the necklace with a pair of silver tongs tricked out with some extra knobs, lights, and bumps. The moment the hyperspanner touched the necklace, the air instantly got lighter, as if a thunderstorm had passed. Lono disappeared in a puff of green dandelion fuzz. Pele hissed at us, raised her hands above her head and disappeared in a spout of flame that scorched the ceiling.

"Wow," said Bill.

He was standing at the door to the spirit chamber with Busy, Gone-out and Medium Rare, all looking as if someone had just told them they were going to hang the next day. Against the wall, Avoirdupois began to laugh. It was a deep, energetic laugh, and it rolled up and down the hallway alone for a long time.

"You are a wonder, sir, make no mistake. You have tied this thing up neatly, I'll give you that, even if, to tell the truth, it did not work out entirely to my benefit." More basement chuckling. "But having said all that, I will further say this: Perhaps we are all better off." He smiled and kicked the kitchen mitten, then experimentally lowered his hands. I let him. I emptied his pistol, kept the bullets, and gave it back to him.

I said, "Come on, Bill."

He waddled to me, and we walked together toward the staircase.

Behind me, Avoirdupois went on. "What shall it be then? Shall we stand here weeping, or shall we begin another gallant crusade?"

"What do you mean, we, you hack-bot?" Busy said.

I looked back, waiting, too curious to descend.

Avoirdupois lifted his hands and twiddled his fingers, feeling the air. He said, "Come now, my friends. Shall we not allow bygones to be bygones? Shall we stand radiating hostility toward each other when we could be," he smiled, "searching for a statuette of a black bird?"

I walked slowly toward him. Questions wanted out. I let them want. Let somebody else do some work for a change.

Arm wrestling her curiosity and losing, Busy said, "What's that?"

With his hands flat at his sides, Avoirdupois began to raise and lower himself on his toes. He said, "It is said to have been carved from a single power crystal by the simple native craftsmen of the ancient and fabled island of Mu. It is said to either bring immortality or cure baldness."

I was standing to one side of Avoirdupois, and I was able to see him frown. "Or perhaps it improves one's sex life. Or it insures that your tax returns will not be audited, no matter how outrageous your deductions." He shrugged and smiled again; this was just a private joke between friends. He said, "The ancient scrolls are not very clear on this point."

Medium Rare said, "What incredible garbage," and walked back into her spirit chamber. She lifted a sheet of velvet and let it fall.

When I left, Avoirdupois was still trying to convince the others to join him in the search for the black crystal bird. I got out before whatever infected Avoirdupois crawled onto me.

31

The Other Painting

When Bill and I got downstairs, Medium Rare's gang was still doing magic at each other, though with less enthusiasm than when I had entered the house. The wind was still blowing, and it had blown pine twigs into the vents in front of the Belvedere's windshield. As I rolled through Changehorses and down the hill, they skittered like dry insects up the windshield and flew away.

While I drove back to the Magic Palace to pick up Captain Hook, I thought about the rogue's gallery that had wrangled in Medium Rare's house that night.

Busy Backson had stolen something from aliens, but they now had it back and were not likely to press charges. Medium Rare had briefly stolen the thing from her, but didn't have it any more, and it had not belonged to Busy in the first place. Pele and Lono had stolen a truck but had given it back. Besides, I don't think California had an extradition treaty with Yewpitz. Busy had tried to murder me twice. But it was nothing personal, she said, and with the spine gone, I didn't think she'd try again. In any case, I didn't want the police or anybody else straining themselves on my behalf. There was nobody at Pasadena Tech I wanted to meet.

What did all this add up to? Zero, zip, zilch. Bupkis. Wipeout. It meant as little as the space between stars.

Some weary hours later, I arrived at the Magic Palace. Above it, the Hollywood Hills were dark. The air smelled as it had out beyond the city—jazzed up with the odor of night flowers and with the invigorating non-odor it had only when it was clean. I filled my nose with it while I could. The next day, just being itself, Los Angeles would foul the air again. I guessed that when day came, geologists would go over the Santa Monica Mountains as if they were looking for a contact lens, and find nothing that hadn't been there for ten thousand years.

The Magic Palace was open, but just barely. The receptionist and some very large boys in tuxedos were in the lobby nodding and smiling as late revelers stumbled out. The large boys had bulges under their arms that probably were not rabbits. Captain Hook was sleeping in the receptionist's chair with his head on the desk. When I woke him up, he was glad to see me.

I opened the windows of the Belvedere and drove that way. The smell of the wind helped keep me awake. Captain Hook stretched out on the back seat and snored out tiny paper umbrellas that popped like bubbles when they touched the ceiling of the car.

When we got to Malibu, we all went into the house, and Captain Hook went to bed. I wanted to sleep more than anything I could think of at that moment. But I had one job to do first.

Bill and I went into the kitchen. I pulled over

a chair for him so he could see out the window.
The hat was still out on the beach. But dull
light was throbbing gently all around it with
the cadence of a human heartbeat.

Much too early the next morning, Will came
in and said, "Some very heavy dudes are here
to see you." I nodded and walked, half awake,
to the bathroom, where I splashed water on
my face and did what I could to make myself
presentable. I looked like last year's bird nest
and felt like a cheese rind, but short of taking
a week or two in the country there was nothing
to be done.

It was Pele and Lono, of course. They were
dressed again in their clothes designed like
tropical explosions, and stood in the living
room looking more relaxed than I'd ever seen
them. They were standing with Captain Hook
in the center of the room. The Captain tried to
keep his hands in his pockets, but every so often he pulled one of them out, and a rabbit with
it. There were a lot of rabbits in the room.

I was surprised to see Jean-Luc Avoirdupois,
but he greeted me as if we were all buddies
and this whole business with the spine had
never happened. "Come to make sure they go
home?" I said.

Avoirdupois liked that. He said, "You are a
kidder, sir, and no mistake. A man after my
own heart. And I'll tell you straight out, I never
kid a kidder." His voice got very low and confidential. Only those people in the room could
hear him when he said, "I am not, as you suggest, seeing them off. I'm going with them—to
search for the black crystal bird."

"Mighty forgiving, aren't they?" I said.

Avoirdupois chuckled and shrugged.

Lono said, "He has the clues and the map. If
we want a chance to find the black bird, we
have to take him. And we do want it. If we find

it, it'll sort of balance our, er, undistinguished record here on Earth."

"The search is all very much in the line of duty, sir, I assure you. My only interest in this matter is as special correspondent to *The Interstate Eyeball.*"

Pele's mouth was a tight line. She seemed very calm for a woman with such a short fuse, especially if she was about to be featured in an *Eyeball* exclusive. I'd be very surprised if Avoirdupois ever had a chance to file his story. But that was none of my business.

"Better you than me," was all I said.

"We were just waiting for you," Pele said and shined her smile on me like a searchlight.

I said, "Let's get to it before the rabbits outnumber the sea gulls."

Pele nodded, gripped Captain Hook by the arm, and said, "Stand here." He looked confused, but he smiled at Pele hopefully. Captain Hook stayed where he was as Pele took a step back.

She looked at me. I nodded. Whipping her arm, she threw a green ball of fire at Captain Hook. He closed his eyes tightly, but didn't move when the fireball hit him in the chest, didn't seem to feel it at all. Green lightning crawled all over him, then burrowed into the carpet and was gone. Captain Hook collapsed. Lono caught him just in time and lowered him to the floor.

We stood over Captain Hook as if he were a fish pond. He blinked and opened his eyes. He said, "If you dudes are so stoked on watching me sleep, maybe I ought to charge."

"Sounds like the old aggro captain to me," Thumper said.

"Bitchen," the surfers said as with one voice and a little awed.

The captain climbed to his feet, stiff as an old man. He looked at me, the challenge back in his jawline. He said, "That hat really drilled me, dude."

"More than you know," I said.

"Yeah. So what about it?"

"It's leaving." I said.

He nodded without smiling and said, "Bitchen." He cocked his head at Pele and Lono and said, "Who are these dudes?"

"They go with the hat."

"They better cruise before I remember how dissed I am."

"Yeah."

Bill and I led Pele and Lono and Avoirdupois out the back door, across the little brick patio, across the public walkway, and onto the sand. We marched through the hot, still air, bobbing along until we got to the hat. A gull sat on top of it, watching. Now it took off, and soared along the edge of the water. It landed and lost itself in a group of other gulls who were patrolling the beach.

Only two other people were nearby, and each of them had a video camera. There was nothing between them and us, nothing between us and the hat. Nothing to stop them from getting some really terrific pictures. They were so intent on looking through their machines, I didn't think either one knew the other was there. After those two, the closest people looked like match heads in the distance.

I shook hands all around. Bill shook hands too, and for once didn't make a production out of it. I wished Pele and Lono and Avoirdupois luck, but what that meant, exactly, I didn't know. If they actually found a black crystal bird, I had the feeling they would be disappointed. I didn't know they would, but I also didn't see how any one crystal statue could be equipped with all the accessories they wanted it to have. On the other hand, just because I didn't know how to do it didn't mean it couldn't be done.

A circular door opened in the side of the hat where no door had been, and the brave little band got aboard.

"Come on, Bill," I said. As we strode back to the house, I said, "How are you fixed for magnetism?"

"You mean my magnetic personality?"

"I know all about your personality. Anything else?"

"Sure, boss. I'm full of the stuff."

"Let it all hang out."

"Right, boss."

When we were about halfway between the two camera people, I called out, "How you doing, Busy?"

Busy briefly looked away from her viewfinder and said, "What?"

The other cameraperson was Gone-out, of course. He didn't even turn his head from his camera when he cried out angrily, "What are you doing here, Busy?"

Busy sniffed and said, "What's it to you? You don't have exclusive rights to any of this."

"Medium Rare will share her knowledge with the world."

"Yeah, for a swift profit. I just want to show this to my club."

"We will rent you a copy."

"Rent nothing. I have my own original right here."

They went on, bickering like chickens while they shot pictures, getting in nice and tight with telephoto lenses.

A few seconds later, the top hat collapsed down onto itself. It stayed that way for a moment. Then, with a loud snap, it suddenly opened to its full height, and the crown pulled the rest of the hat into the sky. It was out of

sight in seconds. After a while, I became aware
that I had been holding my breath.

Busy and Gone-out lowered their cameras
and glared at each other. Busy backed up a few
paces, then ran for the highway, her camera
banging against her leg. Gone-out cried, "This
is an outrage," and was after her.

"Come on, Bill," I said and followed them as
fast as I could.

We were all handicapped by the thick, dry
sand that tried to bury our feet at each step,
but it was quite a race even so. Gone-out
caught up with Busy and tackled her to the
ground. While she fought him, he wrestled the
tape cassette out of the camera and passed us
as he ran back toward the water with it.

In the few seconds it took Busy to get to her
feet, Gone-out was halfway to the ocean. With
a mighty heave, he flung the cassette. It
plopped into the water a little beyond where
the waves broke. He stood on the shore, looking out at the place where it disappeared.

We joined Gone-out for a contemplative moment. I stroked the door to the compartment
that held Gone-out's videocassette and said,
"Nice material, isn't it, Bill?" I thought I knew
what would happen next, and Bill did not disappoint me. He stroked the door too.

He was interrupted by an "Oof!" from Gone-
out as Busy hit him from behind and knocked
him onto the sand. Gone-out didn't fight her,
he just curled around his video camera and
tried to keep his back to her.

"Come on," I said. Bill and I walked toward
Will's House as Busy and Gone-out continued
to struggle.

"What now, Boss?" Bill said.

"Nothing, if your magnetic field was strong
enough to erase Gone-out's tape."

"No problem, Boss. Feel this muscle." He
held up his arm in the classic pose. It was just

a metal arm, but I felt it anyway and told him how impressed I was.

We went back into the house, where Captain Hook was sitting on the couch and the surfers were sitting around him, explaining what had gone on the past week. He didn't want to buy it, but the rabbits were hard to argue with.

Bill said, "I want to show you something."

"Go ahead. I have nothing but time."

He wanted to chose a movie from Whipper Will's videotape library, but I wouldn't let him touch any of them. "You'll erase it," I said.

"No way. I can turn that magnetism stuff on and off. Or shield it, anyway."

"You sure? What about your magnetic personality?"

"No problem, boss."

I let him pull a tape, and he fired up the television. It wasn't long before we were watching *The Wizard of Oz*. I didn't understand a lot of it—there are all kinds of alien cultures—but most of the surfers seemed to know the thing word for word.

When Dorothy got to Oz and everything was suddenly in color, I freeze-framed Munchkinland. The picture quivering on the screen looked just like the other one of Medium Rare's paintings I'd recognized at the Aquaricon. It looked just like Yewpitz.

I said, "It looks like one of Medium Rare's paintings."

"I told you," Bill said. "Oz."

"Close enough," I said.